"But I'd really like to kiss you."

And then she did, and Gabe's universe expanded to include the sensation of soft lips on his own, the exchange of warm breath, and a throb in his lower belly that was near pleasure/pain. He had no idea why he let her do it except that she seemed so precious and fragile, so vulnerable, as though she offered him her loneliness and her sorrows along with her body.

Heaven help him, he could not help but drink them in.

Closer she moved, and closer still, until her breasts were against his chest, and it was this that broke the spell; the desire to put his arms around her and drag her even closer came over him like a wave, and with it came the knowledge that if he let it, he would drown.

Abruptly, he jerked his head back, ending the kiss. "Stop," he whispered, looking into her eyes. "You must stop."

D0395419

05 FEB 2012

Romances by Terri Garey

A DEVIL NAMED DESIRE
DEVIL WITHOUT A CAUSE
SILENT NIGHT, HAUNTED NIGHT
YOU'RE THE ONE THAT I HAUNT
A MATCH MADE IN HELL
DEAD GIRLS ARE EASY

ATTENTION: ORGANIZATIONS AND CORPORATIONS
Most Avon Books paperbacks are available at special quantity
discounts for bulk purchases for sales promotions, premiums,
or fund raising. For information, please call or write:

**Special Markets Department, HarperCollins Publishers,
10 East 53rd Street, New York, New York 10022-5299.
Telephone: (212) 207-7528.   Fax: (212) 207-7222.**

TERRI GAREY

A Devil Named Desire

AVON

An Imprint of HarperCollinsPublishers

This is a work of fiction. Names, characters, places, and incidents are products of the author's imagination or are used fictitiously and are not to be construed as real. Any resemblance to actual events, locales, organizations, or persons, living or dead, is entirely coincidental.

AVON BOOKS
An Imprint of HarperCollins*Publishers*
10 East 53rd Street
New York, New York 10022-5299

Copyright © 2012 by Terri Garey
ISBN 978-0-06-198640-6
www.avonromance.com

All rights reserved. No part of this book may be used or reproduced in any manner whatsoever without written permission, except in the case of brief quotations embodied in critical articles and reviews. For information address Avon Books, an Imprint of HarperCollins Publishers.

First Avon Books mass market printing: February 2012

Avon Trademark Reg. U.S. Pat. Off. and in Other Countries, Marca Registrada, Hecho en U.S.A.
HarperCollins® is a registered trademark of HarperCollins Publishers.

Printed in the U.S.A.

10 9 8 7 6 5 4 3 2 1

If you purchased this book without a cover, you should be aware that this book is stolen property. It was reported as "unsold and destroyed" to the publisher, and neither the author nor the publisher has received any payment for this "stripped book."

Acknowledgments

It's impossible to tell a story about angels and demons without touching on some spiritual issues, but this book—at its heart—is a love story. Whatever belief systems the characters have, and whatever actions they take, came straight from the slightly skewed depths of my imagination, and are not an attempt to convert *or* corrupt.

Like any storyteller, I'm just out to tell a good story.

Thanks, as always, to the people who keep me grounded while I reach for the stars: my family, my friends, my editor, and my agent. Most special thanks to those who read my books; I couldn't do it without you.

A
Devil Named
Desire

Prologue

"So it's true," said the Archangel Gabriel, "criminals always return to the scene of the crime."

Samael the Fallen, Ruler of the Abyss, turned his eyes from the leafy green valley nestled in the hills below. Up here, on the windswept heights, the howling of the wind had disguised the rustle of feathers that might've warned him of Gabriel's approach, and masked the scent of sandalwood that clung to his old friend's person.

His onetime brother, born of the same womb, that of the universe itself. Fellow angels, created in the image of the One, now as different and distant as the Earth from the sun; Gabe clothed in Light, he steeped in Darkness.

"Nothing to say for yourself, old friend?" Gabriel moved to stand beside him on the edge of the cliff. "Has the guilt finally gotten to you? Centuries of pain and suffering for all mankind, caused simply by your inability to control the most basic of urges. Was it worth it, this need you had to bury yourself within the softness of a woman's thighs?"

Samael turned back to regard the vista he'd been beholding and answered simply, "Yes."

Gabriel made a noise of frustration, which was ignored.

"She was down there"—Sammy pointed—"by that waterfall." A silver ribbon in the distance, glistening in the noonday sun. "Naked as the day she was born. Eve, mother of your precious mankind, born to tempt both man and angel alike with her sweet juices." He gave a low laugh. "The epitome of forbidden fruit."

"You didn't have to take her, Samael." The wind whipped Gabe's brown hair, clubbed in a ponytail at his neck. "You could've left her untouched, pure. She was created to be man's helpmate, not your plaything."

A harsh bark of laughter came from Sammy's throat. "*Take* her? The moment I alighted she ran to me, throwing herself into my arms. I could no more resist the softness of her flesh than the ocean could resist the tides." He shook his head ruefully. Turning to look Gabriel full in the face, he added, "*I* was the innocent, old friend. Eve did exactly what she was created for, and I responded. Yet *I* am the one forever damned; where's the justice in that?"

Gabe shook his head, frowning. His eyes were brown, unlike Sammy's, which were as blue as the sky, the heights from which he was forever banned.

"Why are you here, Gabriel? To chide me for doing what came naturally, or to gloat for tricking me into doing what you wanted me to do when last we met?"

"I didn't trick you, Samael. You showed mercy of your own volition, proving that your heart is not as black as you—and the world—believe it to be."

Sammy smiled, but it was a bitter smile. "Given that you are here alone, without the backing of a heavenly choir singing my praises, I take it that the One was neither swayed nor impressed by my recent show of mercy?"

Gabriel didn't look away, but neither did he speak.

Sammy, reading the answer in his onetime

brother's eyes, despised himself for asking the question.

"Ah, well," he said, turning away. "Life goes on."

And on, and on, and on . . .

"You should have resisted the temptation to introduce sin into the world," Gabriel insisted stubbornly. "You were divine, Eve was not."

"Sin," Sammy sneered, curling a lip. "Such a small word for such a big concept." He raked a hand though his blond hair, cropped short, jagged as his temper. "What happened with Eve was sex, nothing more, yet instantly I'm to blame for all the world's evils."

"It's not too late, Samael." Gabriel looked out over the Garden. "Try again to open your heart, to show mercy more often on the One's behalf. He'll see it—He'll heed me eventually, I know it."

"You know nothing of the kind," Sammy told him coldly. "And mercy is in short supply in the world I inhabit. It's also, I might add, something He's never shown me."

"Let go of your anger, brother," Gabriel said impatiently. "You're chained to it, a rabid dog, growling and snapping at the world."

Sammy set his jaw, remembering the pain of that long-ago day when he'd been stripped of his wings. "Of course I'm angry," he growled. "I didn't ask to be born; I didn't ask to be made ruler of the Kingdom of the Damned. The One created me to do *exactly* what I did, don't you see? He knew those bumbling fools in the Garden would lose their innocence eventually—he knew that both good and evil must exist to maintain a balance in the universe. Yet they're offered eternal forgiveness, while I'm not."

He'd been cast off, abandoned, forced to make his way among the humans . . . the same primitive, foolish creatures who'd caused his downfall.

"Stop feeling sorry for yourself," Gabriel snapped, "and get over it."

Sammy's fists clenched as he whirled, ready to unleash Hell upon his brother.

Gabriel stood his ground. "How old do you have to be before you stop behaving like a spoiled child?" He crossed his arms, planted his feet. "Life isn't perfect," he insisted. "Life *happens*." The wind ruffled the feathers on the tips of his wings. "We weren't created with a guarantee that everything would work out just the way we wanted it to. It's not what happens to you, Samael, but how you deal with it."

"Ever the philosopher," Sammy said scathingly, furious at how pointless it would be to give in to the urge to push his old friend off the cliff. A use-less endeavor that would result only a painful display of the flight he could no longer achieve, earthbound and damned as he was. "One who knows nothing of which he speaks. Everything's worked out well for you, hasn't it, Gabriel? You got your guarantee. Right-hand man of the One, Chief Servant to the Universe; how's the view from up there?"

Biting off his diatribe, Samael the Fallen, once at the right hand of the universe himself, spun to walk a few feet along the cliff's edge. He betrayed himself with emotion, and knew better than to reveal any chink in his armor to Gabriel.

He was too late, however, for Gabriel said, "My heart aches for you, old friend."

"Fuck your heart!" Sammy shouted, no longer trying to keep his temper in check. "Take it and go!"

There was a silence, broken only by the harsh cry of an eagle, circling the valley below. Gabriel sighed, and waited.

"You think temptation is so easily avoided, so easily denied?" Sammy's glare would've sent the shadowy denizens of the Underworld scurrying for cover, but against one who'd known him since the beginning of time, it had no effect. "You think that only because you've never been tempted," he spat.

"Not so," returned Gabriel mildly. "Like right now . . . I'm tempted to kick you soundly in the ass, except that my foot would collide with your head, which seems permanently lodged there."

Sammy fought an errant urge to grin, despite the anger and bitterness Gabe had so easily provoked. Gabriel had never been frightened of him, even in those dark days following the Fall, when he'd raged against Heaven and all its occupants. "I meant by a woman," he clarified wryly. "By the softness of her breast, the curve of her belly . . ."

"Spare me the details," Gabriel interrupted, raising a hand. "I need not partake of such pleasures to know they exist."

Something in his voice caused Sammy to narrow his eyes in speculation.

"I've seen humans procreate," the Archangel said defensively, noting the look. "Physical closeness is obviously important to them, particularly when they're in love."

Sammy made a rude noise, noticing the heightened color in Gabriel's cheeks. "*Love*," he scoffed. "Why does everyone speak so freely of love?"

"Because so it is written, and so it will remain."

Gabe quoted, " 'These three shall abide: faith, hope, and love; but the greatest of these is love.' "

Sammy shook his head in disgust, denying both the sentiment and the verse.

Love was pain, and love was madness.

He'd had eons to learn that lesson.

Eons, alone.

Gabriel sighed wearily, bringing him back to reality. "Have you ever truly loved anyone, Samael?"

"No," he answered shortly, not even having to consider his reply.

"Don't you want to?"

The simplicity of Gabe's question took his breath away. He turned toward the cliff, his mind's eye suddenly filled with the image of a young woman with smiling eyes and dark hair, streaked with pink highlights. *Nicki, my love . . .*

"Absolutely not." Crossing his arms, he eyed the eagle who soared, even now, over the valley. "I learned a long, long time ago that the only person you can rely on is yourself." Keeping his back firmly to his brother and his past, he added, "Go away, Gabriel, and leave me alone."

A long silence answered him. Then, in a low voice, full of regret, he heard Gabe say, "I'm so sorry, Samael."

He didn't answer, and finally, mercifully, he heard a brief flutter of wings as Gabe departed. When the silence became absolute save for the keening of the wind, only then did Sammy begin his descent into the valley.

Following a narrow but well-worn path, the Devil made his way to the place of his undoing. This pocket of green, tucked deeply away in the Mediterranean hills, truly was a paradise, as wild and untouched as it had been in the Beginning. There was no reason to rush; there was nothing and no one waiting for him in the garden, save his own memories, both bitter and sweet.

As he walked through the grove of olive trees that lined the path, a shadow slipped up behind him. Black-winged Nyx, Chief Servant of Darkness. Eight feet tall, with eyes that glowed red, Nyx took his customary place at his master's shoulder. Though the demon made no sound, Sammy knew he was there, for Nyx was the other half of his soul. The dark, twisted half that fed on the miseries of others.

"Master?"

"What is it?"

"Let me kill the Lightbringer."

"Gabriel's immortal," Sammy replied, deep in

thought, brushing his fingers against the leaves of a tree as he passed, "an archangel. There's nothing you can do to him physically that he can't overcome."

A low growl of frustration came from the demon.

Sammy continued talking almost idly as they passed through a patch of wildflowers, threaded with weeds. "My onetime brother dares insult me with his pity, and is in need of a reminder of how little I need it," he told Nyx, over his shoulder. "He thinks himself above me, both literally and figuratively." The eagle, soaring high above his head, gave a harsh cry, drawing his bright blue gaze upward. "Like that bird"—he pointed—"who is currently annoying me with its shrieks." He paused in the middle of the path, resting his hands on his hips as he looked up at the bird. "Silence it."

Instantly Nyx spread his blackened wings and took to the sky, the veritable shadow of death itself. A few seconds later he snatched the eagle midair and wrung its neck, the bird's fierce talons no match for those of a demon. Then he cast it away, the bird's lifeless body plummeting like a stone.

Sammy watched it fall, watched, too, the handful of loose feathers that fluttered, far more slowly, toward the ground.

"Faith, hope, and love, indeed," he muttered to himself contemptuously. "Gabriel puts his precious humans on a pedestal, but I think it's time for him to get a more close-up view of humanity."

Chapter One

The water in the bathtub was warm, soothing, and a beautiful shade of red. Sangria shades, of wine and blood.

The steady *drip, drip, drip* of the faucet echoed against the tiled walls, reverberating in Hope Henderson's ears as she lay in the tub. It was peaceful here, in this warm, red space between life and death. The voices of guilt and regret were finally quiet, elusive thoughts of what-might-have-been and what-should-have-been blessedly silenced.

Drip, drip, drip.

Closing her eyes, Hope wondered dreamily how many more drips it would take before it all went away.

"Hello, Hope," came a voice, deep and smooth

as honey. "What a bad girl you are." Someone took her hand, lifting it from the water. "Look what you've gone and done to yourself."

She could barely open her eyes now, and didn't want to anyway, but the voice kept on.

"So pretty," the voice said, "such delicate skin. This will leave scars, you know, scars you will never be rid of."

"Go away," she murmured, refusing to look at the man who held her hand. She would've pulled it from his grasp, but hadn't the strength.

"I can't do that," he replied gently. "And you don't want me to, not really. Open your eyes, pretty little Hope. Open your eyes and see what lies ahead."

So compelling, so gentle. Promising something just out of reach . . .

"Open your eyes," he said, more forcefully, and her eyelids fluttered open.

An arresting face, one she'd never seen before. *Beautiful.* He was so beautiful. Blond hair, blue eyes, high cheekbones, and a strong chin. He was kneeling by the side of the tub, cradling her hand in his, ignoring the sluggish trickle of blood that ran down her arm.

"That's it," he crooned softly. "Look at me."

Something fluttered behind him, a dark

shape . . . the featherlike rustle of what might've been wings, black as the darkness she craved.

"Time to wake up, my darling," he said, smiling a wicked smile, and with that smile she was lost. She would've done anything for him in that moment, because he was here and he was beautiful and he was everything she'd ever wanted and was never going to have.

"What's this?" he murmured, reaching to wipe away the tear that she hadn't even known she'd cried. "No need for tears, surely. Salvation is at hand." But the way he said it told her she was anything but saved—she was damned, damned to Hell for all the things she hadn't done, all the mistakes she'd made. And when he took his hand from her face and picked something up off the floor—something that broke her heart—she was absolutely certain her damnation was never going to end.

"I know where your sister is," he said, gently, looking at the photo in his hand. "Charity isn't dead."

Hope moaned, feeling a prickle of sweat break out on her forehead as she stared at Charity's sweet, beautiful face . . . her baby sister, whom she was supposed to have taken care of, supposed to have kept safe. *Dead. Charity was dead, and it was all her fault.* The feelings of guilt and failure that had driven her to this bathtub, razor blade in hand, rose up again, threatening to drown her in a tide of red-tinged grief.

"Master." A whisper of sound, one she wasn't certain she'd even heard. "Let me take her, Master. The Darkness awaits."

Fear, so far removed a moment ago, squeezed her heart, but she shoved it away. *Let the Darkness take her, let it swallow her whole the way it had swallowed Charity—she deserved it.*

"No," said the man, to someone she couldn't see. His blue eyes were trained on hers. "She stays here."

Hope tried to speak, tried to beg—whether to help her or to let her die, she wasn't sure, but he turned his head and spoke sharply to someone in the shadows behind him.

"Leave us," he said, and her world went black.

She awoke to light, streaming golden through tall windows, reflecting the gleam of skyscrapers. A strange room, a strange bed. The pillow beneath her head was soft, the room tastefully decorated in shades of cream and cocoa. Her wrists hurt.

"You're awake," said a man, and there he was

in the doorway; the man of her dreams, the beautiful blond angel she'd seen as she lay dying.

"Just in time for breakfast." He was carrying a tray, smiling as he set it beside her bed.

Crisp white button-down shirt, no tie. Dark gray trousers that fit him in all the right places. A well-dressed, handsome stranger, who'd pulled her back from the edge of the abyss.

"Don't be afraid," he told her easily. "Everything's going to be all right."

She didn't believe him, knowing nothing would ever be right again, but had no will to argue. Her body felt strange, heavy. She licked her lips, unable to summon the energy to even care about where she was, or how she'd gotten there.

"You're dehydrated," he said, "but that will pass. Let me help you sit up." He bent, slipping an arm beneath her shoulders. The familiarity surprised her, but she hadn't the strength to pull away. He smelled of something warm and exotic; cloves maybe, cinnamon.

Quickly, impersonally, he rearranged the pillows behind her back so she could sit up.

"Here. Have some orange juice."

Her hands shook as she took it. Both wrists were bandaged, and at the sight of them, she winced.

Raising the glass, she was nearly overcome with

despair. *She was supposed to be dead.* The orange juice tasted good, cool as it slid down her throat, and she hated the part of her that wanted it.

"Good girl." He took the empty glass and set it on the bedside table.

"Where am I?" She let her head fall back against the pillow. "Who are you?"

"My name is Sammy, and there's no need to worry. You're safe with me."

Safe? She'd tried to kill herself. All the memories came rushing back: the warm red water, the quiet drip of the faucet. The man, the shadow . . . had there been whispers?

"My sister. Charity." She snatched a moment of clarity from the haze. "You said she wasn't dead."

He nodded. "That's right. She's alive."

She wanted desperately to believe him, but the prickle on the back of her neck warned her not to get her hopes up.

She couldn't go through it, not again.

"Where is she?"

"All in good time, Hope."

Not the answer she wanted, and her wariness increased, because she hadn't told him her name. "Do . . . do I know you?" She was absolutely sure she didn't—a face like his would be hard to forget.

"Not yet," he replied, with a lazy curl of a lip,

"but you'll soon know me better." He cocked his blond head. "In the meantime, I know quite a lot about you, Hope Henderson. Your parents died in a fire when you were twelve, and both you and your younger sister grew up in foster care. Charity, your sister, has been missing for two years. You were told just last week that her purse had been found in a washed-out ravine in the middle of the Sonoran Desert. The police think she's been murdered."

The starkness of the words took her breath away. She turned her head toward the window, eyes filling with tears. The police theorized that her beautiful, vivacious sister, off for a weekend of fun in Las Vegas, had been murdered and dumped, a piece of human garbage left for the coyotes to ravage. As far as the police were concerned, the search for Charity was over; no contact for two years, no use of credit cards or ATMs, no sign of her at all, until now. The slim thread of hope she'd clung to had been severed, driving her over the edge to despair.

Not even a body left to bury.

"I know you were told otherwise, but trust me when I tell you, Charity isn't dead."

Hope's eyes snapped back to his; pale blue, and despite his seeming kindnesses to her, completely devoid of emotion.

"How would you know?" She bit her lip, willing the tears not to fall.

"The abandoned purse was just a cover," he replied calmly. "She's alive and well, and living in Las Vegas." Moving toward the tray, he picked up the coffeepot and poured some into a cup. "And that's all I'm going to tell you for the moment. First, let's get your strength up, put some food in you. Milk? Sugar?"

Stunned, she shook her head, raising a bandaged wrist to swipe at a tear that spilled over anyway.

"Black it is, then," he said lightly, and offered her the cup. "Drink up." His voice was firm, inflexible, the voice of a man used to being obeyed.

She did as he said, and took the cup, using both hands to keep it steady. The coffee smelled good, and in the hopes it would help dispel the sense of unreality that had settled over her, she took a cautious sip. She'd expected to wake burning in Hell, yet here she was, nestled in goose down, sipping coffee with a guy who should be gracing the cover of *GQ* magazine, and talking about the possibility that her sister could still be alive.

"Colombia's finest," he said approvingly, lifting his own cup. "None of that mocha latte shit." His blue eyes twinkled, both knowing and compelling; a gaze that frightened and reassured at the same time. "Take a moment, enjoy."

And because she needed a moment to wrap her brain around the situation, she did, and immediately found him right about the coffee; a couple of sips and she felt stronger.

"Tell me more about Charity. Why hasn't she called me? What's she doing?"

"So many questions." He gave a short laugh, amused. Then the look in his eye turned calculating, making her nervous. "What a waste your death would've been."

Remembrance of those moments in the tub left her silent as she stared into her coffee cup. "I haven't thanked you for saving my life," she told him stiffly, aware that thanks were called for. "I—I was depressed, it was stupid . . ."

"You're welcome," he interrupted dryly. "But you may want to hold on to your thanks, because now you owe me."

The prickle on the back of her neck turned to ice, slipping down her spine.

"What?"

"You were going to die, and I saved you," he said simply. "You called out to me, and I came."

Her normally agile brain finally clicked into gear. The guy was gorgeous, but insane. Hot coffee to the face was a possibility, but there was no way she could bolt past him in her weakened state. He'd catch her in an instant, and then she'd have made him mad.

Something told her she didn't want to make him mad.

"You wanted the Darkness." He lifted the lid of a salver on the tray, releasing the heavenly smell of fresh baked bread. His actions were unhurried, but his words struck fear into her heart. "I *am* the Darkness." Silverware rattled as he picked up a knife. The blade gleamed, mesmerizing her.

She tore her eyes away from the knife and put them back on his face, wanting to be able to describe him to the police if she made it out of this alive.

"Describe me to the police all you like," he said, making her jump. "They're not going to be able to find me, because I don't exist." He smiled, but it didn't reach his eyes. "I'm like the bogeyman . . . gone the moment you turn on the light."

He didn't *look* like the bogeyman, yet for one teeny second she allowed herself to hope that the whole surreal situation was a nightmare, a figment of suicidal delirium . . .

"Ah, the lies we tell ourselves when we're under stress," the man said, as though he'd read her mind. He cocked his head to the side, giving her a bemused grin. "Don't you know who I am yet, Hope Henderson? Haven't you figured it out?" He shook his blond head, making *tsk*ing noises. "It's so disappointing not to be recognized these days; modern media almost always portrays me as dark-haired and goateed, with a decided preference for horns and a red cape. Truth be told, I prefer Armani."

Unsure of what to say to that, she said nothing.

"You've been given a blood transfusion, by the way, as you lost most of your own in the tub. The doctor said not to worry; you're young and otherwise healthy. A little rest, some food . . . you'll be feeling better soon." He dipped the knife in butter and lavished it on a piece of toast. "Don't look so frightened, pretty little Hope. It's not as though I'm going to eat you." He chuckled. "If the rumor mill is to be believed, I prefer small children, lightly roasted."

The coffee in her hand threatened to spill, and she lowered the cup to her lap.

"I'll spell it out for you then, shall I? I go by many names—Satan, Beelzebub, Mephistopheles—but the only one you need to remember at the moment is Sammy." Inclining his head in a mock bow, he added, "Sammy Divine, at your service."

She focused on her breathing, knowing her best hope was to remain calm and not hyperventilate; despite the depression that had lately possessed her and her currently weak state, she was fit, and she'd hadn't taken a five-week course on self-defense for nothing.

Let the maniac think she was compliant, lull him into thinking she was weak . . . she could use the cup as a weapon . . .

He drew closer, forcing her to look into his face: lean jaw, sharply chiseled cheekbones, coldly handsome in a way that only increased the terror in her heart. "I wouldn't do that if I were you. Hand me the cup."

Heart pounding, she played for time, and handed it to him without a word.

"Still you doubt me." He shrugged. "No matter." He cocked his head. "Allow me to prove it to you."

From the corner behind him came a shadow, getting larger and larger, spreading like a stain across the wall, the floor, the very air itself. It twisted and roiled, turning in upon itself and back again. It rose, getting bigger and bigger, until it was looming over him. He had to know it was there—impossible not to know it was there, but he showed no reaction, no fear.

Hope gasped, scrabbling back against the pillows, but the door was behind him and there was nowhere to go. Horrified, she could only watch as the shadow grew larger.

Then, from the inky darkness itself, something stepped into the room, and her blood ran cold.

Two huge wings, black as night, a lump that coalesced into a head, tipped with horns as blackened and sharp as wickedness itself. Hope cried out when she saw its eyes, red as coals in the dark pit of what passed for the creature's face.

"Meet Nyx," the Devil said smoothly. "My right-hand man."

The thing hissed in response, and Hope shrieked, long and loud, covering her face with her hands.

Silence answered her, a silence that frightened her more than anything else that had happened so far. She felt the bed dip and cringed away, keeping her face covered, too weak and shocked to do more. The scent of spices curled into her nostrils like smoke, telling her Sammy had come closer. His fingers gently encircled her injured wrists, pulling her hands away from her face.

"Yea, though I walk through the shadow of the valley of death, thou art with me," he crooned to her softly, in a profane parody of biblical verse. "Nyx *is* the shadow in the valley of death. He is a soul eater, and he is hungry, as hungry as the Darkness from whence he came."

Afraid to look in the direction of the monster, she trembled, and kept her eyes down.

"Look at me," Sammy ordered.

Afraid not to, she raised her eyes to his face. His eyes were such a pale, pale blue; like ice on a frozen pond. Beautiful, but just like ice, there was death beneath the beauty.

"That's it," he murmured softly, mere inches away. "Look at me. Look into my eyes and listen to me carefully."

Terrified, gasping, Hope didn't move, feeling like a rabbit pinned by a fox.

"You gave yourself into my keeping when you slit these pretty wrists," he told her. "Suicides belong to the Darkness, so you're mine now, do you understand? Your soul is mine."

The demon behind him shifted, just slightly, but it was more than enough to make her flinch in terror. Another tear slid down her cheek.

"It's time to make a bargain, you and I."

Almost against her will, she felt a faint stab of hope. "A ba-bargain?"

"I'm going to offer you a gift—a gift that will help you find your sister—but you must agree to do something for me in return."

Biting her lip, Hope was cognizant of the strength of the fingers that held her bandaged wrists. He held them gently now, but one twist, and she'd be screaming in agony. This was no dream, no suicide-induced hallucination. This was a living, breathing nightmare: the beautiful, terrible Angel of Death and his own personal, eight-foot demon.

Gathering her courage, she swallowed hard, and asked, "How do I know that Charity's still alive?"

Satan smiled, letting her go. He held out his hand, palm up, toward the demon, not bothering to look in the creature's direction.

It stepped forward immediately, placing an object into its master's hand. It was a polished disc of stone the size of a CD, black marble veined with white, perfectly flat and smooth. It was rimmed in gold, etched with a pattern of crosshatches.

Holding it between his thumb and forefinger, Sammy held it so Hope could see it clearly. "Look at it," he told her. "Watch."

Before her eyes, the veins of white within the stone began to move, all swirling in the same direction, blending together to forming a type of vortex. Frightened but fascinated, she watched as the vortex became larger, covering the entire surface of the disc.

"The Eye of Caradoc," Satan murmured silkily. "Look deeper, and tell me what you see."

To her shock, the swirling vortex within the stone began to change, revealing an image, misty and unformed. The image became clearer and she gasped; it was the face of a woman, fluffing her hair and putting on lipstick as though she were looking into a mirror, unaware she was being watched.

The honey blond hair, the hazel brown eyes . . . they were as familiar to Hope as her own reflection. *Charity.* Her sister.

Unable to stop herself, Hope cried out, reaching for the stone, but Sammy pulled it back, beyond her reach.

"Keep looking," he told her coldly, and she did, transfixed by how the image grew sharper the longer she stared.

It was like looking through a camera lens. Behind Charity she could see tile walls, marked with lewd graffiti. A single stall, door open to reveal a dingy toilet. Charity kept glancing over her shoulder, appearing nervous as she applied yet another coat of garish pink lipstick. The door behind her opened, and a hulking figure filled it. Hope couldn't make out his features, but it was clearly a man, one who gestured impatiently, saying something she couldn't hear. Whatever it was made her sister's shoulders slump, and her eyes fall. She turned from the mirror, tucked away her lipstick, and left the bathroom. The man followed a moment later, but before he did, he leaned in and took a quick look around the ladies' room, as though assuring himself it was empty. His jacket gaped open, revealing a gun strapped to his chest.

"Your sister's in trouble," Sammy said, and lowered the stone. "Don't you want to help her?"

Weak, terrified, and emotionally drained, she could only stare into pitiless blue pools of ice, and accept the inevitable, just as she had last night when she'd picked up a razor blade. Bowing her head, she whispered, "What is it you want me to do?"

"Good girl," Satan murmured silkily. He reached out to tuck a stray strand of hair behind her ear, casually claiming her as his own. He cocked his head, observing her closely. "You're a Web designer, aren't you?"

Hope nodded, unsure what that had to do with anything.

"Well, then." He rose from the bed, and as he did, Hope saw that the disc was just a stone again; the image of Charity was gone. "I want you to build me a Web site."

She frowned, looking up at him through her lashes. "A Web site?"

"Not just any Web site." The Devil smiled. "A very special Web site, just for my followers."

"You're kidding, right?"

His smile disappeared. "Do I look like I'm kidding?"

"But . . ." She swallowed, trying her best not to make any kind of eye contact with the dark figure that loomed over Sammy's shoulder. "There are tons of satanic Web sites all over the Internet already."

"True," Sammy said softly, "but none of them contain the words of power necessary to let my legions enter the world en masse." He shrugged an elegant shoulder. "A demon here, a demon there . . . some of the faithful have figured out how to occasionally call them up, but demons are fickle creatures, and notoriously hard for humans to control; they usually end up killing the one who summoned them." He shrugged again. "It's a very inefficient system."

Her blood ran cold.

"One or two demons at a time are all well and good for creating occasional havoc, but I think it's time to up the stakes. You will be the means with which I provide the key to the gates of Hell, my pretty little Hope." He chuckled, and to her horror, the creature behind him chuckled, too, a dark sound that made her breath catch in her throat.

Noting the look on her face, he glanced over his shoulder, smiling. "She doesn't understand the joke, Nyx." He handed the stone disc back to the demon and said, "Fetch me the key."

The demon melted back into the corner, returning almost at once. In one black-clawed hand, it held a small book, which it offered to its master.

Sammy took it; a notebook the size of a diary, plain binding, no title. "The *Ars Goetia*," he said, offering it to Hope. "Otherwise known as the Key of Solomon."

Afraid to touch it, she merely stared.

"It contains the words of power given to King Solomon by the angels themselves, in the long-ago days when the war between good and evil was newly won. The key to controlling demons lies within these pages."

"I—" Hope's voice cracked. "I don't understand."

"It's simple, my dear." Sammy tossed the book on the bed, where it lay on the covers beside her. "The words of power have kept my legions contained for thousands of years, but reversed, and in the right hands, they can set them free."

Greatly daring, she asked, "Why don't you just put it in the right hands yourself?"

He shrugged. "Alas, some things are indeed beyond my abilities. The Key can only be read by someone pure of heart, and I'm afraid that neither I nor any of my followers fall into that category. Once it's transcribed, however, all bets are off."

"Why me?" She felt desperate, confused. "I'm hardly Mother Teresa."

"Oh, Hope." The Devil cocked his head, eyeing her in a disturbingly friendly fashion. "You're sweet and kind and goodhearted to a fault. Losing your parents at such a young age could've left you bitter and angry, but instead it left you mistakenly carrying the weight of the world on those delicate little shoulders. Unfortunately for you, your misplaced guilt over your sister's fate brought you to my attention. I hate to put it so bluntly, but it's my nature to exploit that which is good, and use it for evil. It's what I *do*."

The shadow creature she feared gave a raspy chuckle, then melted back into the corner, retreating as though it had never been.

"It's time to bring the power of social networking to bear." Turning, he strode toward the door, where he paused. "I'll give you two weeks. You'll make these words available to my followers, or you'll never see your sister again." He smiled, the curl of his lip like wickedness itself. "Do we have a bargain?"

Hope bit her lip, eyeing the book. *Two weeks.* A lot could happen in two weeks, including figuring out a way to satisfy the terms of the bargain without putting the actual words out there; she could easily mess up a phrase or leave something out. And somewhere, deep in her heart, lurked the thought that if all else failed, she could destroy the book before anyone else did what she herself was being asked to do.

After all, if she was going to burn in Hell for being stupid enough to offer herself to the Darkness, maybe Hell would be easier to bear if the world she left behind was safer for it.

"Yes, we have a bargain, but—" She stiffened her spine, digging deep for the strength that had kept her going in the years since her parents died, the strength that had deserted her the evening before, during her dark night of the soul. "I want my sister back as soon as the Web site goes live, and then I want you to swear to go away and leave us both alone. Forever."

Sammy laughed. "Dictating terms now . . . not quite dead yet, are you, Hope?" He gave a short nod. "Agreed, but allow me to give you a final word of warning: that book is very, very important to me. It's the only copy in existence. If anything should happen to it . . . well, let's just say that I'll be watching, and so will Nyx."

Chapter Two

Gabriel sat in the sunshine outside Moonbeans Café, listening to New Age music and sipping coffee while he watched the world go by. A few doors down was the vintage clothing store run by the woman who'd captured Samael's heart, and unbeknownst to his angry, stubborn, onetime brother, he liked to stop in every now and then to check on her. In keeping a protective eye on Nicki Styx, he'd discovered the eclectic Atlanta suburb of Little Five Points, Georgia, where he would occasionally linger and people-watch.

Sammy had liked the funky little neighborhood, too, though Gabriel doubted he'd come here again. *Beautiful, terrible, troubled Sammy.* It saddened him still, what they'd lost; once brothers, now foes, each the other's nemesis in the ways of the soul. Still, Sammy had shown mercy instead of vengeance when Nicki chose a mere mortal over him, and it was this crack in Samael's hardened heart that had led Gabriel to believe he could one day find his way out of the Darkness that consumed him.

Now, after their last conversation on the hill overlooking the Garden, he wasn't so sure.

With a sigh, Gabe pushed the vintage sunglasses he'd just bought higher on his nose. Ray-Ban Drifters, a name he found amusing, for a drifter was what he was, going here, there, and everywhere imparting grace and comfort in his role as an angel. Nicki Styx, her chocolate brown eyes twinkling, had told him they made him look "cool." It was a shame, really—her kindhearted zest for life would've been good for Samael, who'd lived too long with his rage and bitterness.

Gabe took a sip of coffee, wondering yet again, as he had many times through the ages, what it was like to truly love a woman. He'd seen many men fight and die for a pretty face, risking their lives for a sloe-eyed glance or a night of pleasure. There was no denying the existence of feminine appeal—the One had designed women to be pleasing to the eye for a reason—but he'd personally never found himself tempted to do more than just admire, much as he admired the beauty of nature, art, and sculpture. He'd had many opportunities to *be* tempted, of course; women clearly found him attractive in human form, whether it be third-century Rome or twenty-first-century Manhattan. Even now, on the streets of Little Five Points, he drew continued admiring glances from the tattooed and pierced young woman behind the counter of the coffee shop, as well as several women browsing in and out of the stores along Moreland Avenue.

"Can I get you anything else?" The young woman had left her place behind the counter, and now stood next to him, holding a tray filled with pastries. She had a small ring in one nostril, three studs in her right eyebrow, and colorful tattoos on both forearms. "We've got some killer muffins today, and these brownies are epic."

"Epic?"

"Awesome. Delicious." The girl smiled at him. "Totally yummy."

He didn't need to understand the vernacular in order to know he was being flirted with, but he wasn't interested in food or flirtation, and shook his head with a smile. "No, thanks."

She arched a pierced brow, still proffering the

tray. "You sure? Because I think you'd like what I have to offer."

"I'm sure I would," he told her, giving in to a full-blown grin, "but no thanks."

She quirked her lip in disappointment and turned away, taking her goodies with her, while Gabriel went back to his people watching.

A woman came around the corner, striding quickly along the sidewalk. She was attractive: delicate features and blond hair, cropped short as a boy's. She would've been more so save for her expression, which was sad and preoccupied, as though her thoughts were not to her liking. She glanced briefly at him in passing, and for an instant, it seemed that the world changed. He saw her, a small woman in jeans and a long-sleeved shirt, then saw *past* her, into the soft white glow that surrounded her like a nimbus. Then he saw past *that*, noting with a chill the darkness that swarmed around that nimbus, desperately seeking a way in.

Gabriel blinked, and it was gone; she was just an attractive woman on the sidewalk.

She crossed the street, ignoring him while he eyed her narrowly behind his sunglasses. He'd never seen an aura attacked in such a way, never seen such sharp contrast between black and white. The warrior in him, battle-scarred from the age-old fight between good and evil, stirred, his protective instincts immediately roused.

When he saw the shadows slinking along on the ground behind her, he knew his instincts were correct. Smoky smudges of black, weaving in and out beneath of the feet of unsuspecting passersby, who would see them merely as shadows from the trees lining the sidewalk, caused by passing clouds or differing angles of sunlight. Gabriel, however, knew them for what they were: purposeful, evil harbingers of trouble, trailing after the woman like hounds on a scent.

He rose, leaving his coffee behind, and began following. Weaving his way through slow-moving cars, he crossed the street behind her, keeping her in sight as she passed several small shops, a T-shirt vendor, and an open-air fruit market. She paused, as did the shadows, which were trampled beneath her feet as she turned and walked back to the market, where bins of fresh fruits and vegetables were displayed for purchase.

Gabe entered the market area himself, pretending interest in a bin of Fiji apples while the woman grabbed a small basket from a nearby stack and began perusing some bananas, checking for bruises. She added a small bunch to her basket, then moved on to the vegetable area. A quick check of the sidewalk showed that the shadows kept their distance, blending seamlessly into the shade of a neighboring tree, but the prickle on the back of Gabe's neck told him they were still there. He'd seen them before, usually just before the death of a person whose soul was in jeopardy. They were like flies, with no powers of their own, attracted by the prospect of feeding on whatever scraps a soul eater might leave behind, and as such, were indicators that a soul eater was nearby.

Of all the demonic denizens of the Underworld, soul eaters were the ones Gabriel hated the most. In particular, he hated Nyx, Sammy's red-eyed second-in-command, whom he'd dealt with before. Part of him hoped Nyx would show up now, here, today, so he could put the filthy abomination in its place once and for all.

"Good morning, Hope. How are you today?" A plump woman in a straw hat and apron emerged from an open storefront that looked out over the fruits and vegetables. "I've got some lovely seedless grapes to go with those bananas. Add some apples and some fresh yogurt, and you've got yourself a feast."

The blond woman—whose name he now knew was Hope—answered the fruit vendor rather listlessly. "Hi, Mrs. Rodriguez. That sounds great; I'll take whatever you recommend."

"Oh," said Mrs. Rodriguez knowingly, "I definitely recommend the apples." She gestured toward the bin where Gabe was standing, deliberately drawing Hope's attention that way.

Gabriel made a point not to acknowledge that he'd overheard the remark, recognizing a blatant yet well-meant attempt at matchmaking when he heard one. Fine with him; he could easily charm his way into the blond woman's good graces, maybe buy her a coffee and keep her close while he found why she'd been marked as prey by the Darkness. He picked up an apple and examined it closely, feeling Hope's eyes rest on him briefly before she turned away, heading for the grapes.

"That's okay," she told the fruit vendor. "I'll just have some grapes and bananas. I'm not a big fan of apples."

He was a bit surprised at the summary rejection, and took a quick glimpse at her left hand to see if she wore a wedding ring. She didn't.

"I'll be right with you," the fruit vendor said to him, in a friendly fashion. She followed Hope toward the grapes, plucking a big bunch from the pile and placing them in a plastic bag she pulled from her apron.

"I need some extra bananas for my neighbor, too," Hope said. "Poor Mr. Qualey hasn't been feeling well lately, and I promised to make him homemade banana pudding."

"No offense, chica," said Mrs. Rodriguez, eyeing her customer with motherly concern, "but you don't look like you're feeling too good yourself. You doing okay?"

Hope turned away with a shrug. In profile, Gabe could see faint shadows beneath her eyes, her skin so pale it seemed translucent. "I'm fine," she answered, using her free hand to tug on the sleeve of her shirt. "I've been working pretty hard, having a little trouble sleeping."

"I've got just the thing," answered Mrs. Rodriguez. "Lavender oil. A few drops on your pillow and you'll sleep like a baby."

"Sounds great. I'll take it."

Mrs. Rodriguez bustled off into the tiny storefront. Through the open doorway Gabe could see a wall of shelves, a single refrigeration unit, and a small counter that held a cash register—not much room for danger to hide.

Hope moved on to the plums, ignoring him while he picked up an orange and brought it to his nose, enjoying the sharp scent of citrus.

"Here you go," said the fruit vendor, returning

with a small bottle in hand. "On the house. Consider it a bonus for doing such a good job on the Web site. You'll sleep good tonight, I promise."

"No, I'll pay you for it."

Mrs. Rodriguez waved away Hope's protest, dropping the bottle into her basket. "That online coupon idea was genius. We've already got over one thousand names on our Garden of Eatin' mailing list, adding more every day."

"Thanks, Mrs. R."

"You're welcome, chica. Get some sleep, eh?"

Gabe lingered while Hope finished her shopping, which didn't take long. When she stepped inside to pay her bill, he meandered a few feet down the sidewalk in the direction she'd been going, keeping an eye on the patch of shadows beneath the tree while pretending to window shop at a neighboring bookstore.

He watched her reflection in the glass as she passed behind him and saw, too, that the shadows still followed. Keeping some distance between them, he trailed along behind, on the lookout for anything that might threaten the woman's safety: a mugger, an out-of-control car, anything out of the ordinary. Human life was so fragile, something that could be taken in an instant, and while he accepted that, he never took lightly the idea of losing a soul to the Darkness. From what he'd seen of her aura, this woman's soul burned brightly at its core, yet was clearly beset; should she die today, he would do what he could to guide her toward the Light.

A couple of panhandling teenagers with spiked hair and nose rings approached her, and he tensed, but Hope freely handed over some change and went on. About a block later the Little Five Points business district was left behind, and they entered a more residential area, with a few low-rise apartment buildings and a scattering of houses.

They weren't the only two people on the sidewalk, as an elderly woman swept leaves across the street, and a young couple passed them by, hand-in-hand, so Gabe didn't feel too conspicuous. The neighborhood would've been pleasant if he hadn't been on high alert; big oak trees, green lawns, blue and pink hydrangeas in full bloom.

About a block later, Hope headed up the stairs to a small, two-story apartment building, disappearing inside. A small orange and black sign in one otherwise bare window read FOR RENT. The shadows that trailed her still followed, oozing their way in around the lobby door as it closed behind her. Gabe quickened his step, bounding up the short stairs and going in. He came to an abrupt stop at the sight of Hope, facing him in the lobby, just a few feet away. She flung out her hand, and something wet hit him directly in the face.

"Get away from me!" she shrieked, throwing the now-empty lavender oil bottle at him as hard as she could. He ducked, barely able to dodge it; it hit him on the back of the arm, just missing his head. Luckily his new sunglasses had protected his eyes from the brunt of the oil, but they were still stinging, his nose filled with the reek of lavender.

She whirled and bounded up another short flight of stairs. "Mr. Qualey!" she shouted, at the top of her lungs. "Mr. Qualey, help!"

Gabriel stayed where he was, wiping oil from his face, stunned at how easily he'd been caught off guard. Despite her small size and vulnerable air, the woman was a bit of a tigress. He heard the frantic rattle of a doorknob, followed by more shouting. "Mr. Qualey!" There was a *thump*, followed by several lesser thumps as a purple plum came rolling down the stairs to lie, bruised and battered, at his feet.

He could go away, disappear as though he'd never been, but a prickle on the back of his neck told him he'd be giving the Darkness exactly what it wanted if he did. Now that she'd seen him, he decided to stop skulking and make the best of the situation.

"I'm not going to hurt you," he said loudly, wishing Hope had chosen something less oily and smelly to hit him with. He was drowning in scent, and his attempts to wipe it away merely made it worse.

More frantic doorknob rattling and a muttered "Shit" preceded more yells for the neighbor, who apparently wasn't home.

"I said I'm not going to hurt you," Gabe repeated, irritated to feel a trickle of oil on his scalp; he'd never liked perfumed oils in his hair, even though it had once—centuries ago—been the fashion. "Lost your keys?"

There was a silence, during which he took off his sunglasses and used the hem of his T-shirt to mop his face, smearing oil all over it.

"Why are you following me? What do you want?" From the note of fear in her voice, Gabe surmised that not only was she locked out, there was no way out of the building unless she came back down the stairs. "I'm calling the police on my cell phone, right now!"

"My name is Gabriel," he told her calmly, "and I'm here to protect you."

Another silence, longer than the first. Lavender oil dripped from his sunglasses onto the lobby floor; it was even on his jeans, which was unfortunate, because they were his favorite pair.

"If I wanted to hurt you I would've done it by now," he pointed out mildly, knowing she could hear him just fine. "Being drenched in lavender oil is not much of a deterrent; it's not like it's sulphuric acid or something."

He looked up, and there was Hope's face, peeping cautiously over the edge of the stair rail. She had a cell phone in her hand.

"Protect me from what?"

"I'm not really sure," he told her honestly. "I just know you need protecting."

Her eyes, which were a startlingly vibrant shade of green, narrowed in suspicion. "Right." She cocked her head, eyeing him closely. "You need to get out of here right now, before the cops show up."

"Let them come." he said, fairly sure he knew a bluff when he heard one. "I haven't done anything."

"This is private property."

"It looks like a lobby to me. For all they know I came in to see someone about renting an apartment."

"You followed me home," she accused.

He shrugged, using the back of his arm to wipe oil from his forehead. "I'm telling you the truth when I say you need protecting. Calling the police won't change that—it may even make things worse."

"Are you *threatening* me?"

He had to admire her courage, because if he *had* been threatening her, there wouldn't be a thing she could do about it; she couldn't be more than five-four in her stocking feet, and he outweighed her by at least fifty pounds.

"I'm not threatening you." With a sigh, Gabriel told her the truth, or at least part of it. "Just the opposite, in fact . . . I'm a Guardian."

"A guardian." Her skepticism was unmistakable.

"It's true. There's no reason to be afraid of me."

"Sorry, but when a strange man follows me home, I tend to be a bit suspicious of his motives."

"I'm not *that* strange," Gabriel said, venturing a bit of humor in hopes of easing the tension. "At least I wasn't until you made me smell like a girl. This stuff is really pungent."

She didn't smile. "What are you *really* doing here?"

"I told you . . . I'm here to look after you."

"Who says I need looking after?"

He could tell her the truth, but she'd have a very hard time believing that he was an angel. Besides, revealing his angelic state was something he reserved for the very young and the very elderly, for it upset the order of the universe, turning what was meant to be a matter of faith into certainty. So, using a trick he'd learned long, long ago, he turned the question around and gave it back to her. "Think for a moment . . . is there anything going on in your life right now that frightens you?"

She went pale, two spots of color high in her cheeks. There was no mistaking the flicker of fear in her eyes as she stared down at him.

"I'm afraid you're just going to have to take my word when I tell you I'm here for a reason."

Hope stared at him silently, her mind obviously working.

"*He* sent you, didn't he?"

Gabriel said nothing, letting her believe what she liked, as long as it worked to his advantage.

"You even look like him, in a way; too fucking perfect to be real. Is that part of your deal with him, pretty boy?"

The hostility of her reply confused him, but more than that, he found himself troubled by the sound of profanity on the woman's lips, for he was oddly certain it didn't belong there.

The glare she sent him was decidedly un-friendly. "He didn't send you to protect *me*, he sent you to protect his own interests."

"Regardless," Gabe replied, taking shameless advantage of an opening. "Here I am."

"I guess I should be grateful you're not some kind of monster."

More confused than ever, Gabe chose to agree. "I guess you should."

She bit her lip, then put her hands on the stair rail and straightened. "You're not going to hurt me?"

"Hurting you would be counterproductive." Gabe was able to say the words with conviction, for that much, at least, was completely true.

"Okay, so you're my guardian." She stopped leaning over the rail and straightened, giving a shrug. "It's not like I have a whole lot of choice in the matter, now do I? Make yourself useful, Guardian, and find my keys."

Chapter Three

As it turned out, Hope found her own keys, right where they should've been, in her purse. Considering what she'd been through during the last few days—and the last few minutes—it was no wonder she'd been too rattled to find them the first time. She kept a wary eye on her new "guardian" as he picked up her bruised fruit, thinking furiously about this latest development. After twenty-four hours in an unknown bed, being transfused, fed, and frightened within an inch of her life, she'd awakened to find herself back in her own apartment. It had looked the same—no sign of her aborted suicide attempt, no blood, no razor blade—and she'd nearly been able to convince herself that it had all been a bad dream until she removed the bandages on her wrists and saw the cuts, still red and sore, indisputable reminders of failure and folly.

Then, of course, there was the book, which she found sitting squarely in the middle of her desk, just above her keyboard. So far she'd been unable to touch it, even to move it, and consequently had been unable to work.

For the last two nights, she'd lain awake, re-membering burning red eyes, whispers of dark-ness, and the rustle of blackened wings. If she hadn't promised a few days ago to make Mr. Qualey that banana pudding, she wouldn't even have ventured out today, but she'd steeled herself to move forward, act normally, hating the feeling of being paralyzed by fear.

Evidently the Devil was tired of waiting for her to get a move on, because now he'd upped the pressure by sending her some kind of sa-tanic babysitter. There was no earthly reason that anyone would be following her otherwise, and certainly no reason anyone would claim they'd been sent to look out for her.

No one ever looked out for her—ever—at least not since her parents died.

"The plums got the worst of it," he said, offer-ing her the bag of fruit.

She snatched them from him, still angry at how he'd managed to frighten her half to death. "You can cut the nice guy routine," she told him, unlocking her apartment with her free hand. "Just because I have to put up with you doesn't mean we're going to be friends."

A beautifully arched masculine brow shot up in surprise, and the sight made her even angrier, because there was no *way* any guy this gorgeous should be on the wrong side. When she'd seen him sitting at a table at Moonbeans, chin-length brown hair tucked behind his ears, wearing those awesomely cool sunglasses, her inner jaw had dropped. She'd noticed him at Garden of Eatin', too, but figured it was just a coincidence, one she didn't have time to appreciate or enjoy. It wasn't until she'd noticed him trailing along on the sidewalk behind her that she began to wonder if there wasn't more than coincidence involved, and seeing his sprint up the steps to her apartment had sent her over the edge into full-blown panic.

She didn't like full-blown panic, so now she was just pissed.

"Well," she told him shortly, "don't just stand there . . . come in, but you should know that if you lay one finger on me, *your* plums will end up just as bruised as these."

She hadn't taken that self-defense course for nothing, and she'd kick him where it hurt without a second thought if he touched her.

"I'll keep that in mind," he told her dryly, and followed her into the apartment.

Her heartbeat kicked up a notch as he closed the door behind him. She went directly to the kitchen, using action to try and drown the voice in her head that told her she was crazy for inviting a stranger into her apartment, but what choice did she have? At least he was a *human* stranger, instead of that blackened *thing* who did Sammy Divine's bidding.

A plaintive meow caught her attention, and she looked down to see Sherlock, her cat.

"Who's this?" asked Gabriel, behind her. He bent, offering his hand to the biggest gray and white feline snob on the face of the planet. Sherlock took a dainty sniff, and then, to Hope's disgust, rubbed his furry face against Gabe's fingers.

"That's Sherlock," Hope answered sourly. "He doesn't usually like strangers. It must be the lavender oil."

"Animals sense what people don't," Gabriel said, scratching the cat beneath the chin.

"Then my cat has clearly taken leave of his senses," she returned, plopping her fruit bag down on the counter a bit too hard. "Either that, or he's just hungry."

Sherlock meowed again in response.

"See? That settles that."

Her new guardian straightened, glancing around her kitchen. "Nice place. Very homey."

"Gee," she returned, opening the tiny pantry to pull out a bag of dry cat food. "I'm *so* glad you like it."

"Listen, I'm sorry if I scared you. I didn't mean to; I was just worried about letting you out of my sight."

"How reassuring." Hope wasn't interested in apologies. "I would think that scaring me would be a big part of your job."

Gabe looked puzzled, crossing his arms and placing a lean hip against her kitchen counter. "Why would I want to scare you?"

"To get me to do what you want, of course." Hope slammed the pantry door a teensy bit harder than she needed to. "But first I've got some banana pudding to make, so you're just going to have to wait." She could hardly even bring herself to look at him, although when she did, she noticed his shirt, smeared with oil, as were his cheeks and hair.

"No offense," she said, clearly meaning just

the opposite, "but maybe you should go sit in the living room. You reek."

"Whose fault is that?" A note of testiness crept into his voice.

"Yours," she said flatly.

"I'm not sure what you're so hostile about—I'm the one who was assaulted."

"Assaulted? Like you said, it's lavender oil, not sulphuric acid."

"It stinks," Gabriel said, lifting the neck of his shirt to sniff it. "I've never been a fan of lavender."

Hope rolled her eyes, pouring dry food into Sherlock's bowl. "Yeah, I'm sure brimstone would be more up your alley."

"Brimstone?"

"Never mind," she told him irritably. "Just go in the other room. I've got stuff to do." Rational or not, she'd decided to do a good deed before doing the Devil's bidding, and damned if she was going to let anything stop her. She pulled the bananas out of the bag and put them on the counter, then turned on the oven, mentally going over what she needed for the pudding: Nilla Wafers, eggs, bananas, pudding mix . . .

Checking the rack where she kept her spices, she picked up a small bottle of vanilla oil.

"Whoa." Gabriel took a step back, raising his

hands. He gave her what she would ordinarily consider one of the sexiest grins she'd ever seen, if it hadn't come from some kind of Satanist freak. "You're not going to throw that on me, too, are you?"

"Get out of my kitchen," she snapped. "I don't think you're funny, and I don't want to be your friend. If you have to be here, then stay quiet, and stay out of my way. Go read a book or something."

The look on the guy's face was almost comical. He seemed honestly offended, but Hope didn't care. The more she looked at him, the more pissed she got, because he was just so damn *perfect*. Even with oil in his hair and smears all over his clothes, he was so gorgeous it made her stomach hurt; it wasn't *fair* that he was one of the bad guys.

"Fine," he answered stiffly. "I'll just go drip lavender oil on your living room furniture, shall I?"

"Sit on the floor," she told him stonily.

"That isn't going to happen," he told her flatly. "I said I was a Guardian, not a guard dog."

Sherlock proved the guy's point by giving a soft meow, and rubbing up against his jean-clad legs.

Hope bit her lip, feeling both oddly betrayed and completely vulnerable. Throw in the fact that she was completely, utterly exhausted, and she knew full well that she was being a complete, utter bitch. Not her normal MO, and not a state she enjoyed.

"Look, I—" With a sigh, she let her shoulders slump. "The bathroom's the first door on the right," she said, gesturing down a short hallway. "Go clean up. There's soap, towels . . . everything you need." She hesitated, then added, "If you drop your shirt outside the door, I'll throw it in the washer. But"—she held up a finger in warning—"don't get any ideas, and stay away from me until it's clean and dry and I've given it back to you."

While Gabe had no objection to washing off the increasingly sticky lavender oil, he wasn't all that keen on leaving Hope alone, for he hadn't forgotten what had drawn him to her to begin with. Somewhere nearby was a soul eater who'd marked her as its target. Now that he'd openly proclaimed himself her guardian, it might stay away, but then again, it might not.

Sensing his hesitation, Hope made an exasperated noise. "I'm not going anywhere, all right? This is my house, not yours, and I'll be right here when you're done cleaning up. Now go away and let me get to work; I'm not touching that book until I'm good and ready."

Gabe, who'd restlessly prowled over to investigate a small alcove just off the kitchen, only to find it contained nothing more than laundry items, answered absently, "What book?"

When Hope didn't answer, he turned to look at her, noting how her eyes had narrowed in suspicion. "Never mind," she told him shortly. "Just give me some space."

Gabe looked down at Sherlock, who, having finished his meal, lay sprawled at ease on the kitchen floor. He found the sight reassuring, for not only did cats sense things, they saw things humans didn't, and the furry little beast's relaxation level seemed pretty high.

"Okay," he said, "but I need to check the rest of the apartment first." *The shadows could be anywhere; better safe than sorry.*

She bristled, but instead of arguing, she merely pressed her lips together for a moment, then bit out a "Fine." Marching past him, she gave him a quick tour of her apartment. "This is the living room, which as you can see, is empty." Buttery yellow paint on the walls, lots of light. The furniture was an eclectic mix of old and new, a brown leather couch and a worn velvet armchair, brightly colored throw cushions, and gleaming hardwood floors.

He trailed her down a short hallway, keeping an eye out for the shadows.

"This is the bathroom." She flipped on the light. Small, mostly white, shower curtain open, leaving nowhere for anything to hide.

"This is my bedroom, which is completely off-limits." A big room, with a comfortable-looking bed and a large, somewhat messy desk taking up an entire corner. The curtains were open, sunshine streaming into the room.

He started to push past her, intending to check the closet, but she blocked him with one slender arm. "What part of off-limits didn't you understand?" she asked him tartly. This close, she had to crane her neck to glare at him, the top of her head barely reaching his chin. Her breath smelled like pomegranates, the skin of her cheek appearing peach-soft and rosy with color.

"The closet," he murmured, strangely fascinated by how dark her lashes were, and how perfectly they framed her green eyes.

She blinked, then turned to stalk toward the closet, which she jerked open, giving him a clear view of the contents. Just some clothes on hangers, shoes on the floor, boxes on the top shelf. "Nothing there, see?"

He nodded, a bit disconcerted by how easily he'd been distracted by her closeness.

"You want to look under the bed, too?"

A soft meow came from Sherlock as the cat brushed past him, leaping onto the bed as though claiming it for his own. Yellow feline eyes met his in perfect understanding.

"No need," Gabe answered, no longer concerned that danger had followed Hope into the apartment.

"Good." She waved him away from the door, then went past him, heading back to the kitchen. "Don't be stingy with the soap."

He waited in the hallway until he heard the rattle of pots and pans as Hope rummaged in a cupboard, and took the opportunity to run his hand lightly over the front door, leaving a trace of himself there as a warning to the shadows. Then he stepped into Hope's bathroom, closing the door behind him.

Turning on the water, he stripped off his clothes, glad to be rid of his shirt, in particular. He opened the door just wide enough to drop it in the hallway outside. Showers were one of the things he truly enjoyed while in human form, so he took his time, soaping his body thoroughly and shampooing his hair twice. Then he stood beneath the hot water, letting it sluice over him as he wondered about the woman on the other side of the bathroom door, and how he could best help her.

Her hostility was unexpected, even though he'd bungled things a bit by charging up her front stairs. Every bit of evidence he'd seen pointed to her being a kindhearted soul: the whiteness of her aura, the friendliness and concern of the fruit vendor, her solicitude toward an elderly neighbor, even her offer to wash his shirt. Yet she didn't seem to like him very much, and it wasn't a reaction he was used to. In his experience, women were usually grateful for whatever help he offered, in whatever form he offered it. Hope's response to his presence left him puzzled.

When the water began to run cold, he shut it off, and moved aside the shower curtain to step from the tub. It was then he saw the edge of a photo, sticking out beneath the bathroom rug. Carefully, not wanting to ruin it with wet fingers, he lifted the rug to see it better.

Two young women, smiling and happy, one of them Hope. She looked younger in this picture, more carefree, her arm looped loosely around the shoulders of the other woman. It was plain they were sisters, both blond, though Hope's eyes were green and the other's brown.

Somewhere outside the bathroom door, she'd turned on some music, and he cocked his head, listening. Strings, horns, a woman singing in a low contralto. He found it pleasing, unlike much of the discordant noise that passed for music these days.

Drying his hands carefully on a towel, Gabe picked up Hope's picture and put it atop a nearby clothes hamper, propping it where he could see it. Then he turned to the mirror, steamy from his shower. There was a comb and a brush on the counter by the sink, so he picked up the comb and used it, wincing as he worked some of the tangles from his hair. He'd trimmed it recently, for long hair was not the current fashion, but truth be told, it was his one vanity, and he didn't like wearing it short. Consequently, he was still able to tuck it behind his ears. Shaving was easy—he'd seen a disposable razor in the shower, but merely passing a hand over his face removed any trace of stubble.

Naked, clean, and oddly relaxed, Gabe stared at his reflection in the mirror for a moment, wondering what was like to live in a house like this, surrounded by the small touches that made it a home: damp towels, steamy mirrors, pictures of those you loved. A nest of sorts, a place of safety to be shielded from the world.

It was a peaceful here, in this home Hope had made for herself. Whatever darkness gathered, regardless of her unexplained hostility, he would drive it back, or his name was not Gabriel, Angel of Light.

He could not, however, gain Hope's confidence naked, and lack of clothing suddenly became a minor problem. Despite her admonition to stay away from her until his shirt was dry, he had no intention of doing so, shirt or no shirt. With a shrug, Gabe pulled on his jeans, wrapped a towel around his neck, and left the bathroom in search of his destiny.

Chapter Four

Hope did her best to get her emotions under control while Gabriel was in the shower. Once she'd heard the bathroom door close a second time, she'd put his reeking shirt into the washer and had a long talk with herself while slicing bananas, mixing up the pudding and layering a baking pan with Nilla Wafers. Whipping egg whites and sugar into a froth for the topping was therapeutic, and she had to stop herself from overdoing it and ruining the meringue. Once the pudding was in the oven, she'd turned on some music to drown the voices in her head, the ones screaming that she was crazy for inviting a stranger into her apartment, the ones that told her she'd lost her mind the night she tried to kill herself. Now she stared out the tiny kitchen window at the hummingbird feeder she'd put there, hoping for a distraction, but the hummingbirds stayed away.

Good-looking guys made her nervous; every time she'd been around one he'd turned out to be a loser. She'd never been a party girl like Charity; it seemed as though her sister had only to smile, and guys would fall at her feet. Unfortunately, Charity had a way of choosing the *wrong* guys, usually based on how pretty they were, and she'd mopped up a lot of her sister's tears when they'd all turned out to be faithless jerks.

Her own track record wasn't much better, though much more limited. She could claim only two serious boyfriends in her whole life, if you counted Jimmy Macafee back in high school, which she wasn't sure she did. They'd never done more than kiss, and the rumor at her last high school reunion was that he'd come out of the closet after his mom died.

She'd had opportunities to date, but she'd never had the *time*. Working two jobs to put herself through college, acting as mom to her wild-child younger sister . . . men, and the emotional turmoil that came with them, had been on the bottom of her list, particularly after Boyfriend #2 had dumped her for the boss's daughter after taking a job at a law firm in Boston.

Lost in thought, Hope vaguely realized that the shower, along with the washing machine, had stopped.

"How's the baking coming?"

Hope jumped, then could only stare, stupefied, as Gabriel walked back into her kitchen.

Broad-shouldered, beautifully muscled. What she could see of his chest was smooth and broad, tapering to a flat belly. A faint line of dark hair trailed downward, disappearing into his jeans.

Bare feet. Very *big* bare feet. Very *male* bare feet.

"Sorry about the towel." Gabriel smiled at her, showing white, even teeth. "But it was better than nothing."

Not by much. Aware her mouth was open, Hope shut it.

"I really enjoyed that shower. I feel like a whole new man."

Uncomfortably aware that he probably felt better than most, Hope turned away, clearing her throat.

"There's no need to be afraid of me, Hope. I'm harmless, I swear."

He looked about as harmless as a damp, half-naked satyr set loose among the vestal virgins, none of whom would be able to resist him.

"Your shirt just finished washing." She jerked a thumb toward the washer. "You can put it in the dryer now."

"Thanks." He walked over, and her eyes were drawn like a magnet to his ass.

Damn eyes.

"Ummm . . ." Clearly having mastered the "helpless male" routine, he glanced at her over one towel-clad shoulder as she quickly looked elsewhere. "I'm not really sure how to work these things."

Great, she thought, *probably lives with his mother.* She opened the oven and checked on the pudding, glad she hadn't yet burned the meringue. "Just a second," she told him, sliding the pan out and putting it on rack to cool. *Probably how he got into this "dark side" crap to begin with . . . too many games of Diablo in his mom's basement.*

Mocking him in her mind helped steady her, so after she closed the oven door she was able to ease past him and go through the mundane motions of moving his T-shirt from the washer to the dryer without any problems.

"Whatever that is, it smells great," he said. "Looks good, too."

"You can't have any," she told him shortly. "It's for my neighbor."

"Kind of you to do that for him."

She shrugged.

"What happened to your wrist? Did you hurt yourself?"

Frozen with her finger on the dryer button, Hope stared at the bandage on her wrist. It was crusted with dried blood, an indisputable reminder that no matter how many banana puddings she made or elderly neighbors she brought the paper in for, she was going to burn in Hell one way or another. Here she was thinking about all the guys she'd never loved and lost, when none of it mattered, not the slightest bit. Even the bloodstain on the bandage was in the shape of a lopsided heart, reflecting her entire lopsided life, and Hope was seized with a sudden, inappropriate need to laugh. She wanted to laugh, and laugh, and never stop laughing. Then maybe she could be left alone, in a quiet room, where no one could ever expect anything from her, ever again.

"You've been bleeding," Gabriel said quietly.

Yes, I have, for a long, long time.

She turned on the dryer and lowered her hand, tugging at her sleeve until the gauze was covered. "It's okay. I'm okay."

"What happened?" he asked again. "Tell me." His voice was kind, but she didn't want his kindness.

She shrugged. "I was stupid, that's all." Brushing past him, she went into the living room, immediately changing the subject. "When the buzzer goes off your shirt will be done. It shouldn't take long. You can watch TV while you wait."

Then she walked to the couch and plopped down on it, but instead of reaching for the remote, she stared blindly toward the window overlooking Mr. Qualey's rooftop garden. The sweet old man was one the reasons she'd rented the place, actually . . . she could've afforded a bigger apartment, but the place was cozy and the neighborhood was nice, and when he'd shown her around he'd been so kind, so fatherly, that she hadn't bothered to look anywhere else.

"Hope." Gabriel followed her into the living room. He took a seat in the chair opposite her. "I know something's troubling you. Tell me what it is. Maybe I can help."

She turned her head to look at him. The light from the window streamed over the bare skin of his shoulder, catching the glints of gold in his damp brown hair. What in the world would a guy like him *ever* know about how it felt to carry the weight of the world on his shoulders? What would he ever know about hopelessness and despair?

"It's none of your business," she told him bluntly, unwilling to expose any more of herself. "I've been going through a rough time, that's all."

"Okay." He took her rebuff with equanimity. "If you can't talk to me, is there someone else you can talk to?"

She shook her head, wishing he'd stop talking.

"What about your sister?"

Her already racing heart gave a thump. She hadn't said a word to him about Charity. "What about my sister?" She put hopelessness and despair aside, and sat up straight. "What do you know about Charity?"

"Nothing, really." He shook his head. "I found a picture on the bathroom floor," he said. "You two look too much alike to be anything but sisters."

"Oh." *The picture.* The one she hadn't been able to find once she got home, the one taken by the fountain in Little Five Points the day she'd gotten her computer engineering degree.

A not-so-subtle reminder from Sammy Divine, no doubt, left just where Gabriel would find it.

"You looked happy in that picture," he told her gently, "but you don't look happy now."

"I'm fine," she said tonelessly, hearing the lie in her words. "I'm just feeling a little . . . weird today, that's all."

He glanced again at her wrist. Even though she'd already pulled her shirtsleeves down over the gauze, they both knew the bandage was there. "You hurt yourself on purpose."

She met his eyes, gold-flecked brown sparked with light from the window.

"You blame yourself for something," he murmured, and reached out across the small space that separated them to put his hand atop one of hers. "Tell me what it is."

His skin touched hers, and for Hope, it seemed time stood still. The heat of his palm felt like the sun, bathing the back of her hand with liquid warmth. She swallowed hard at the sensation, and stayed quiet, unmoving.

There were smile lines at the corners of his eyes, though he wasn't smiling now. He smelled of soap and dampness, and she wanted more than anything to have met him under different circumstances; circumstances that didn't involve a missing sister, suicide, Satan, or his demons of Darkness.

But the Devil called the tune these days, and she could do nothing but dance to it.

"I really don't want to talk about my problems," she told him calmly, and withdrew her hand.

Gabriel leaned back, considering. Hope's behavior was erratic, veering from hostile to quiet and subdued. There was a definite sadness in her eyes, but she was clearly not going to offer any confidences.

So be it; he enjoyed a challenge.

Rising from the chair, he turned his back to look out the window. "Somebody has a green thumb." There was a garden on the roof opposite, full of potted plants and flowers: bursts of reds, oranges, pinks. A vine-covered trellis bloomed white, sprays of yellow from hanging baskets. A couple of wicker chairs sat in the shade of a small awning, a book and a cup evidence that someone sat there recently.

"That's Mr. Qualey's garden." Gabe caught the quick flash of a halfhearted smile reflected in the window before Hope lowered her head. "The man I baked the pudding for. He's out there at the crack of dawn every morning, just like clockwork. Calls it his own little Eden."

Gabe was quiet for a moment, remembering the indescribable beauty of the original garden, knowing it could never be duplicated.

The music she'd begun listening to while he

was in the shower still played, a woman's voice, low and exotic, a rhythm that spoke of love and longing. "I like this music," he said. "It's very soothing. Who is it?"

"Sade."

"That's a beautiful name. Is she a friend of yours?"

Hope gave a small snort of laughter, her first. "Hardly."

"Yet you refer to her by her first name."

"You've never heard of Sade?"

"I haven't." He looked over his shoulder, grinning at her tone of disbelief. "I don't get out much."

"Just as I suspected," she murmured, with another little laugh.

He shifted the focus of his gaze, letting the window act as a mirror, reflecting Hope on the sofa. She looked different when she laughed, younger, her face open and unguarded.

She couldn't be more than thirty, and he wondered about her: Who were her friends? What did she do for a living? Why had she tried to take her own life?

He had no illusions about the wound on her wrist—the way she'd shut down when he asked about it told him more than she realized.

"I like your apartment," he told her, making

small talk to keep her at ease. "What do you do for a living?"

She gave him a sharp upward glance that she wasn't aware he'd seen, and cautiousness returned to her gaze. "Not very informed for a guardian, are you?"

"Just making conversation," he answered lightly.

"I work with computers," she told him shortly.

For a moment, he stayed quiet, merely watching her in the window. Her short blond hair suited her, displaying the bones of her face to advantage. Her features were anything *but* boyish: small and delicate, elegantly feminine.

He turned to face her, arms crossed over his chest. "You look tired."

"Gee, thanks." There was no mistaking the sarcasm that crept into her tone.

"I think you should go to sleep."

She rolled her eyes. "Yeah? I don't think that's going to happen."

"Yes, it is."

She frowned, but before she could say anything further, he exercised a power that was as easy as breathing, and sent a wave of calm to wash over her, bathing her in peace. It wouldn't last, of course, but it was enough to cause her eyes to close, and that was all it took; she slumped to the side as though drugged, sleeping the sleep of the truly exhausted.

Sherlock padded into the living room, furry gray tail held high, and leapt onto the couch beside her. Gabriel smiled at the faithfulness of such a fickle creature, further evidence of Hope's kind nature.

"You were a stray, weren't you?" he murmured to the cat, who answered him with half-closed eyes and the twitch of the tail.

Knowing patience was a virtue, Gabe took a seat in the chair opposite, content to watch over his charge while she slept. Perhaps, if he was lucky, she'd be in a better mood when she woke up, and might even cease to snap at him. His eyes roamed the room, lighting on yet another picture of Hope with her sister. Charity, she'd said her name was, and Gabe smiled grimly as he realized the irony: Hope and Charity, together as one. The one thing required, yet conspicuous by its absence, was Faith.

He looked at her, so pale and slight against the cushions, and saw again her aura, surrounding her with a faint white glow. The black swarm he'd seen was absent, but he didn't fool himself into believing it was gone. This woman had her own demons, and until she confronted them head-on, they would never go away.

Chapter Five

"He's taken the bait, Master."

Samael, Prince of Darkness, did not stir from his contemplation of the fire. He spent many hours here, in this hard-backed chair, carved with arcane symbols and blackened with age. In this chair he heard nothing but the crackle of flames, and thought of nothing save the yearnings of his own heart.

"Did he now?" he asked Nyx idly. He knew exactly who Nyx was referring to, having arranged the meeting between Hope and Gabriel himself, and chosen the Throne of Nothingness to await the results. Gabe thought himself so clever, keeping an eye on Nicki Styx while thinking Sammy none the wiser; he would learn that Little Five

Points, Georgia, was no safer for an angel's heart than it was for a devil's, and maybe even learn to mind his own business in the process. "Why am I not surprised?"

Nyx edged closer, stepping from the shadows into Sammy's line of sight. The tips of his wings quivered, a sure sign of anticipation, eyes glowing red in the firelight. "The Lightbringer is in her apartment," the Chief Servant reported. "Shall I challenge him now?"

"No." Unconcerned, Sammy leaned back in the chair, extending his long legs toward the fire and hooking bare feet at the ankle. His robe, woven from cobwebs by the Dryads of Doom, kept him warm when all else about him was cold. "The game is barely begun, my friend, and all the sweeter for it."

"I don't understand."

"I don't expect you to."

Of course Nyx wouldn't understand; the delicate dance between man and woman was far beyond him, for when Sammy created him, he hadn't understood it himself.

Now he did, perhaps too well.

The walls of the bedchamber, his private sanctuary, were hung with tapestries that had once adorned the palaces of kings. Gold and silver thread caught the glitter of firelight, deceiving the eye into thinking the pageantry they depicted— colorful jousts, processions, hunting scenes, mythical creatures—were real, and important, when in actuality they were flat, lifeless memories of days long past.

"But the Darkness, my lord," Nyx made bold to protest, disturbing Sammy's reverie. "It's hungry. The ethereals are sorely depleted in number, as are the imps. The demon Ashtaroth has traditionally been given the souls of suicides to replenish himself; he needs them now more than ever."

"The hounds of Hell are always baying, old friend. There's not enough blood on Earth to satisfy them."

The door to Sammy's bedchamber flew open, banging loudly against the opposite wall.

"Where've you been, Father?" Cain, Sammy's nine-year-old son and the current bane of his existence, burst into the room with no regard for his father's privacy. "Where did you get that robe? Is it velvet? Can I have one, too?"

Wincing at the sudden assault to both his ears *and* his nose, Samael the Fallen regarded Cain with exasperation, unable to explain the sudden lift he felt in the region of his nonexistent heart.

"You reek of brimstone," Sammy told the

boy shortly, answering none of his questions. "I thought I told you to stay away from the pit."

Cain, his son by Persephone, the fey, amoral Goddess of the Underworld, was every bit as elusive and impulsive as his mother. Sammy had known of the boy's existence for only a few short weeks, and among the first things he'd learned were that the little hellion liked to roam, and didn't take orders well.

A careless nine-year-old shrug answered him. "The imps are the only ones who will play with me." Cain moved toward a bowl of fruit on a nearby table and snatched an apple in one very dirty hand. "Everyone else is afraid."

"As well they should be," Sammy agreed. "You're a troublesome little son of a—"

"They're not afraid of *me*," Cain interrupted him, talking around a bite of apple. "They're afraid of *you*, and what you might do to them if anything happened to me."

"I'd reward them handsomely," Sammy lied, "and don't talk with your mouth full."

"You had Thamuz torn limb from limb for losing me in the Canyons of Despair," the boy said cheerfully, "and you almost destroyed the Dread Demon Ashtaroth with flaming serpents of fire for trying to claim my soul." Blithely, the boy clambered onto the goose down coverlet atop his father's bed, leaving streaks of soot in his wake. "Tesla told me all about it."

"Tesla is a gibbering fool, who had best watch his tongue, or I'll have it removed much the same way Thamuz's was." Privately he despised the imps, but they were a necessary evil.

The tinge of ice in Sammy's tone did not go unnoticed by the boy, whose pale blue eyes—so like his father's—widened. "No! Don't do that!" He swallowed his bite of apple, looking contrite for the first time. "Please don't hurt Tesla . . . he's my only friend!"

Annoyed to find himself troubled by the real fear in the boy's voice, Sammy looked away, toward the tapestry of a mythical unicorn, so pure and white in its garden of green, unaware that the beautifully embroidered bushes surrounding it held hunters, moving in for the kill.

"Tesla can't help the fact that he talks too much," the boy went on. "The imps are trained to cause trouble, you know they are!"

Sighing heavily, Sammy rose from his chair. "Get off the bed, you filthy little beast."

Cain obeyed with uncharacteristic alacrity, smearing soot into the coverlet even more deeply than before.

"You will bathe, and then we will eat together at table, you and I," he told the boy sternly. "It's time you learned some manners." Well aware that his second-in-command watched him closely, Sammy resisted an urge to ruffle his son's white blond hair. "But before that, we need to have a chat." Casting a deliberately careless glance in Nyx's direction, he clipped, "Leave us."

The demon didn't hesitate, bowing smoothly in agreement before leaving the room, closing the door gently behind him.

Cain looked at him warily, clutching his half-eaten apple as though he might need to throw it. The sight pained the poor excuse for a heart Sammy no longer had.

"You must guard against forming friendships among the imps, my son." He was still unused to the phrase, but found it easier to utter each time he said it. "They're bred to take advantage of weakness, and not to be trusted."

"You're the one who made them that way."

Sammy was unsure if such directness was common in nine-year-olds, or whether it was part of what made Cain unique unto himself. "Yes, I did," he agreed. "They're unscrupulous and amoral. Their job is to see inside the souls of the damned to find what thoughts most torment them, and to exploit those thoughts without mercy." With no one to witness it, he gave in to the urge to touch Cain's hair, as tousled as his own, but not nearly as clean. "Which is why you can't trust them. In fact, you can trust no one here in Sheol—it's not a place where you can let your guard down."

"Why do you live here, then?"

Sammy smiled a bitter smile. "Better to rule in Hell than serve in Heaven."

"Have you ever been to Heaven?"

The stab of pain the question brought was an old one, as familiar as his own reflection in the mirror. "Yes."

Skies without end, the laughter of his brother angels as they played hide-and-seek among the clouds.

"The humans claim it's a beautiful place." The boy's eyes were far too shrewd for those of a nine-year-old. "But you like it better here?"

"Yes," lied the Father of Lies.

"Then I like it here, too." *Dirty, defiant, and too naïve to be afraid—how much the boy reminded him of himself, once upon a time.*

"It doesn't matter if you like it or not." Sammy gave his son a tired smile. "For here is where we are, and here we shall remain."

* * *

An hour later, bathed and dressed, Cain looked at his father across a table strewn with gilt plates and heavy crystal and stated, "I'm not hungry anymore. Can I go now?"

"No, you cannot," Sammy answered calmly. They were in the most formal of his dining rooms, the one he privately found the most soothing. Deep red walls and black furniture, spare and simple, candlelight instead of electricity. "Pick up your napkin and spread it in your lap."

Cain gave a long-suffering sigh, but did as he was told. Freshly scrubbed and glowing with health, he was a beautiful child...cherub-cheeked, with hair that held his mother's curl. "There are too many forks," he complained, frowning down at the table. "And the food looks weird."

Sammy arched a brow. "Weird?"

"There are no rolls," the boy went on, "and no fruit. What's that gloppy black stuff?"

"That"—Sammy smiled and picked up a small triangle of toast—"is caviar." With a tiny spoon, he heaped a small portion of roe onto the toast, and handed it to the boy. "Normally we would have it as an appetizer—it's best with champagne, which you're not allowed to have, by the way—but I wanted you to try it. You'll love it."

Cain took the toast, making a face as he examined the caviar closely, taking a sniff. "It smells like fish."

"It is fish. Raw fish eggs, in fact."

"Ew." Cain put the toast down without trying it. "That's disgusting. I'm not eating that."

Sammy blinked, unused to his wishes being so summarily dismissed. "It's a delicacy," the Great and Mighty Satan explained, in an utmost attempt at patience. "Meant to be appreciated in small bites. Taste it."

"No." There was no truculence in the boy's tone, merely a calm statement of refusal.

Sammy's brow darkened, storm clouds gathering, but before they burst there came a *whoosh* of wind that set the candles aflutter. Sammy and Cain both looked toward the door, newly opened, and the dark-haired woman standing in it.

"Really, darling," the woman drawled, stepping into the room, "you can't possibly expect the child to enjoy caviar—it's an acquired taste, and his taste buds have yet to develop." She was beautiful, sloe-eyed, and curvaceous, clad in spangled robes of midnight blue.

"Pandora," said Sammy, with an affectionate grin, "how lovely to see you." He rose, coming around the table to take her by the hand, placing a kiss on one alabaster cheek. She accepted such tribute as her due, looking every inch the goddess she was, gold dripping from her ears, neck, and fingers. The torque around her neck gleamed with jewels that caught the candlelight and reflected it back into the eyes of the beholder.

"I beg your pardon, Master," said Nyx, at Pandora's shoulder. "She slipped past me."

"Pooh, go away, you ghoul." Pandora gave the Chief Servant of Satan the back of her hand, not deigning to turn and look at him. "I'm as fast as I was three thousand years ago, while you're getting to be an old man. Leave us."

Nyx's eyes flared red, but his master gave him a nod, and he faded back into the shadows.

"And as for you," she said to Sammy, with mock severity, "how long were you going to keep the wonderful news of a son and heir from your Pandora?" She reached out one plump, beringed hand, and poked the Prince of Darkness quite firmly in the shoulder. "I'd given up waiting for your invitation to visit, and decided to issue one for myself."

Sammy, amused as always by Pandora's careless impudence, allowed himself to be brushed past as she focused on Cain, sitting silent and wide-eyed at the table.

"And this must be the princeling," Pandora

crooned, reaching out both plump arms. "Get up and give your Aunt Pandy a hug."

Cain—who, Sammy had noticed, already had an eye for the ladies—obeyed with alacrity, and immediately found himself engulfed by soft, fragrant female flesh, spangled in blue.

"Yes, yes," Sammy said, unsure of whether to be proud or concerned over the boy's enthusiasm, "Pandora, meet Cain. Cain, meet Pandora."

"He's *adorable*, darling," Pandora exclaimed. "Your very image! Look at those eyes."

"We were just about to eat." Samael redirected her attention to the table. "Why don't you join us?"

"I couldn't possibly," she demurred, immediately moving toward a seat.

Instantly Nyx materialized, pulling the chair out for Pandora with all due respect. She ignored him, settling herself with a sigh of pleasure. Her napkin went into her lap with a flourish, an action Cain watched with interest.

Sammy resumed his seat, and indicated that Cain should do the same. "Pandora is an old friend of mine," he told the boy.

"Tut, tut," she said, raising a perfectly manicured finger. "Never use my name in a sentence that contains the word 'old.' "

"I beg your pardon," the High Prince of Darkness murmured, with a smile. He'd always had a soft spot for Pandora. She was cheerful, and clever, and relentlessly curious, which made her not only useful, but a wonderful bed partner. They'd enjoyed each other many times over the eons, spacing their visits by decades, even centuries, so they never tired of each other.

He didn't trust her, of course, but then he trusted no one.

"What are you feeding this child, you ghoul?" This remark was addressed sharply over Pandora's shoulder, to Nyx, who waited in the shadows. "Boys this age don't want fish eggs, they want meat!"

"I don't eat meat," Cain quickly interjected. "But I do love bread and fruit."

Sammy raised his brows at this new bit of information. "You don't eat *meat*? Since when?"

"Since I realized it was once living flesh," the boy told him boldly, looking him directly in the eye. "I'm not a cannibal."

"Oh my," Pandora murmured, "the cub is much like his sire, in a 'don't tell me what to do' kind of way. How amusing."

Not as amused as his guest, Sammy shot her a look.

"Don't glower so," she told him. "Of course the

child has his hackles up . . . what kind of setting is this for a boy his age?" She lifted her hands to indicate the formality that surrounded them. "He's full of energy, and needs to run and play, not be stifled by gilt and crystal."

Cain nodded vigorously, looking worshipfully at his new Aunt Pandy. "I'm not even hungry," he offered eagerly. "I told him that, but he didn't listen."

It was Sammy's first experience at being double-teamed, and he wasn't sure he liked it.

"I have a suggestion," Pandora said, reaching out a soft, perfumed hand to lay atop Sammy's. "Why don't you let Cain run along, and we'll have dinner together alone"—her thumb stroked the back of his—"the way we used to in the old days."

Annoyed as he was by being crossed, as he looked across the table at his son's hopeful face, Sammy could find no real reason to make him stay.

Pandora's hand squeezed his again, giving him a real reason for the boy to go. "Perhaps"—she dimpled at him, arching a brow coyly—"if you're very, very nice to me, I shall visit more often, and help you turn this young princeling into a prince."

Since Sammy privately admitted that he had absolutely no idea what he was doing when it came to rebellious nine-year-old boys (never having been one), the idea was tempting. "Very well."

Cain leapt to his feet, ready to bolt.

"But I will see you in your chamber at eight, and you will read me a full chapter from Leviticus."

"Yes, Father," the boy said. "I will." He paused by Pandora's chair. "Good-bye, Aunt Pandy," he told her. "I hope I see you again."

"You will," she told him, pulling him in for another hug. "Go, and have fun."

And then he was gone, racing from the room.

"Nyx," said Sammy shortly, "make sure he stays away from the pit. It won't hurt him to be separated from the imps for a while."

"As you wish, Master," said the demon, interpreting his instructions correctly as a dismissal. He faded out of the room, closing the door gently behind him.

"Really, darling . . . Leviticus?" Pandora dropped his hand and regarded him with lazy amusement. "Why would you give the child such dreary reading material?"

Sammy shrugged, reaching for his half-empty wineglass. "So that he knows his history, and knows his enemies."

"He's a charmer, that one." She smiled and

leaned back in her chair, deliberately displaying her ample bosom to advantage. "You must be ecstatic."

" 'Ecstatic' is not quite the word for it," he murmured, taking a sip of his wine.

"The Great and Mighty Satan, now father to a nine-year-old boy," Pandora mused. "How will it change you, I wonder?"

Sammy's hand stilled on his glass. He didn't want to change, he didn't *need* to change, and damn Pandora's curiosity for making the leap across that particular chasm. "What do you mean?" he asked abruptly.

"Oh, darling, of course you'll be changed, all parents are." Pandora shrugged, a graceful shrug that made her jewelry glitter in the candlelight. "I don't have firsthand knowledge, of course, but it's a well-known fact that offspring are both a challenge and a responsibility. The experience can't help but change you." She rose from her chair, trailing a beringed finger along the table as she moved toward him. "No need to worry about it, though. You'll be fine." She'd reached his chair, and came up behind him, running her plump hands over his shoulders, and up, though his hair. Her lips were against his ear, her breath fragrant on his cheek. "You are Ruler of the Abyss, Lucifer,

Son of Morning. There is no challenge you cannot meet, no responsibility you cannot bear."

Sammy relaxed a bit, leaning his head back against the seat. Pandora not only knew how to use her femininity to advantage, she knew the value of stroking a man's ego along with his organ.

Her fingers were busy on his chest, undoing the buttons of his shirt to touch his bare skin, removing any obstacles in their path. "I've missed you, my darling," she breathed in his ear. "It seems eons."

"It has been eons," he agreed, closing his eyes to the feel of her hand on the fastening of his trousers. "Several centuries at least."

His cock, already thickening, was released into her plump, warm hand. Rewarding her with a growl of pleasure, Sammy stayed quiescent, allowing her to press heated kisses to his neck and ear as she squeezed and stroked, bringing his staff to full hardness. When he'd had enough of that, he stilled her hand, lifting it for a kiss as he rose from the chair.

Pandora was a soft armful of woman, and he thoroughly enjoyed the feel of her bottom through her blue spangled dress. He enjoyed even more lifting that dress until his fingers could slip beneath it to touch the silk of her skin. Standing, his hardness pressed to the softness of her belly, he did some squeezing and stroking of his own, sliding his fingers down and between the crease of her ass, seeking the damp heat between her legs, until Pandora was gasping against his throat. Her delicate little hands clutched his shoulders, kneading and pulling, her lush breasts against his chest.

Soon, the delightfulness of her bottom was no longer enough, and with the sweep of an arm, he cleared room on the table.

Pandora shrieked with delight, laughing up at him as he caught her about the waist and lifted her onto the table. She threw back her head as he tugged down the midnight blue straps of her dress, revealing her full, round breasts, capped with caramel-colored nipples, pointed and erect.

Burying his face between those ripe mounds, Sammy pressed the softest of kisses to each before laving them both with his tongue.

Pandora gasped in pleasure, clasping the back of his head with beringed fingers. Her legs came up, the fabric of her dress like spangled midnight spilled across her thighs and belly, sliding upward beneath his hands as he ran them over her warm flesh. Her arms, freed from her gown, came around him, stroking his back before tugging his shirt free from his trousers. A moment later, and it was gone, Pandora's clever little hands warm on his bare skin.

Cupping her full breasts within his palms, Sammy continued to play with them, sucking, licking and kneading. She keened her pleasure as he took one of her nipples in his teeth, biting it gently while tickling it with his tongue. Her throat arched, and she lay back on the table in surrender, giving him full access to her lush body.

Her belly rose against his chest, her legs twining around his hips like snakes as she writhed beneath him, her jewelry reflecting the candlelight, her hair a dark pool of ink, studded with diamonds.

She was the banquet, she the dessert, and Sammy found himself suddenly starving. His cock, hard as iron, sought the soft heat between her thighs, and with a thrust that made them both gasp, found it.

Engulfed by her honeyed warmth, Sammy closed his eyes, imagining—just for an instant— that the woman he held in his arms had eyes the color of chocolate and dark hair, streaked with pink. Would Nicki Styx have felt like all the others, he wondered, or would she have been unique unto herself?

Knowing the answer in his heart, and scarce able to bear it, he wiped all thought from his mind by the simple expedient of moving his hips, driving himself deeper into Pandora's welcoming warmth, and giving himself up to her cries of pleasure, her grasping hands, and her beautiful, luxurious womanhood.

After all, he'd thrown away any hope of Heaven for a taste of this kind of pleasure, so there was no need to deny himself now.

Chapter Six

Throughout what was left of the morning, and into the early afternoon, Hope slept on while Gabe kept watch. When his shirt was dry he donned it, enjoying the brush of clean cotton against his skin. He lingered in her kitchen, noting all the small personal touches that proclaimed it hers: various magnets and photos on the refrigerator, a red and white checked dish towel hanging on a hook, African violets blooming on the windowsill. A flash of movement caught his eye, but it was merely a hummingbird, come to sip delicately from a bright red feeder just outside the window. He smiled at a small wooden plaque above the counter that read, "Blessed are those who can laugh at themselves, for they shall never cease to be amused," but his smile faded as he thought about how Hope had apparently failed to take that particular piece of advice.

In the other room, the music still played, and for a brief moment in time it seemed as though all the world was calm and safe and quiet. Gabe drank in the feeling, knowing it was an illusion, but grateful for it anyway.

Then he stepped back into the living room, and just as quickly, the illusion was over.

Through the window, in the garden opposite Hope's apartment, the shadows were once again on the move.

From beneath the awning they came, moving toward the sliding glass doors that led inside the neighbor's apartment, swarming like sharks to a feed. Gabriel glanced at Hope, still sleeping, and had but moments to make his decision: stay, or go?

Then he thought of the dessert, cooling on the counter, and the care she'd taken with it despite whatever was troubling her, and the decision was made. She cared about the old man who'd planted that garden, and he would do what he could before it was too late.

In seconds, he'd left her apartment and entered the one across the hall. The door was unlocked, and he found himself in a small living room, messier than Hope's and not nearly as cheerful. The air was stale, the curtains drawn, leaving the interior dim.

A small groan came from a room at the end of the hallway, and Gabe wasted no time finding its source. An old man, eyes closed, was lying on a bed. He was fully dressed, the bed neatly made, shades drawn. At Gabe's approach, the shadows, already gathered in a far corner of the room, drew back, but didn't flee entirely, as he'd hoped.

Another glance told him why: the old man was pale as parchment, death clearly stamped on his features. He was portly, his belly high and round, wispy stands of white on his nearly bald head.

There was nothing Gabriel could do, save what he was best at, so without a word, he went to sit at the old man's side, and took his hand.

At his touch, the man's eyes opened, struggling to focus.

Gabe smiled at him reassuringly, letting the man see—for an instant—his true form, making sure he saw his own precious grace reflected in Gabe's eyes.

" 'Yea, though I walk through the valley of the

shadow of death, I will fear no evil,'" he murmured softly, feeling a faint twitch as the old man tried to squeeze his hand.

"I—" A blink, then another, from the man on the bed. Shock, recognition, and then, inevitably, a sort of grateful acceptance. "I've sinned," he whispered to Gabe hoarsely.

"No man is without sin," Gabriel told him softly. "By grace are you saved; a gift of the One, freely offered."

The shadows began to recede, swarming angrily into a small knot, like bees returning to the hive.

A gasp of pain came from the man, a hitch in his breath. Gabe held his hand tighter, keeping his voice low as he repeated the Twenty-third Psalm, having done it so many times he'd lost count. Dying was an inevitable part of life, but the transition was often frightening; the visual imagery of the psalm soothed as much as the words themselves.

"I was wrong," rasped the man. "So wrong. Unfaithful. My wife, she didn't deserve it; when she found out, she left, took the kids with her." A tear slipped from his eye, running down his temple toward the pillow. "Never forgave me, until the day she died. I ruined everything."

Gabe bowed his head, hearing the old man's pain and regret in his words, letting him speak them while he had the chance.

"Always loved her," the man whispered. "So sorry."

There were photos on the dresser, old and faded: a smiling young woman in a gingham dress, dark hair carefully styled, candid shots of her holding a birthday cake, a swaddled baby, two small children posed before a Christmas tree.

"You'll see her again," Gabe told him quietly, "and she won't be angry anymore." There was no room for anger where the old man was going—if he'd died alone, his guilt and fear might've made him susceptible to a soul eater, but no longer, for Gabriel flooded his dying soul with Light, letting him see what awaited him on the other side.

"Muriel?" the old man whispered, his eyes no longer seeing Gabe, or the darkened room in which he lay. "Muriel, is that you?" A look of joy and wonder spread over his tired, wrinkled face, and in the next instant, he was gone, hand going limp in Gabriel's grasp.

The shadows were gone, the corner empty, but Gabe sat there for a while anyway, letting the Light that flowed from his face and hands continue to bathe the old man's body. Then he let the

Light dim, resuming human form, and rose from the bed. He went to the dresser and picked up Muriel's photo, studying it.

The old man had loved her, yet hurt her anyway, then carried the guilt of doing so for the rest of his life. He looked at the children's faces, so bright with happiness as they posed on Christmas morning, and wondered how, once having known such trust, such joyous responsibility, a man could throw it all away for a night or two of pleasure. Tracing the outline of Muriel's cheek with his finger, he imagined how she must've looked on her wedding day when the world was full of hope, her smile when she lay in the arms of the man she loved, her expression when she'd held her first child. Somehow, though the face in the portrait was a stranger's, the face he saw in his mind's eye was Hope's, who lay sleeping across the hall. An ache formed in the region of his heart, for he would never see such things firsthand, and a part of him—for the first time—regretted it.

Love was beautiful and terrible and strange, but he—not being human—would never experience it.

He could do nothing but marvel at its power, and wonder.

* * *

Hope woke up to find herself alone, save for Sherlock, curled in a gray and white ball on the couch beside her. A glance at the sun outside the living room window told her it was early afternoon. She sat up cautiously, a bit stiff, and looked around for Gabriel.

"Hello?" Her old afghan had been draped over her legs. She shoved it aside and sat up, alarmed to think she'd actually fallen asleep in front of a stranger, leaving him free to snoop through—or steal—everything she owned. A quick check of the kitchen proved it empty, as were the bathroom and her bedroom. "Gabriel?"

Her front door was unlocked, when she was always careful to lock it. "Some guardian you are," she muttered, oddly disappointed to find him gone. Not wanting to think about why that could possibly be so, she locked it again, then went into the bathroom to freshen up. Her reflection in the mirror made her wince; she looked like death warmed over, dark circles beneath her eyes, not a stitch of makeup. Cursing her own vanity, she took a couple of extra minutes to apply some concealer, a little color on her lids, and a quick dab of lip gloss.

Coming back into the hallway, she looked toward her bedroom, where the book still waited, sitting squarely on her desk. Knowing she couldn't put off the inevitable much longer, she put it off as long as she could by going into the kitchen and pulling out the aluminum foil, putting a large piece of it over the top of the banana pudding, now completely cooled.

"Be right back, Sherlock," she told the cat, just to have someone to say it to, then went across the hall to knock on Mr. Qualey's door, which she found open a few inches. It didn't surprise her, for he often left it cracked, in part—she was sure—so he could hear her comings and goings. He was lonely and enjoyed a chat; it was common for him to pop his head out to say hello when she climbed up or down the stairs.

"Mr. Q?" She stuck her head in, speaking softly in case she caught him napping. There was no answer, but she came farther in anyway, knowing he was a bit hard of hearing. A light at the end of the hallway went out, drawing her attention. "Mr. Qualey?"

A man stepped into the hallway, holding something in his hand, and it took Hope no more than an instant to realize that it wasn't her neighbor.

She began to shake, for it was Gabriel, in a place he didn't belong, holding something that wasn't his.

"You're awake," he said quietly, stating the obvious.

"Where's Mr. Qualey?" The pudding suddenly felt as though it weighed fifty pounds. "What are you doing here?"

He took a few steps toward her, light glinting on what he held in his hand: a picture frame, some kind of family portrait.

"Your neighbor is gone," Gabriel said.

"Gone?" she repeated, stupidly.

"Passed away."

"No." Hope shook her head, denying the dark thoughts that were taking shape inside her brain. "No."

"I'm sorry."

"Sorry?" She backed up, not even conscious of doing so. The edge of the front door hit her in the back, stopping her short.

The whole scenario, the whole day, suddenly made some kind of weird, twisted sense—Satan wanted to up the pressure on her, and up it he had. "You killed him."

Gabriel's face went blank.

"You killed him, didn't you?" The rational part of her brain, the part that could still think, wanted to shriek, to scream, to throw something, but instead she merely gripped the bowl of pudding tighter. The weight of it was familiar, like a millstone around her neck. Everyone she loved met the same fate: her parents, Mr. Qualey, even Charity, who—even though she wasn't dead—might as well be.

And every single time, it was her fault.

She'd left the candle burning when she was twelve, even though she wasn't supposed play with her dad's lighter. She'd been too hard on Charity when—seven years later—she'd finally gotten them both out of foster care, playing hard-ass mom instead of sister. And she'd been the one who insisted on making banana pudding instead of doing what she was supposed to do, which was translate the damn book and put it on the Internet.

Mr. Qualey was dead because of her.

"It was his heart," Gabriel said, but she didn't believe him.

"You're a liar," she told him softly, "just like your boss." Tears threatened, but she blinked them back, because tears got her nowhere.

"Hope, I didn't—"

"Shut up," she snarled. "Just shut up." Even knowing him for a murderer, she found herself unafraid, cocooned in numbness. If he'd wanted to, he could've killed her anytime he chose—particularly as she'd lain sleeping on the couch—but death was apparently too good for her these days. The Devil wanted her alive, so she could transcribe his book, dance to his tune, torment her with worry, and tantalize her with glimpses of a life she'd never have. Pushing past Gabriel, she went to the open door of the bedroom and stood there, needing to see for herself what he'd done to her friend.

Mr. Qualey's body lay on the bed, fully dressed. He looked peaceful, but Hope could tell at a glance that the old man himself wasn't there; the body on the bed was just a shell, slack-jawed and pale.

A hard knot of grief and guilt rose in her throat, threatening to choke her. "Go back and tell him he won, would you? Go back and tell him that I've learned my lesson, just like he wanted."

Gabriel said something, but she didn't listen as she turned away, numbly heading for her apartment, where she would call the police and tell them that she'd found her neighbor—her sweet, kind neighbor—dead in his own home.

And then she'd do what Sammy Divine wanted, and transcribe the Key of Solomon before someone else paid the price for her hesitation.

Gabriel watched her go, stunned.

She thought him a murderer. He'd shown her nothing but kindness, yet she thought him capable of cold-blooded murder. The ache in his heart—the one caused by the photo in his hand,

and the imaginings it sparked—grew sharper, more painful.

He could go after her, try once more to explain, but perversely, he no longer wanted to. Let her think the worst, since she was so eager to think it.

Mouth grim, he turned and walked back to the bedroom, placing the photo of Muriel Qualey and her children back on the bureau where it belonged. Then he left the apartment, ignoring Hope's closed door, and made his way down the stairs.

There were plenty of humans in the world who needed his help, and no reason to stay where he wasn't wanted. The scent of lavender permeated the lobby, a scent he would now forever associate with disappointment. Drawing his new sunglasses from his back pocket, he opened the front door and went out into the sunshine.

"Well, hey there, Calvin." Coming up the walkway to the apartment building, heading directly for him, was a familiar figure. Wearing a short plaid skirt, plain white tee, and hip ankle boots, Nicki Styx gave him a cheerful grin. "I knew those Drifters would look good on you, and when I'm right, I'm right."

He grinned in return, unable to help himself, for he truly liked her.

"Hey yourself," he answered easily. "But my name's not Calvin."

She laughed, coming closer. "I know—it's just a little nickname my partner Evan gave you, because he thinks you look like a Calvin Klein model. It's Gabe, right?"

He nodded, eyeing her curiously. "What are you doing here?"

She shrugged, pausing to talk. "Just visiting a friend."

He couldn't help but ask, "Hope?"

Nicki shook her head. "No, I—um—" She looked around, as though expecting to see someone else standing there. "My friend Muriel . . . well, she asked me to stop by and check on her husband."

A tingle ran down his spine. "Muriel."

"Yeah, Muriel Qualey." The grin Nicki gave him now was a bit more forced than the one she'd given him earlier. "She says he hasn't been feeling well lately."

Gabe, who already knew the secret that Nicki tried so hard to keep from the world, decided to speak honestly with her. "Mr. Qualey passed away a few minutes ago. His wife, Muriel, passed away long before that."

She paled.

"I know you see the spirits of the dead," he told her gently. "I know you often help them with their unfinished business. You were going to tell that kindly old man that his wife forgave him for what he'd done, and that she still loved him."

"How did you . . ." Nicki took an uncertain step backward. "How did you know that?"

Gabriel sighed, less surprised than ever that his onetime brother Samael had been so drawn to this woman. In her own way—her own *human* way—she, too, was an angel, just as Samael himself had once been. "It's complicated," he told her, resting his hands on his hips. "Let's just say that I have some gifts of my own."

"The knack," Nicki said faintly, clearly taken aback. "That's what my grandmother calls it." She sighed, shaking her head. "Muriel wanted me to tell him that she forgave him; she regretted leaving the words unsaid. She knew he was dying, and was afraid that his guilt would allow him to be swallowed up by the Darkness, when what she really wanted was for them to be together in the Light."

"She got what she wanted," Gabriel said softly. "Trust me on that."

Nicki smiled, a sweet smile that lifted his heart. Then she turned her head sharply to her right, as though listening to something Gabe couldn't hear.

"Muriel says, 'Thank you for being with him at the end.'"

In the corner of his eye, Gabe caught a quick flash of light, as familiar to him as his own name.

"She's gone," Nicki said softly. "It's finished." With a sigh, she looked back to Gabe, and resting her own hands on her hips, asked, "So who are you, really?"

Gabriel laughed a little under his breath, shaking his head. "You wouldn't believe me if I told you."

"You'd be surprised by what I'd believe," she told him, eyeing him closely.

Tempted as he was to reveal himself, Gabe knew it was a bad idea. Better to let her live her life the way it was going, for the One clearly had plans for her.

"Another time, perhaps," he said, certain he'd see her again, one way or another.

"Why are good-looking guys always so cryptic?" she muttered, clearly dissatisfied with his answer.

"That's a question for your husband to answer," he returned with a grin.

Her face lit up. "You know my husband?"

"No." Gabe shook his head. "But it's a safe bet that he's good-looking."

Nicki inclined her head graciously in acknowledgment. "I'll take that as a compliment."

"Do." He turned to walk away, thinking once again of his brother Samael, experiencing genuine regret on his behalf.

"Gabe, wait."

He paused, looking over his shoulder.

"Muriel told me something else, just then . . . at the end."

"Yes?"

"She said not to abandon hope."

His breath caught. *Hope, who thought him a murderer.*

"Does that make any sense?"

He pictured her, upstairs in her cozy little apartment, all alone. In the distance, he heard the wail of a siren, and knew they were coming for her friend Mr. Qualey. The ache in his chest returned, and with the memory of big green eyes, breath that smelled like pomegranates, the way the skin of her cheek looked like peaches.

"Yes," he told Nicki, "it makes sense, but I'm not quite sure how to go about it."

Nicki took a step closer to him. "Listen, I . . .

I usually try really hard to stay out of people's business, but is there anything I can do to help?"

"Not unless you can convince a certain some-one that Mr. Qualey's death had nothing whatso-ever to do with her, or with me."

"Ah." Nicki's brown eyes crinkled at the corners when she smiled. "Girl trouble, hm?"

"In a way."

She came up, slipping her hand through his arm as though they'd known each other forever. "Walk with me," she said. "Luckily for you, I'm pretty good at getting people to believe the unbelievable."

Chapter Seven

The police and the ambulance were gone, and the building was once again quiet. Hope lay on her living room couch, Sherlock cuddled to her chest, and cried.

Impossible to believe she'd never see the old man again—inconceivable she'd never wake up in the morning, groggy with the need for coffee, and see him through her living room window, puttering in his garden. How many mornings had he waved her over? How many mornings had she gone, coffee cup in hand, still in her pajamas, picking up his newspaper on her way across the hall?

Life was so cruel, so unfair. The bandages on her wrists seemed suddenly too tight, and she debated ripping them off and leaving them that way, stitches or no stitches. What did it matter if the wounds reopened, anyway? The scars would never go away, and now she had a brand-new one—the death of a friend on her conscience—to add to her collection.

There was a soft knock on her door, but she ignored it, hoping whoever it was would just go away.

It came again, and Sherlock, who'd been content to let her hold him, struggled to be free. She let him go, watching as he padded quickly to the door, gray tail held high. Reaching it, he looked over his shoulder at her with big yellow eyes, as though asking, *What are you waiting for?*

She sighed, barely bothering to wonder why he hadn't pulled his usual disappearing trick under the couch; she had so few visitors that knocks on the door usually sent him running. Sitting up, she grabbed a new tissue from the box on the coffee table and wiped her eyes and nose.

The knock came again, and thinking it probably had something to do with Mr. Qualey, she got up and shuffled to the door.

"Yes?" Putting her eye to the peephole, she saw a dark-haired young woman. "Who is it?"

"My name's Nicki Styx," the woman said, speaking directly into the keyhole. "I'm looking for Hope."

Cautiously, Hope opened the door. There was no one else in the hall, and the woman looked harmless, but one could never be too careful.

"Hi," said the woman named Nicki. She looked far too cool to be a cop, pink streaks in her hair, short skirt, ankle boots. "Can I talk to you for a second? It's about your neighbor."

Hope swiped at her nose again, not really up for it, but shrugged and opened her door wider. "Come on in," she said.

Nicki came in, checking out her apartment with a quick glance. "Nice," she said. "Great view."

Fighting back another onrush of tears, Hope didn't answer at first. Then she took a deep breath and asked, "What can I do for you?"

"Can I sit down?"

"Sure." Listlessly, Hope led the way to the couch, where Nicki took a seat. She took a chair opposite.

Sherlock, fickle as ever, leapt up beside Nicki, sniffing curiously at her skirt.

"Beautiful cat," Nicki said. She let him satisfy his feline curiosity, then scratched him under the chin. "What's his name?"

"Sherlock," Hope answered. "Because he's so nosy."

Nicki smiled, and Hope couldn't help but notice

how pretty she was. There was a sparkle in her eyes that reminded her of Charity, even though this woman and her sister were total opposites, looks-wise.

"Listen, I know you're having a really bad day," Nicki said, "and you don't know me from Adam, but I've got something to tell you—something that you may have a hard time believing."

Hope leaned back in her chair, resting her head against the cushion. "Go ahead," she said, too tired and depressed to have any patience with beating around the bush. "What is it?"

"What happened to Mr. Qualey wasn't your fault," Nicki said softly. "He had heart problems, had them for years. Today was . . . well, it was just his time."

The hair rose on Hope's arms, leaving her flesh goose pimpled. She straightened, still clutching her tissue.

"You knew Mr. Qualey?"

Nicki shook her head, dark eyes full of sympathy. "No. I knew his wife."

Increasingly confused, she responded, "He didn't have a wife."

"Yes, he did, years ago."

"But she—" Hope thought back to the very few times Mr. Q had ever mentioned his wife.

He'd gotten teary every time, and she was one-
hundred-percent certain that he'd told her his
wife had died young. The woman on the couch
in front of her couldn't be more than thirty, tops.
"He said she died a long time ago."

"She did," Nicki said simply. "But she came to
see me this morning, regardless."

Any other day, any other time, Hope wouldn't
have hesitated to show Nicki to the door, and tell
her not to let it hit on the way out. But today, after
everything she'd been through, she just didn't
have it in her.

"So you're saying . . ." She moved to sit on the
edge of the chair. "You're saying you see dead
people."

"That's what I'm saying."

Oddly, or perhaps not so oddly, Hope found
that she almost—*almost*—believed her.

"Muriel Qualey came into my store this morning," Nicki said, "and told me that her husband
was about to die. She said she'd been hanging
around for years, wanting to tell him something,
but had never been able to reach him. She was
afraid that if he died without knowing what she
had to say, he'd give up, and his soul would be
taken somewhere she couldn't go."

Hope stared at her, remembering whispers and

reddened eyes, being on the verge of a Darkness
that had nearly claimed her.

"You know what I'm talking about, don't you?"
Nicki stroked Sherlock rhythmically as she talked,
the motion as soothing as her voice.

Numbly, Hope nodded, then looked away,
toward the window, where light streamed in and
left bright patches on the floor.

"His death had absolutely nothing to do with
you," Nicki said, with conviction. "It was just his
time," she repeated, "and he's fine now, just fine."

Hope put her head in her hands, wanting to believe what she was being told.

Nicki leaned across the coffee table, and put a
gentle hand on her shoulder. "He and Muriel are
together now, and that's all he ever wanted. You
don't have to worry anymore."

If only that were true, Hope thought. *If only that
were true.*

Drawing a deep, shuddering breath, she once
again raised her head, and looked into Nicki's face.

It was a kind face, an open face, with no shadows or secrets. Only compassion in those brown
eyes, understanding and concern.

"Why are you telling me this?" she asked,
grateful, in that moment, that she wasn't alone.
"You didn't have to come here."

Nicki shrugged. "It's what I do," she answered
simply. "Evil wins when good does nothing—if I
can do *something*, no matter how small, then why
shouldn't I do it?"

She stood up, giving Hope's shoulder a final
pat. "Here." She reached in the pocket of her skirt,
and pulled out a small card, which she handed to
her. "If you ever want to talk . . . here's my phone
number."

The card read HANDBAGS AND GLADRAGS:
A VINTAGE BOUTIQUE. NICKI STYX, PROPRIETOR.
"Better yet, stop by the store sometime—we're
just a few blocks away, in Little Five Points."

Hope knew exactly where it was, having
walked past it many times. She'd never gone in,
always too busy, and not much of a shopper. A
memory surfaced, of Charity dashing in the door
to show off a frilly new skirt she'd just bought.

Come out with me tonight, she'd said. *Let's go to
the Vortex and have some fun; you're wasting the best
years of your life in front of that computer.*

That computer pays the bills, she'd retorted, but
her little sister had tossed her head and rolled her
eyes.

You'll be sorry one day when you're old and gray,
Charity had singsonged. *Life is short, you've gotta
grab it while you can.*

Then she'd left, and Hope had gone back to work.

How she wished she'd gone, while she had the chance.

"Thank you," she said to Nicki, through a throat suddenly tight. "I'll stop in sometime, and say hello."

"Good," Nicki said, giving Sherlock one more chin scratch before heading for the door. "People can never have too many friends. Life is short, and you've gotta grab it while you can."

Chapter Eight

Gabriel sat in Mr. Qualey's rooftop garden, alone in the dark, watching Hope through the window of her apartment. The police and the ambulance had come and gone hours ago, and all was quiet.

The night wind set the plants rustling, and lifted his hair. Gabe stayed in the shadows, wondering about the woman who thought him a murderer, and what had happened to make her so quick to see evil where there was only good.

He was drawn to her, perhaps more than he should be. Her boyish blond hair and her air of tragic fragility should've inspired nothing more than protectiveness, but Gabriel the Archangel, Servant of Truth, never lied to himself, and knew that despite the hurt and anger that had almost driven him away, what he felt for Hope was something more than mere protectiveness. He'd aided many beautiful women through the centuries, yet not once had he pictured them the way he'd pictured her in his mind's eye, those few moments after the old man's death. Women were mortal, and he was not. Women were human, and he was not. Why, then, had he imagined her smiling up at him over a bridal bouquet, lying in his arms, perhaps even holding his child?

Troubled, he chose to put his momentary lapse aside and concentrate instead on keeping her safe, even if he had to do it from a distance. He'd watched her for hours after the police left: first as she'd moved around her apartment, occasionally weeping, then as she sat at her computer, her face illuminated by whatever she was looking at on her screen. He'd seen the cat leap into her lap, observed how—as it grew dark—she'd gone through the apartment room by room, turning on all the lights. She was still afraid of whatever had driven her into his company today; he could see tension in the set of her shoulders, wariness in her eyes. Strangely, she hadn't closed her drapes, almost as though she were afraid to hide herself away from the world, perhaps for fear something else might creep in.

"I see I'm not the only one with a weakness for gardens," came a familiar voice, and his old friend Sammy stepped from the shadows. "Or is it a weakness for something else?"

Unfazed by his old friend's appearance, Gabe regarded him silently before he spoke. Samael looked every inch the Prince of Darkness this evening, clad in a crisply tailored black suit, eyes hooded. The only light thing about him was his hair, cropped short and carelessly mussed, and the glint of silver from an earring in one ear.

"Why are you sneaking around in the dark, Samael? Haven't you tired of it yet?"

Sammy didn't answer, and it was this that told Gabe his barb had struck home, so he pressed a bit further. "You look as though you have a party to go to . . . Black Mass at Dante's Inferno, perhaps? Virgin sacrifice at dawn, champagne to follow?"

"I came to check on my newest recruit," Sammy said smoothly. "How's our darling Hope this evening?"

The hair on the back of Gabriel's neck rose, for he knew a challenge when he heard one.

"You can't have her," Gabe said flatly. "I'm going to drive the Darkness away from this one."

"You're too late," Sammy answered, with a smile. "She's already mine."

The surge of anger Gabriel felt surprised him. He rose from the chair, willing his warrior side to calm. "I beg to differ," he said to Sammy politely, though tension coiled itself inside him like a spring.

Sammy sighed, slipping his hands into his pockets. "Oh, Gabriel, you know as well as I that the rules of the universe cannot be broken. Hope Henderson called out to me, and I came. We've already made a bargain, she and I."

"No." Gabriel's warrior side surged again. "I don't believe you."

"Why would I lie about something like that, Gabriel?"

Gabe stepped closer, the better to see his one-time brother's face. "To provoke me," he said, keeping his voice low, "and to make me go away and leave her to the Darkness."

Sammy met his eyes, and the gleam of malice in them told Gabriel that his suspicions were true; whatever danger Hope was in, Sammy was clearly at the heart of it.

"I'm very sorry to tell you this, old friend"—though His Infernal Majesty was obviously not sorry at all—"but the girl has chosen to put her feet upon the path that leads to Sheol. She isn't the innocent you believe her to be."

"Her soul is pure," Gabriel said, between his teeth. "I've seen it."

"Your eyes deceive you," Sammy stated.

At a stalemate, as usual, the two stared at each other across a chasm of bitterness and regret, a chasm growing ever wider by the moment.

"Not all humans choose lives of quiet desperation, you know." Sammy's teeth gleamed white in the moonlight; Gabe knew that particular smile, and disliked it intensely. "Some people seek the power they weren't given as mortals, and they come to me to get it. It's quite simple, really . . . they do something for me, I do something for them."

"You provide a service for the underprivileged, is that it?" Gabe didn't try to keep the sarcasm from his tone.

"Exactly."

"How noble of you."

"Come, come, Gabriel . . . you can't win them all, now can you? A soul for you, a soul for me . . ." Sammy trailed off with a shrug. "It all works out in the end." He moved casually toward a hanging plant, lifting a bloom to his nose. "If only you'd been minding your own business instead of enjoying that coffee in Little Five Points this morning, you wouldn't be sitting here in the dark, pining for something you can never have."

"Ah." Gabe began to see Samael's twisted game more clearly. "You put her in my path deliberately, didn't you?"

"Oh, Gabriel." Sammy let the flower drop. "Why would I do that?"

"Because I can speak to Nicki Styx without seeing fear in her eyes, and you can't."

The look he received in return for that statement would've reduced a human to ash.

"You knew I would see how Hope's soul was beset by darkness," Gabe went on. *"You're* the 'he' she kept referring to—you're the one she thought sent me to watch over her." He eyed the Father of Lies narrowly.

"She mentioned me?" Sammy said lightly, as though anger were the furthest thought from his mind. "I'm touched."

"You'll regret this, Samael," Gabe told his onetime brother coldly. The warrior within him raged, seeking to be released. It was all he could do to keep his wings furled, and his face impassive. "Now that I know how you've used this poor woman to your own ends, there's no power on Earth that will stop me from saving her."

"Give it your best shot, Sir Galahad," Sammy said, with the careless wave of a hand. "Risk your life to save the pretty blond princess in the tower."

He turned away, giving Gabriel his back as he strolled into the shadows. "But you might want to check your facts first. Not everyone *wants* to be saved, and *she* came to *me*."

And between the first and second Circle, which thou shalt thyself have drawn with the Instrument of Magical Art, thou shalt make four hexagonal pentacles, and between these thou shalt write the four terrible and tremendous Names of God.

Holy crap, thought Hope, *this is unbelievable.*

Rubbing her eyes, she leaned her head back against the sofa, wishing the nightmare would just go away. All those B horror movies about pentacles and candles and calling up demons had some kind of basis in reality after all, if the Key of Solomon, the *Ars Goetia*, were to be believed.

She'd always hated B horror movies, and she'd never had any desire to call up demons. Now it looked like she was going to be the one who told the world how to do it.

Exhausted and drained, she sighed and stared at the ceiling, wondering if she really had it in her to transcribe the instructions outlined in Solomon's Key.

Could demons really be called forth and controlled?

It was mind-boggling, fantastic.

She looked at the book again. *Come ye, come ye, Angels of Darkness; come hither before this Circle without fear, terror, or deformity, to execute our commands, and be ye ready both to achieve and to complete all that we shall command ye.*

Just reading the words on the page brought chills to her spine.

And then, perhaps because she was exhausted and drained and completely, utterly tired of being a pawn in someone else's game, another mind-boggling, fantastic thought occurred to her: if demons, like the one she'd seen at Satan's shoulder, really could be controlled, maybe *she* needed to be the one calling the shots.

Steeling her resolve, Hope stood up. There was a lot of information here about the stars and the planets and the best times to cast which spells, but she needed to cut to the chase. The Key emphasized the need for bravery and confidence first and foremost when dealing with the spirit world. Since she was feeling the absolute opposite of brave and confident, she decided a little bit of practice couldn't hurt; she wasn't anywhere near ready to call up any demons yet, hadn't drawn anything or lit any candles, but she could work on her attitude. She needed to be tough, not a wimp.

Standing in the middle of her living room, Hope practiced reading the passage aloud. "Come ye, come ye, Angels of Darkness; come hither before this Circle without fear, terror, or deformity, to execute our commands, and be ye ready both to achieve and to complete all that we shall command ye."

Definitely bad B movie script material.

Clearing her throat, Hope made sure she stood up as tall as she could (which wasn't very), and made her voice more forceful as she read aloud the next paragraph.

"I conjure ye, and I command ye absolutely, O Demons, in whatsoever part of the universe ye may be, by virtue of—"

A loud hiss startled her. It was Sherlock, who wasn't looking at her, but staring fixedly at a point somewhere behind her. She twisted, and there, outside her window, was a sight that turned her veins to ice: two glowing red eyes, surrounded by a darkness so black it blocked the lights of the city from her view. Blackness in the shape of wings, gently flapping as they held the demon aloft, holding him in place as he stared at her from the other side of the glass.

With a shriek, Hope forgot all about spells and incantations and words of power. She threw the book down and took off running, fear having taken her in a mindless grip. Behind her, glass shattered, and she shrieked even louder as she pounded down the short hallway that led to her room. Dashing inside, she slammed the bedroom door behind her without daring to look back, and immediately realized the futility of her actions, for she had nowhere to go.

The sounds of all Hell breaking loose came from her living room; an earsplitting tinkle of glass, then another, thumps and bumps and crashes, each more frightening than the last. Terrified, Hope dived for the room's only hiding place, a tiny closet barely big enough to hold her own meager wardrobe. There she cowered, panting with fear, as the noises in her living room seemed to go on and on.

The demon was on a rampage, and it was only a matter of time before it found her.

Please, God, don't let me die. Hope barely knew where the thought came from, because she'd long ago stopped praying to a God who didn't care. If He cared, he wouldn't have let her parents die in the fire that had taken everything they owned. If He cared, He'd wouldn't have let her and Charity go into foster care, wouldn't have let them be separated for even a day, much less seven years. If He cared, He would've shown her how to be a better big sister to the wild child Charity had been when she'd finally regained custody. If God had cared, He would've helped her be a better role model to a vivacious, precocious, beautiful young woman in her teens and twenties, and maybe both of their lives would've turned out differently.

The events of the last ten years flashing through her head was further proof to Hope that she was about to die.

And then, suddenly, unbelievably, all noise in the apartment stopped. Her own breath, harsh in her ears, was all she heard.

With a gulp, not daring to move, Hope did her best to get her breathing under control. After all the crashing and breaking, the sound of silence was deafening. She waited, straining her ear for some sound, no matter how faint, but heard nothing. Her heart was pounding, palms clammy with fear.

And then, finally, came the sound she'd been dreading: footsteps, coming down the hallway from her living room. The handle to her bedroom door turned—she hadn't bothered to lock it in her terror—and there was a familiar creak as it opened. Squeezing her eyes tightly shut, no longer daring to breathe, Hope crouched in the darkness of her closet.

Chapter Nine

When Gabriel saw the demon hovering outside
Hope's window, he didn't hesitate, and launched
himself from the wall of the rooftop garden.
Wings unfurled, he was right behind the creature as it smashed through the glass in pursuit
of Hope, who was screaming in mindless panic
as she bolted from the room. He had the element
of surprise on his side, and hit the sulphurous,
blackened beast with his full body weight, pinning it against a far wall before it knew what hit it.

The demon fought him, throwing itself backward, thrashing, flapping its wings, and raking
viciously at him with blackened claws. It made
no sound, but was no less dangerous for its silence; it was a Dronai, a soldier, and having no

will of its own, needed no voice. Gabriel held tight as it writhed and thrashed, whipping its serpentine tail in every direction. A nearby lamp was knocked to the floor, as were several tables and the chair beside the couch. The cheerful, sunny living room Gabe had enjoyed earlier in the day became a battleground in the war between good and evil, its cozy furnishings the first casualties in a war Gabe had no intention of losing.

He held on, countering the creature's every move, letting the abomination know his strength as they grappled. It was a minor demon only, and no match for an archangel. He could've killed it easily, letting the Light within him burn it to a crisp, but contented himself with proving his mastery, trapping its night black wings against its body as it weakened. Finally the creature stilled, quivering with unholy rage, powerless in his grip.

"You will go back to the Darkness from whence you came," Gabe ground out, in what passed for the demon's ear, "and you will tell your master that the Archangel Gabriel has laid claim to this house. Should any more of your filthy, corrupt brethren attempt to enter, they shall meet the point of my sword." And with that, he shoved the creature away. It twisted, turning on him like an adder, and earned a powerful blow to the face for its trouble. Stumbling back, it hit the far wall, where it slumped, glaring at him balefully. Gabriel brought his sword forth from nothingness, where it was always close at hand, and wielded it so that light gleamed along its razor-sharp edge.

The demon cowered, shading its red eyes against the light, and seconds later it was gone, out the broken window, wings flapping soundlessly as it disappeared into the night.

Gabe stepped to the window and watched it go, letting any of its brethren who might be hiding in the shadows see him, his snow white wings unfurled, the gleaming Sword of Righteousness in his hand. Both physically and symbolically, he staked his claim, and took Hope's life—as well as her soul—into his hands.

Murmuring the words of power that would set an invisible barrier over the window, Gabe used two fingers to inscribe it with his mark. Turning, he cast his hand over the entire apartment, using a soft gleam of light to claim every inch under his protection. The magical barrier he'd set in place wouldn't stop a determined demon who wanted to get in, but it would definitely slow it down.

Then he looked around at the destruction the demon had caused, his eyes narrowing at the

sight of an open book, lying on the floor. Sheath-
ing his sword back into nothingness, he bent, and
picked it up.

Scanning the pages, his heart sank.

The *Ars Goetia*, the Howling Art, the secrets of
which he himself had given to Solomon in those
long-ago times when the war between Darkness
and Light had been newly won; a way to prove
the One's mastery over the Dominion of Darkness, any time the King of the Jews chose to do
so. Those pages, marked with names and symbols
he couldn't help but recognize, contained knowledge of the Black Arts not meant to be shared, and
could prove disastrous in the wrong hands.

Samael, Father of Lies, had told him the truth
about Hope, for her possession of the book proved
she'd already opened her heart to the Darkness.

Surprised to find his disappointment so keen,
Gabriel squared his shoulders yet again, for he
was still resolved to save her, even if he had to
save her from herself.

"It's all right, Hope. You can come out now."

A perfectly normal male voice, muffled but familiar, reached Hope's ears as she lay huddled in
the closet.

Unsure, still terrified, she stayed quiet.

The door to her closet opened, revealing her hiding place.

"Gabriel?"

He was surrounded by light. After her time in the dark closet she had to squint; the glow around his head and shoulders was blinding. "Are those . . . are those *wings*?"

He reached down, offering both hands to help her to her feet. She gripped his fingers tightly, terrified, disbelieving, and he pulled her up easily.

"Are you all right?" He looked rather fierce, different somehow, but she was in such shock that she hardly knew how to answer him.

"Here, sit down." He urged her gently toward the bed. She was trembling like a leaf, knees weak, so she did as he said.

She was seeing things . . . she had to be seeing things . . .

Covering her face with her hands, she took a deep breath. When she lowered them again, the glow she'd mistaken for wings was gone.

"It's all right," Gabriel said. "You're safe now."

She wanted to believe him so badly it hurt.

"You don't understand," she told him, shooting looks toward the door. "There was a *thing* . . . it was a *thing* . . ." She couldn't quite bring herself to use the word "demon." "It came in through the window—"

"A Dronai," Gabriel said, "one of the lowest order of demons in Satan's army. Soldier imps, little more than lizards with wings."

Stunned, she stared at him blankly. *The bad B horror movie had just turned into an episode of* The Twilight Zone. "What?" she asked faintly.

"You invited it in when you read aloud from the Key," Gabe told her grimly. "That was very foolish of you."

Her jaw sagged. He was right, of course he was right, but how did he *know*?

"We have to get out of here." Panic fluttered in her chest. She'd find out later how he knew so much; right now she just wanted to go someplace safe.

Gabriel shook his head, clearly taking charge. "We're safest here."

A quizzical meow announced Sherlock's arrival on the scene. The cat leapt up on the bed, sniffed her briefly, then went straight to Gabriel, shamelessly seeking his attention.

Gabriel stroked him, and he immediately began to purr. "You see?" Sherlock's purr grew louder. "Your cat knows the creature's gone," he told her. "Listen to him."

She stared at him, willing her mind to go faster and her heart to slow down. A silence grew between them, growing increasingly more awkward.

"How—" She blew out a breath, letting some of her tension go with it. "How do you know about the Key, about the d—" She still couldn't bring herself to say the word.

"I know many things," he said to her gently, "and I am not your enemy."

A stab of shame pierced her. Everything she'd accused him of earlier in the day was wrong. He really *had* come to look after her, even if she didn't know why.

"I didn't mean to do it," she told him, not quite able to look him in the eye. "I didn't know what would happen."

"Which time?" he asked. "In the living room, when you called up the demon, or when you made your original deal with the Devil?"

Her eyes flew to his.

His gaze was direct and matter-of-fact. *He knew everything.*

She looked away, ashamed of herself.

"You've made some bad choices, Hope." Gabriel stood straighter, squaring his shoulders. "You've put your soul in peril," he said, "and I've sworn myself your protector."

"You can't protect me," she whispered, shaking

her head. Sherlock was in her lap now, and she scooped him up, needing the comfort of his warm, furry body. "Nobody can protect me." She looked up at him from her seat on the bed, filled with a sense of the surreal. "Who *are* you, anyway?"

"Listen to me," Gabe murmured. He took a seat next to her, and reached out a hand, cupping her face.

It was a big hand, warm and strong. Hope wanted to lean into it, and never move.

"I'm the Archangel Gabriel," he told her, "and I will protect you from the Darkness."

Deep inside, Hope trembled. Was it possible? If demons existed—and she now knew they did— so too, then, must angels. The conclusion wasn't all that far-fetched.

And if anyone looked like a modern-day angel, Gabriel did. In some indefinable way, he radiated confidence and power.

She stared into his eyes. Brown eyes, shot with gold. The kindness, the gentleness she'd sensed in him earlier were both still there, but so was a steeliness, a ruthlessness that she hadn't detected earlier.

"Why didn't you tell me this earlier, when I . . . when I was being so mean to you?"

"Would you have believed me?"

Deep inside, she was forced to admit that the answer was no. She wouldn't have believed him.

Gabriel shrugged. "We take human form often, coming and going as we please, rarely revealing our presence. We mingle, we watch, we do our best to inspire the good in people."

"*We?*"

"The Darkness has its army, and so does the Light."

The Darkness had its army, all right—both the demons she'd seen, and the unseen ones, like the depression she'd fallen into after Charity's disappearance. She should've gotten help for herself while she'd had the chance.

"It's too late," she whispered, knowing in her heart that it was true. She was too far gone, too frightened of Sammy and what lay in store for her if she didn't do as he asked.

Despite Gabriel's claim he would protect her—even if he *were* an angel—Hope had no faith in angels anymore, and could see no other solution.

Chapter Ten

"The solution is simple, darling." Pandora stretched like a cat, basking in the sun. "The child needs a tutor. His studies shouldn't interrupt your leisure time." She was sunbathing, naked, on the deck of a private yacht. They were alone, the boat a tiny white speck in the vast blue waters of the Aegean. "He could use a companion, as well, someone his own age to play with."

Sammy turned his head, admiring Pandora's ample curves, enhanced by the wearing of a large sapphire in her belly button. Even naked, the shamelessly wanton goddess could not forgo her bling.

"I'll admit that having a playmate can be fun," he returned equally, "but it's not as though children grow on trees in the Underworld. Their spirits are too pure for them to end up in my domain, and the ones that do, well"—his lip curled in an involuntary expression of dislike—"they are not the ones I want my own child spending time with."

"That ghoul you call a lieutenant is a useless companion for a boy his age . . . not a speck of spontaneity in him."

"I should hope not," Sammy murmured dryly, returning his eyes to the sparkling blue water. "Spontaneity is not an attribute I expect among my legions. They are to obey, not take the initiative. I don't want them to think for themselves."

"Is that what you want for Cain?" Pandora eyed him archly, and he was forced to admit that he didn't.

"The boy is chafing under your restrictions," she told him, adjusting her Fendi sunglasses against the glare. "He needs a companion, someone his own age, with whom to run free."

Sammy frowned, remembering what happened the last time Cain had "run free." He'd gotten lost, kidnapped, and nearly been turned to stone by a basilisk. "The child has no fear," he told Pandora, "and I trust no one save Nyx with his safety."

"Then you must teach him fear, darling." Pandora reached for her drink, tall and fruity, and sipped it through a straw. "Ah, ambrosia," she murmured, after she'd swallowed. "You must have the sylphs of Circe give me the recipe."

Sammy answered her absently, his mind on the concept of fear. "The sylphs would never do that, my dear, and you know it. You're far too generous in your curves, which they envy madly."

Pandora gave a throaty chuckle, and took another sip. "They do, don't they?"

"Why must I teach him fear?" Sammy's mind was still on Cain. "Why would I want to crush the boy's spirit?"

"I said nothing about crushing his spirit, darling." Pandora put her drink down and turned over, exposing the round globes of her bottom to the sun. Her breasts dangled like ripe fruit as she rested herself on her elbows. "The child must learn that actions have consequences, and children learn by example, not by rote. If you wish him to be more prudent about his safety, you must give him *reason* to be prudent."

Sammy's Ray-Bans hid his expression, but Pandora smiled, knowing she had his attention, in more ways than one.

"I'm not sure I should be taking parental advice from you, my delightful Pandora," he said, reaching out a finger to trace the line of her shoulder, plump and warm. "You're one of the least prudent, and least motherly, women I've ever known."

She laughed, genuinely delighted. "Thank you, Majesty." Tiny bells, worn on an anklet, tinkled as she kicked her feet, wiggling her toes rapturously.

"In fact," Sammy went on, his voice shifting to a lower timbre, "I'm quite certain I could never fuck anyone's mother the way I'm about to fuck you."

Pandora's generous lips curled into an entirely different kind of smile. "Please do, my prince. Please do."

And there, between the blue of the heavens and the blue of the sea, Sammy slaked himself once again on warm, female flesh. The smooth skin of Pandora's back became a playground for his lips and tongue, the rounded globes of her ass delectable targets for wicked nips from his teeth. He teased her with his body, crushing his naked loins against her, letting her feel the hard length of his cock. Mercilessly, sensually, he rubbed his hardness all over her softness, all the while withholding its entrance to her body.

Pandora gasped her pleasure at every turn, her mews of delight turning to those of mock frustration as he kept her pinned on her belly, leaving her hands unable to reach him.

Aroused, Sammy trailed his kisses and nips to the back of her neck, laying his full body weight upon her hips. His hands came around her, grasping her breasts. He squeezed and fondled them as he bit her neck, hands full of luscious flesh and nose full of the sun-warmed scent of flushed skin.

And in the end, he took Pandora from behind, slipping into her heated femininity and surging against it, time and again, as she cried out her pleasure, moaning against the cushions of her lounge chair.

When it was over, Sammy rolled to lie flat on his back. Beside him, a beautiful woman lay exhausted and well satisfied, while he . . . he stared up at the vaulted blue sky, and wondered if the satisfaction he felt in that moment would ever be enough.

Later, as Nyx gave him a report of Cain's activities during his absence, he had reason to recall Pandora's parental advice.

"The boy truly *is* the spawn of Satan," Nyx told him, with a long-suffering shake of his shadowed head. "If he were mine, I'd have him beaten." The blunt opinion demonstrated a familiarity Sammy would never have allowed anyone else.

"What's he done now?" snapped the High

Prince of Darkness, irritated at how the thought of punishing Cain annoyed him.

"He set fire to his own bedding with the Crystal of Khartoum," Nyx told him, "and then escaped like an eel as I put out the flames. He was gone for several hours, and when he came back, he reeked of brimstone."

"And how did he get the Crystal of Khartoum?" asked Sammy, with exquisite politeness. He kept all his magical treasures in one place, and it was a place no one was allowed to enter without his sanction.

"He raided the treasure room when he was supposed to be bathing," Nyx answered flatly.

Sammy gave his second-in-command a dire look. "You were supposed to be watching him."

Nyx drew himself up stiffly, a soldier, ready to take his punishment. "I'm not a wet nurse, my lord." His wingtips quivered, whether trepidation or outrage, Sammy couldn't say. "During his bath, I left him in the care of the water nymphs, who were pleased to be of service."

"I'll bet they were," Sammy murmured, not entirely thrilled with the idea of the amoral, aquatic nymphs cavorting unsupervised with his son. They knew Satan for their master, it was true, but that would not stop them from teasing an impressionable young princeling with their sloe-eyed, dripping beauty. Or, apparently, being taken in by his childish charm. "Where is Cain now?"

"I confined him once again to his room, Great Shaitan. I knew you would want to deal with his disobedience immediately."

"That I do," Sammy agreed grimly. He strode toward the door, on the way to his son's room. "Fetch me the imp known as Tesla."

Nyx disappeared like smoke, but Sammy walked, hearing his footsteps echo coldly against hallways of stone. He'd always taken perverse pleasure in his home—an ancient temple, hidden in plain sight by magic that had endured through thousands of years, and would endure for thousands more, but for the first time, he saw it as a child might see it, and found it coldly imposing.

Just as it should be, he reminded himself.

When he opened the door to Cain's room, he expected defiance, and wasn't disappointed.

"I hate you," the boy shouted, just as a pillow hit him in the face.

Completely taken aback, Sammy froze, giving Cain time to leap from the bed and charge him. Almost immediately, the boy realized whom he was facing, and froze as well.

"Father!" Cain was clearly stricken. "I didn't

mean to hit you . . . I didn't know it was you! I thought it was—"

The boy broke off, the expression on the face of His Satanic Majesty obviously a bit too much for one of even his great courage.

"You defy my second-in-command?" Sammy's dignity demanded he keep his tone even. "You strike my emissary? You disrespect my wishes?"

Cain looked crestfallen.

"You rifle through my possessions?"

Cain seemed to shrink, becoming even smaller.

"You set fire to my house?"

"Not the house," Cain interjected hastily, "just a blanket."

The withering look he received in return silenced him.

Sammy crossed his arms over his chest, knowing a line needed to be drawn. Pandora had been right, and the child needed to know that actions had consequences.

"The imp known as Tesla, my lord." Nyx materialized, holding a scruffy, dirty, scrabbling imp in one hand. The little creature was doing his best to bite and claw at the eight-foot demon, who disregarded his efforts as though he were an insect.

"Tesla!" Cain's face showed his apprehension

clearly. "Put my friend down, you creep!" His anger was directed toward Nyx, but Sammy was the one who answered him, using his voice like the crack of a whip.

"Silence!"

Cain looked at him fearfully, biting his lip, then looked at his friend, who'd gone still in Nyx's grip.

"I'm told you left the safety of the temple yet again while I was gone," Sammy said to the boy coldly. "I've warned you about going near the pit, have I not?"

"You didn't actually *forbid* me," the boy dared answer, splitting hairs hopefully.

The Great Beguiler was not beguiled, however, and kept his face impassive.

"I've clearly been too lax with you, as was your mother." Persephone, fey and flighty, treated her offspring as the birds did, nudging them from the nest the moment they could fly. "You no longer live in a place where it's safe for you to come and go as you please, and I believe I've made that clear to you."

Cain shot another anxious look toward Tesla. The imp was the size of a child, but there any resemblance ended. Ash gray in color, knobby-kneed, long-fingered, with bulbous eyes full of fear and apprehension. To the creature's credit, he said nothing, though his terrified expression spoke volumes.

"Nyx recommends you be beaten," Sammy told Cain mildly.

The boy directed a fulminating look toward the demon. *"Him,"* he said, imbuing the word with disgust. *"He* won't let me do anything—he expects me to sit in my room and read all day! He picks out my clothes and makes me bathe and calls me princeling all the time, even though I've told him I hate it!"

Sammy found himself mildly surprised at the boy's outpouring of complaints, but let the child go on and get it all out.

"He doesn't know the simplest of games, and refuses to learn any because he says it's *beneath* him," sneered Cain. "He treats me like I'm a helpless kid! I know perfectly well how to dress myself!"

"Oh my, yes," Sammy murmured, taking in Cain's tattered, charred T-shirt and shorts. His dirty tennis shoes were better suited to a basketball court than a marble palace. "I can see that. You certainly look like a child of the Great and Mighty Satan."

Nyx gave a grunt that could easily have been taken as an I-told-you-so.

Cain flushed sullenly, looking away.

"My lieutenant was only doing as he was told," Sammy said, "unlike my son, who was doing as he pleased. As I said earlier, Nyx believes you should be beaten, but I have a better idea."

Cain left sullenness behind, and eyed his father anxiously.

"Your friend here, he's your partner in crime, is he not?" Sammy gestured to the imp, who cringed, obviously hoping to remain unnoticed. "It's him you go to see when you go down to the pit, isn't it?"

Cain's eyes, so like his own, grew wide. "Tesla has nothing to do with it," he exclaimed, clearly seeing where the danger lay. "He doesn't *make* me go! I go because I want to, and because there's nothing to do around here!"

"Boredom is no excuse for disobedience," Sammy stated sternly, then turned to the imp. "Is it?"

Tesla shook his head. "No, O Son of Morning," he squeaked, clearly terrified. "Boredom is no excuse."

"And you?" The Great Shaitan gave the imp his frighteningly full attention. "Are you bored?"

Frantically, Tesla shook his head again. "No, O Ruler of the Abyss. I have my duties."

"Your duties." Sammy sensed Cain shifting restlessly, but ignored him. "What are your duties?"

Tesla licked dry, gray lips with the tip of his tongue, bulbous eyes blinking rapidly. "I keep the hellfires stoked, O Great Mephistopheles."

"A lowly fire imp," Sammy mused, as though to himself. "My son defies me for a creature such as this."

"I didn't defy you, Father—"

Sammy cut Cain off with a lift of his hand, never taking his eyes from the imp. He was quaking now, knobby knees clacking, soot-covered limbs trembling. If Nyx weren't still holding him tightly at the nape of his neck, he would no doubt have been cowering in a heap on the floor.

"What say you, imp? Are you my son's true friend? Are you worth a beating?"

"Yes, Most High," Tesla assured him, then immediately countered with "No, Most High . . . I—I am honored by the Prince's friendship, but I would never presume . . ." The creature lifted long-fingered, gray hands to plead his case, opened his mouth, then shut it. Giving Cain a somewhat agonized glance, he shrugged, then said simply, "I'm not worth a beating."

"This isn't Tesla's fault," Cain insisted. "Leave him alone."

Samael the Black didn't take orders well from anyone, much less a nine-year-old hellion. In a flash, he grabbed the imp's arm, wrenching the creature from Nyx's grasp.

"No, Father, don't!" Cain threw himself between them, shielding the petrified imp with his body. "I'm sorry I defied you! I'm sorry I went into your treasure room . . . I'm sorry! I'll do whatever you want as long as you don't hurt Tesla!"

Surprised by the boy's passion, Sammy hesitated. The imp made himself as small as possible, peeping fearfully over Cain's shoulder. The two of them—one fair-haired and blue-eyed, the other blackened with soot—were studies in light and dark, direct contradictions.

"As my son and heir, it isn't fitting that hands be laid upon you in anger," Sammy said quietly. "This creature will take your punishment on your behalf, while you watch. If you are tempted to defy me again, perhaps you will remember his pain, and do the opposite."

Cain shook his head, appalled. "But he's my friend!"

"If he's truly your friend"—Sammy eyed the imp grimly—"then he'll be more than happy to take a beating for you."

"Father, please . . ." This time Cain spoke softly,

laying a hand upon his arm. "The punishment is mine. Let Tesla go."

It maddened him that his son—this beautiful, fair-haired child, heir to the Kingdom of the Damned—would lower himself to plead on this filthy creature's behalf. He'd obviously failed in his duty, showing the child only his better half in the short time they'd been reunited. It was time for the boy to learn who his father *truly* was.

"Cain," he said, hardening his gaze. "Don't you realize how far below you this creature is? The imps are vicious, and untrustworthy—he nourishes no tender feelings of friendship for you, for he is incapable of them! He would throw you into the fire at a moment's notice should I order him to. Tesla, like all his brothers, is my servant. He's *not* your friend."

Cain's expression didn't waver. "Yes, he is."

Eyes narrowed with anger, His Satanic Majesty directed his next question to the imp. "Choose, imp. Shall I punish you, or shall I punish Cain?" He was confident he knew the answer, merely wanting to make his point.

Tesla swallowed, eyes bulging. Slowly, very slowly, one long-fingered gray hand came up to rest on Cain's shoulder, still placed between him and his master. "Punish me, O Son of Morning," the imp quavered. "Punish me."

Astounded, Sammy straightened. A low growl came from Nyx, as though he sensed a threat, though what threat there could be from two such small beings was unclear.

Cain, small though he was, stood straighter, acknowledging Tesla's hand, and his support. Suddenly, despite his dirty clothes and worn tennis shoes, he looked every inch a young princeling. He was clever enough to keep his mouth shut, however, merely looking his father in the eye, and awaiting his verdict.

Chapter Eleven

Gabriel watched Hope from the corner of his eye as she swept glass from the floor. She hadn't wanted to stay in the apartment with the window broken, but he'd insisted. He had, however, closed the curtains, effectively shutting out the night and whatever watchers it held.

So far she'd been subdued and cooperative, seemingly too frightened to do anything else, but he was uneasy. She might very well be a pawn in one of Sammy's twisted games, but her willingness to invoke the Darkness meant that she was on the opposite side, and he needed to remember that.

"Samael tells me that you made a bargain with him," Gabe stated bluntly. He righted a lamp that had been knocked over during the fight. "Is that true?"

Hope straightened, looking puzzled. "Samael?" She'd obviously never heard the name.

"Samael the Black, the Great Deceiver, Father of Lies," returned Gabe, despising the titles his one-time brother had accumulated through the years. "The Devil in disguise, also known as Sammy Divine."

Her skin turned the color of parchment. "You *talked* to him?" Her eyes darted fearfully around the room. "Was he here? What did he tell you?"

Gabriel, noting her terror at the mere mention of Sammy's name, simply shrugged, pushing the couch into place. "Only that you came to him."

"I didn't—" she started to deny it, then stopped. "I didn't mean to," she murmured, turning back to her sweeping.

"Didn't *mean* to? How could something like that be an accident?" She did, after all, have the Key in her possession. "I know all about the bargain," he told her flatly.

Her cheeks, so pale a moment before, flooded with color.

"Nothing to say for yourself?" He wasn't quite sure why he was pushing her so hard, but it seemed important to lay everything on the table.

She drew herself up, gripping the broom, and looked at him, a hint of defiance in her green eyes. "What do you expect me to say?"

"I expect you to start telling me the truth," Gabriel returned. "All of it. So I can help you."

He could almost see her mind working, measuring whether to trust him. It irritated him that she'd even have to think about it; didn't she see that he was her only hope?

"Tell me why you made a deal with him." His anger at Samael burned hot, yet he found himself angry at Hope, too. This pale slip of a girl had dabbled where she shouldn't. She was too young, too beautiful, and too smart to have made the mistake of seeking the Darkness, whatever the reason.

Hope looked away and sighed, staring toward the closed curtains. Her eyes held the sheen of tears, but she blinked them back, as though knowing they were useless.

She looked so bleak, so vulnerable . . . Gabe felt something shift in the region of his heart. The warrior in him rejected the feeling, clamping down on it immediately. Weakness was not a weapon he would use to win this war, so he had no use for it.

To her credit, Hope chose not to wield that particular weapon, either. She squeezed her eyes shut, rubbed her eyes, and made a valiant effort to compose herself. After a moment, she swiped at her cheeks, leaving them damp.

"I did it because of my sister," she said, and he knew that she was finally telling him the truth. "She disappeared from a Vegas casino two years ago, and I've been searching for her ever since." Her face was expressionless, but Gabe could tell there was turmoil behind the mask. "Two weeks ago, I got a call from the cops, saying they'd found her purse in a ravine. I thought she was dead." Her voice cracked on the last word, just a little. "I was really depressed. One night I threw myself a pity party, had a little bit too much wine, and did something really, really stupid." She lifted an arm, shirtsleeve slipping to reveal the gauze around her wrist.

He moved to sit on the edge of the couch, saying nothing, hoping his silence would allow her to go on. The silence stretched and grew; by the time she spoke again, he felt as though they were in a confessional; she the sinner, he the confessor.

"It's funny," she mused quietly, looking down at the broken glass at her feet, "I'm usually so cautious, never impulsive, but I couldn't seem to get the idea of suicide out of my mind. I did the research on the least painful ways to kill yourself. I didn't have any sleeping pills, but it turns out you don't need them. All you need is a razor blade and a warm bath. A few sharp stings, and I could just go to sleep . . . it seemed a good choice, particularly when it came to cleanup."

Her words were so unemotional, so far removed from the turmoil she must've felt at the time.

"I didn't know what would be waiting on the other side."

This, Gabriel understood. The other side of the veil, the other side of the fine line that led to Heaven or Hell. What he didn't know, what he didn't understand, was why Hope had found Darkness waiting for her instead of Light.

"I was lying there, in the bathtub, all but gone, and there was this *thing* . . . this presence, hovering over my shoulder." Her look turned inward for a moment as she remembered, but what she saw clearly frightened her, for she hurried on. "It wanted to take me somewhere, but suddenly *he* was there, and he said no."

"A soul eater." A growing sense of outrage caused Gabe to clench his fists. Suicide was a gray area. When a person full of sadness or insanity threw away his life, his soul could be misled, but he was usually given a choice.

He found it hard to believe that Hope would have chosen the Darkness.

"Tell me," he said to her softly, "did you seek him out?"

She gave him a troubled look. "I suppose I did, in a way. I blamed God for taking my sister away, and for lots of other things." Things she clearly didn't want to talk about. "I didn't believe that there would be anything waiting for me on the other side but blackness." Her slender throat moved as she swallowed. "And I guess that's what I got."

"Not true," Gabriel said, moved despite himself at the set of those fragile shoulders, slumped with guilt. "You also got me."

For just an instant, he saw a faint glimmer of hope in her eyes, but she blinked and looked away. "Lucky you," she murmured sardonically.

"And the Key?" He looked dispassionately at the book, now sitting on the coffee table. "Why do you have it?"

"He . . ." She hesitated, shooting him a guilty look. "He gave it to me. He wants me to transcribe it, put it on the Internet. I was scared; I thought maybe I could use it against him. I thought maybe that if I could control the demons he'd threatened to send after me, I'd be the one with the upper hand, not him."

He wanted to believe her, but her eyes, so green, so clear, still held secrets.

"I was so stupid." She looked toward the curtains, suppressing a shudder. "I don't know what I would've done if you hadn't shown up to drive that thing away."

"I don't know, either," he agreed, remembering the satisfying crack of his fist against the demon's blackened, leathery chin. That particular Dronai was going to have a hard time chewing for the next few days; his only regret was that he hadn't ripped the foul creature's head off.

He rose from the couch, restless and unsettled. "Go to bed," he told her abruptly. "I'll keep watch."

She shook her head, opening her mouth to argue, but he cut her off. "You're safe with me, Hope, safer than you'd ever be with a book of spells you don't know how to use." He took the broom from her, gesturing toward the hallway that led to her room. "You're exhausted. Go now, and we'll talk more in the morning."

She had to crane her neck to look up at him, and he was reminded of how small she was, how delicate the bones of her shoulders, how fragile the line of her jaw. "Why are you doing this?" she asked him softly. "I was awful to you, accused you of"—her voice broke, and she swallowed—"of doing something terrible."

Gabriel hardened his heart. "Yes, you did." He could tell her his own truth, which was that she was a pawn in a game of Satan's choosing, and that he'd taken up the gauntlet before knowing of her Devil's bargain. He could've told her everything, including his history with Samael, his one-time brother. Instead he merely said, "I'm sworn to defend humankind against the Darkness. It's what I do."

"Oh." She sounded slightly disappointed. "So you'd do this for anybody."

"Not anybody," he answered, and left it at that.

She turned and left the room. A moment later he heard her bedroom door close, and breathed an unconscious sigh of relief. He had a long night ahead of him, and just being near her left him on edge. How much of her story was truth, and how much fiction? How steeped in Darkness was she, and at this point, why did he even care?

Pacing the living room, scooping up the remainders of broken glass, he told himself it was because he didn't want Sammy to win this one. Because he was duty bound not to be responsible for a single soul being consigned to Hell, whether it be from his onetime brother's spite or his own arrogance. He'd taunted Sammy into proving him wrong about temptation, and Hope was the tool Sammy was using to prove it.

It wasn't her fault.

Or was it?

It was thoughts like this that led him, hours later, to pad softly down the hall to check on her.

The light from the hallway fell upon her sleeping face as he silently opened the door. On a pillow beside her, the gray cat lifted its head, eyes glowing golden. It, too, kept watch, and the sight comforted him.

Hardly knowing what he did, he stepped into the room, coming closer to the bed. She slept on, one hand palm up on the pillow, the other atop the covers. Her arms were bare save for the gauze around her wrists. Whatever she wore to sleep in had slender straps, white against her shoulders. He wanted to wake her up, to rail at her for being so foolish as to have dealings with the Devil, but he could only stare, like a lovesick boy, at the creamy curve of her cheek, and the lashes that lay like dark feathers upon it.

Then, to his surprise, her eyes opened.

"You're so beautiful," she murmured, still half asleep. "So beautiful."

Gabe's heart rate accelerated.

She was the one who was beautiful, the expression on her face just as he'd imagined a woman in love would have, when the man she loved came to her bed. Languorous, yet knowing. Open, yet willing to be opened further, a bud needing only the slightest encouragement to bloom.

He could never be that man, yet he couldn't seem to stop himself from bending over her, touching his hand to her hair. "Shhh . . ." he whispered, "go back to sleep."

Her eyes drifted shut, but at the same time, her hand came up to encircle his neck. He froze at the sensation, fascinated by the unique experience of her touch, like liquid heat, as she drew him down.

And then she kissed him, and Gabe's universe expanded to include the sensation of soft lips on his own, the exchange of warm breath, and a throb in his lower belly that was near pleasure/pain. He had no idea why he let her do it, except that she seemed so precious and fragile, so vulnerable, as though she offered him her loneliness and her sorrows along with her body.

Heaven help him, he could not help but drink them in.

Closer she moved, and closer still, until her breasts were against his chest, and it was this that broke the spell; the desire to put his arms around her and drag her even closer came over him like a wave, and with it came the knowledge that if he let it, he would drown.

Abruptly he jerked his head back, ending the kiss. "Stop," he whispered, looking into her eyes, now wide with shock. "You must stop."

The look on her face confused him: hurt, surprise, and something else, something he was afraid to acknowledge, for he felt it, too; heat, tension, a sensation that simmered in the air between them like magic.

She swallowed, eyes wide in the dimness. "We don't have to stop," she whispered, keeping her hand in place.

To his shame, Gabriel found he didn't want to. He wanted to kiss her again, and again, until the urges of his earthly body had been sated with the softness of her flesh, the moist heat of her mouth. *Just once—no one would know.* He heard the words inside his head, knowing they were a lie, but understanding, perhaps for the first time, why humans lied to themselves so easily.

"You're not yourself," he told her, speaking for the both of them. He pulled back, stepping away.

In his heart, he knew it was best. He was an angel, and she was human. Neither desire nor temptation was his master.

Until now . . . until *this* human, she of the green eyes and the bandaged wrists, made further mockery of his resolve by sitting up, lifting her filmy top over her head in a simple yet elegantly complex motion of her arms, and sat before him in nothing but her own glory. Her breasts were revealed: tender, rounded drops of feminine flesh, tipped with pale strawberries.

Gabriel's mouth went dry as his body betrayed him, the most basic male part of him stirring, rousing, clamoring its hunger for he knew not what.

"Cover yourself," he said hoarsely, unable to look away.

Hope shook her head, voice shaking. "No."

Despite her seeming bravado, she was afraid.

From deep within, Gabriel summoned his inner self—the faithful servant who stood at the One's right hand—and used it to subdue the human form he currently occupied. He was a protector, not an object of fear or desire. It was his job to save Hope from the Darkness, not throw himself into it alongside her.

"Cover yourself," he told her, harshly this time, and turned away.

* * *

Ashamed, Hope lay awake in the dark, wondering whether it wouldn't have been better if she'd succeeded at killing herself.

If she'd managed to take her own life, she wouldn't be in this position, caught in a battle between Heaven and Hell, balanced on the knife edge of fear and desire, no closer to finding her missing sister than she'd been to begin with. She wouldn't have had to admit to herself that when she'd seen Gabriel standing over her, she'd felt her heart soar, and her soul take wing. She wouldn't have had to acknowledge, deep in her heart of hearts, that she wanted Gabriel for herself, and that no matter what she did, she'd never be able to have him. His golden brown eyes saw straight through her, and she wanted them, just once, to look at her and see a woman, not a lost, pathetic soul in need of rescue.

She sighed, turning on her side. She'd slept alone for so long, yet the bed had never felt emptier. His shoulders had been so broad, as though they could bear the weight of the world without bowing. His hair had spilled partially over his cheek, the light from the hallway gilding one side of his face, while the other had been in darkness.

When she'd opened her eyes and seen him,

she'd felt the way the sirens must've felt, once upon a time, willing men to their doom through songs and the sweetness of their flesh, and she hadn't cared, for nothing had mattered in that moment except the touch of Gabe's lips against her own, and the chance to feel them again.

Then he'd said no, and it had all vanished, like a puff of smoke, leaving her bereft.

Always, and forever, bereft.

Chapter Twelve

"Surely you're not going to let him get away with this, Master." Nyx was outraged, as was the Dronai warrior at his back. They stood in the center of Unholy of Holies, the throne room Sammy used when he had official business to conduct. "He's as much as declared war upon you, my lord. The woman belongs to the Darkness, and the Light-bringer knows it!"

Bored, His Satanic Majesty hooked a knee over one side of his gilded throne, and rested his chin in his hand.

"It's true, Great Shaitan." The Dronai warrior's voice rasped like a rusty saw. "He brought forth a sword, infused with light, and has placed seals upon the doors and windows. I barely escaped with my life."

"Whipped out the Sword of Righteousness already, has he?" Sammy perked up a bit, but not for the reasons his warriors might have thought. "Oh, he's in for it now, is Gabriel." A slow smile brought a diabolical curve to his lip. "How delightful."

"Then we attack? Let me send the Ravenai— they'll tear his human flesh to ribbons before he has a chance to defend himself."

"The Dronai can do it," objected the smaller demon, clearly insulted. "Our honor is at stake! A few dozen of us, and he'll stand no chance!"

Sammy, deep in thought, waved the idea away. "The Ravenai are no match for Gabriel, and neither are the Dronai, no matter how many I send. His corporeal form may be flesh and blood, but his essence is not."

Baffled, Nyx loosed a rumbling growl of frustration. "You cannot let this challenge go unanswered, my prince! He has no right to claim the girl, for we have already claimed her!"

A blond eyebrow arched. *"We?"*

Nyx frowned, casting his red eyes down toward the marble floor. "The Darkness, my lord. I refer to your legions, who act on your behalf. I meant no disrespect."

"I should hope not," Sammy answered silkily. "For though you are a part of me, you are *not* me, and never will be."

The heavy doors of the throne room swung open, admitting childish laughter into the room.

"Come on, Tesla," cried Cain, "Stop being such a wimp! Last one to touch Father's throne is a—"

Silence fell, pregnant with tension. Sammy's son stood in the doorway, and behind him, a small imp, who tried desperately to make himself look even smaller. For a moment, Cain looked worried, but he recovered quickly, pasting a sunny smile on his face. "Father," he said. "I'm sorry, I didn't know you were in here."

"As though it would've mattered," Sammy muttered beneath his breath.

"A fire imp?" questioned the Dronai, clearly astonished. "What is *that* vermin doing here?"

Sammy rolled his eyes, knowing quite well how competitive his legions could be. The Dronai, though mere foot soldiers, thought themselves far above the imps, who were never allowed to leave Sheol. The Ravenai thought themselves far above the Dronai, the Vulturi thought themselves above the Ravenai, and the ethereals thought themselves above all, save the Ruler of the Abyss himself.

"Tesla isn't vermin," shot back Cain, clearly not intimidated by the Dronai's disapproval.

Somewhere, in the nether regions of his chest, Sammy felt a stirring of pride. He fixed a warning eye on his son, nonetheless.

"Take your pet and go play elsewhere, child. This room is off-limits."

Cain flushed, accepting the rebuke. He backed from the room, the imp skittering nervously behind him, and closed the doors as he left.

Nyx gave an inelegant sniff. "The creature reeks of brimstone. He doesn't belong in the inner temple."

"He certainly doesn't," rasped the Dronai, in a rare show of support.

"I don't believe I asked either of you for your opinions," Sammy rapped out sharply. "Have you any other suggestions on how to raise my son?" He stood, crossing his arms over his chest as he looked down upon the two demons. "Perhaps you'd like to tell me how to run my kingdom, as well."

Nyx, far taller than the Dronai, drew himself to attention. "Of course not, O Dark One."

"Of course not," echoed the Dronai, doing the same.

"If I choose to give Cain a playmate, it's no concern of yours," Sammy said, addressing himself mainly to Nyx. "You've proven yourself unable to keep up with him . . . if he's to stay safe, he must stay within my stronghold, not roaming the Underworld."

Too well trained to betray his annoyance at being found wanting in front of a lesser demon, Nyx remained silent.

"The imp keeps him entertained, and out of trouble." The statement wasn't entirely true, as evidenced by the current situation. "As long as he does so, I see no problem."

"Nor do I, Master." Nyx inclined his head, and like a puppet, the Dronai did the same.

"Go," snapped Sammy, unaccountably irritated. "Leave me, both of you. I'll let you know what's to be done with the Lightbringer, but in the meantime, do nothing."

A few moments later, and he was alone, in an empty throne room. The golden columns that encircled the room glittered, as did the chandeliers above his head, reflected in the shining marble floors. Annoyed at himself for being annoyed, Sammy took a deep breath, drinking in the silence.

Had he been wrong to spare the imp? It seemed a harmless enough way to keep the boy occupied, and saved him the trouble of crushing the creature beneath his heel.

Liar, said a voice in his head. To his chagrin, the voice sounded much like Gabriel's. *The Great Deceiver, who deceives even himself. You didn't want the boy to hate you . . . you, who claim to thrive on hate.*

"Damnation," Sammy muttered, and quit the throne room, looking for somewhere less overwhelmingly ostentatious to spend his time.

Knowing just the place, he soon found himself on the shores of an underground sea, where the water was as black as his soul, the sky leaden, scudded with gray clouds. The Sea of Sorrows, he called it, for it was here that the shades of regret lingered, seeking fruitlessly to leave their footprints in the sand. They never would, of course, for by the time they got here, they were incorporeal, mere figments of the humans they'd once inhabited. The wind wailed, and the waves crashed, and in its own way, the sea was as beautiful as the blue-green oceans on the planet above.

Sammy made his way along the rocks that littered the shore, enjoying the thunder of the waves, ignoring the wisps of regret that passed him by, unseeing. He soon found himself in a small cove, sheltered from the worst of sea's fury. There, combing her long, black hair with a comb made of mother-of-pearl, sat a Nereid, singing a song of loneliness and longing, with no one to hear it save the wind and the sea. Half woman, half octopus, the Nereids were treacherous, but beautiful, at least above the waist.

Intrigued, for the Nereids were shy creatures, Sammy stood, and listened.

Weep for the secrets you never revealed
The time you lost while striving,
Mourn the passing of the years
Like the dead, no hope of reviving.
Pearls on a strand were the days of your life
The string now snapped, and broken,
Mourn for the secrets you never revealed
And the words you left unspoken.

Closing his eyes, Sammy let the song wash over him, the words resonating more than he wished, and less than they would had he ever been human. What was it like, he wondered, to know that your existence was finite, and that every step you took led you closer to death? That every decision you made was meaningless in the big scheme of things, and that everything you thought was important was, in reality, nothing?

"Hail and well met, O Prince of Darkness."

Sammy opened his eyes to see that the Nereid had slipped into the water and swum to where he stood. Her black hair flowed around her like ink, darker than the Sea of Sorrows itself, as she bobbed in the water near his feet.

"I thought the stories of your magnificence were exaggerated," said the Nereid, "but now I see the truth of it myself. You gleam like the treasures beneath the surface of the deep."

"Thank you," Sammy replied, amused by the Nereid's flattery. "Your song was lovely."

"I am Galene," she said, "and I am honored. Swim with me, and I will sing for you again."

With a laugh, he shook his head. "Oh no, my pretty one, for I know what would happen. You would seek to entwine me in your coils, and I would be forced to kill you." He tilted his head, admiring her bluish-gray skin, the onyx glitter of her upturned eyes. "What a shame that would be."

"I am what I am," Galene said simply. "You can't blame a girl for trying."

Such modern-day speech from such an ancient creature made him laugh again. "Sing for me anyway," he ordered, and took a seat on the rocks, leaning his back against one of the largest.

The Leviathan stirs, dark currents swirl,
Woe to the man, and joy to the girl
Who spins her web, unknowing of fate
And snares the one who thought himself safe.
Like the dark River Styx
That flows to the sea
Woe to the one who thought himself free.

Sammy stiffened, and sat up.

Love unrequited, yet sweeter by far
Than a kingdom of darkness, ruled by a star
Who once dwelled in the Heavens
Yet now is cast down
Woe to the one who chafes at his crown.

"That's enough," he said sharply, but the Nereid
went on.

Where mercy is shown, mercy is given
Woe to the one, himself unforgiven,
Who pines for that which he'll never possess
Denied her touch, love's tender caress
Kisses like wine, yet to be tasted
His kingdom at risk, his true glory wasted.

"Enough," Sammy roared, and came to his feet. He trembled with rage, and something else— something that felt suspiciously like pain. "Save your words for those who deserve them, for those who come here hounded by regret!"

"*You* came here," Galene said simply. "And I but sing what the sea moves me to sing."

Scooping up a loose rock, Sammy flung it at the Nereid, who dodged it easily, slipping through the water like an eel.

"Why so angry, O Great Shaitan? Everyone has things they regret, and whoever the dark-haired girl was, are you not better for having known her?" Galene eyed him curiously, unruffled by his loss of composure. "What doesn't kill you makes you stronger, you know."

"Then I am a Colossus," he shouted, and raised his arms wide. Staring up at the leaden sky, he let the anger come, let the memories of Nicki Styx flood his brain, and felt anew the rage and frustration he'd felt when he'd finally accepted she could never be his.

Nicki, wide-eyed and frightened, yet refusing to give in when faced with a choice between good and evil. The unconscious sway of her hips as she walked the streets of Little Five Points. Laughing with her friend Evan as they worked together in her store. The Halloween party at the Vortex, the first time he'd laid eyes on her. The scent of her hair, like cherries, the one and only time he'd ever kissed her.

He'd had to let her go to keep her safe, for his world had no room for a kindhearted young woman with pink streaks in her hair. She would have had no defense against the malevolent forces that surrounded him. His one and only selfless act of mercy, which hurt more than anyone would ever know.

"You are indeed a Colossus," Galene agreed, treading water at his feet. "But now you must be wary, for it is the nature of others to mistake strength for weakness. There are those within your kingdom who would snatch your crown from your grasp."

"What do you know of strength?" He lashed out with scorn, seeking to wound. "You're nothing but a cold-blooded freak of nature, with no idea what it means to rule a kingdom."

"I am friend to the Leviathan, and friend to you as well," said the Nereid, unperturbed by the insult. "The Leviathan sleeps, but sees all in his dreams. He sent me here, to tell you in song what you refuse to hear otherwise."

"You speak in riddles," Sammy snapped.

"All the better for you to understand me, O

Golden One. We speak the same language, you and I. Here beneath, I sing my endless refrains as a reminder of what could have been, what might have been, but in the world above, I am a trickster, dragging men and women alike to their doom." She tilted her sleek, wet head, observing him dispassionately. "Unlike you, however, I am content with my fate, for it is all I've ever known."

"You are most fortunate," murmured Sammy, and turned away. Like a match, his anger had flared, then burned away, leaving him spent. "Most fortunate."

"I'm very sorry, my darling, but if your pet's to stay in the room with us while I teach you to read, he must have a bath first." Pandora wrinkled her pretty nose at the imp and waved a hand before her face, rings glittering on her fingers.

"He's not my pet," Cain said. "He's my friend, and his name is Tesla."

"He could be named Terrydiddle Farquart for all I care," she replied calmly, "but if he's to remain, he must be clean."

They were in the temple library, a huge room with floor-to-ceiling shelves, filled with books of every description. One wall held niches stacked with scrolls, some of them already crumbling to dust.

Tesla, who was sitting on the floor, openly gawking at Pandora's plump prettiness, looked to Cain and asked, "What's a *bath*?"

"It's when you get all wet," his friend replied, "except you have to use soap."

"What's *soap*?"

Exasperated, Pandora rolled her eyes. "Heathens, the pair of you." She looked at the imp again, giving a delicate sniff. "What have you been rolling in?"

Tesla, taking his cue from Cain, answered without a shred of self-consciousness. "Brimstone and ashes, my lady."

"Well"—a pair of perfectly tweezed eyebrows rose—"at least it has some manners."

"Tesla's not an *it*," Cain replied, showing a bit of exasperation himself. "He's a fire imp."

"He's a *dirty* fire imp," she returned placidly. "And you could use a bath yourself."

"Ugh."

"Ugh, indeed," said Sammy, strolling in. "I don't know which of you is dirtier."

"Tesla is," Cain answered promptly.

The imp, who a moment before had been quite

talkative, seemed to have nothing whatsoever to say for himself. He eyed Sammy with trepidation, clearly uncomfortable in his master's presence.

"You've frightened the poor creature to death, you bad boy," Pandora said to Sammy playfully. "Just look how he quivers."

Not bothering to look, Sammy addressed himself to Cain. "Where are your shoes?"

Cain, glancing down at his bare—and very dirty—feet, shrugged. "Tesla doesn't wear shoes."

Narrowing his eyes at his son, the Great Shaitan replied. "You are *not* an imp, and *you* do. Those were two-hundred-dollar Nikes, and the third pair you've lost this week . . . where did you leave them?"

Pandora gave a light trill of laughter. "Since when have you cared about money, my most dreadfully handsome lord?"

Sammy gave her an annoyed look. "It's not about the money. It's about the principle."

"What's *money*?" Tesla could be heard to whisper, but Cain shook his head, obviously having no idea.

"Go and bathe," Sammy told his son sternly, "and take that troublesome creature with you. Don't come back until you're clean, *and* wearing shoes."

Cain, ever-resilient, gave a fatalistic sigh. "Come on, Tesla. I'll introduce you to the water sprites . . . they're almost as pretty as Aunt Pandy."

Pandora laughed and clapped her hands. "Bravo, young prince! Flattery is a skill that will always serve you well. How charming that I need not teach it to you." To Sammy, she remarked, "The boy is a natural, just like his father."

Throwing himself into a chair at Pandora's side, Sammy watched as boy and imp scampered from the room. "Of course he is. He has more tricks up his sleeve at nine than I did at nine thousand."

"Pooh," she replied, "you couldn't possibly be a day over eight."

"Cain's not the only one who's full of flattery today." He eyed his lover speculatively, his conversation with the Nereid having made him wary. "Tell me, my dear, why are you being so accommodating lately? It's hardly like you to put yourself out on anyone's behalf."

"True," Pandora answered, not bothering to deny it. The bracelets on her wrist tinkled as she laid down the book she'd been holding. "I'm an indolent creature at the best of times, but one gets bored with one's own company after a while." Coiling a lock of hair around a beautifully mani-

184 Terri Garey

cured finger, she gave him a provocative smile. "You, my darling Devil, are never boring."

"Still, I would never have taken you for a teacher." He glanced around the room, gesturing toward the books. "Or a nursemaid."

She gave a mock shudder. "Perish the thought. Have you seen what nursing can do to one's figure?"

Not in a playful mood, Sammy gave her a sour look.

"All right, all right . . . no need to glower. If you must know, I needed a challenge."

"Did you now?" Sammy knew he was being petty, but couldn't help himself. "I believe the last time you took on a challenge, you failed."

She looked at him archly. "How so?"

"The golden casket containing all the world's ills, my dear. When it was given into your safe-keeping, you were told not to open it, but you did."

"Oh, that." She shrugged, causing her ample breasts to rise and fall. "Curiosity has always been my downfall, darling, as you know quite well. If I hadn't been forbidden to open that box, it would've remained forever closed. It's not as though I knew I'd be releasing nasty things like disease, or war, or famine into the world, now was it?"

"Some would argue that ignorance is no

excuse." Sammy looked away, remembering his own mistake, and what it had cost him.

"Yes." Pandora reached out, placing a plump hand over his. "It's something we share in common, isn't it? We're both blamed for releasing evil into the world."

The Great Shaitan said nothing, but neither did he move his hand.

She squeezed his fingers. "Take heart, my darling Dark One. I closed the box before *everything* escaped, you know."

"Is that so?" he asked idly, not really caring. "What was left?"

"Hope, my dear," she said, patting his hand. "Hope."

He shot her an irritable glance, not in the mood for puzzles. "What is *that* supposed to mean?"

Pandora leaned back, releasing his hand. "It means we all have secrets, Samael, sometimes secrets we hide even from ourselves." She smoothed a hand over her hair. "The universe doesn't care what we seek to hide; it will have what it wills, and occasionally what it wills is in our own best interest. We all hope, in our heart of hearts, that the universe will one day take pity on us, and do as it wills."

Chapter Thirteen

Gabriel spent a sleepless night, but it hardly mattered, for he didn't need sleep. When light began to creep around the curtains in Hope's living room, he opened them, watching the city turn ever paler shades of gray.

Why was he so drawn to her? Why this need to protect her? She'd known what she was doing when she made her unholy bargain with the Devil, just as she'd known what she was doing last night when she tried to seduce him.

Never before had he been tempted. Never.

Lifting his hand, he held it out from his body, the sun a glowing ball behind it. Blood coursed through his veins, a different form of energy from what he was used to when in angelic form. Blood, breath; the pulsing engines that drove the world of the flesh. Mankind had been created in the One's own image; was it wrong for an angel to take pleasure in it?

"Guide me, my Father," he murmured. "I need to be strong, but I've never before felt so weak."

Light bloomed at the corner of his vision, a much brighter light than the sun outside the window. Gabe turned his head to see a corner of Hope's living room become slowly eclipsed by a pulsating, amorphous ball of pure energy that grew, and grew, until the walls surrounding him disappeared entirely, leaving him bathed in Light, warmed through and through by knowledge of its source.

Gabriel closed his eyes, basking in it, soul soaring as the Light took everything he had, and returned it tenfold.

"Gabriel, my son." A Voice, full of love and compassion, came from the Light. "It is through weakness that strength is most often forged."

"Most High." Gabriel inclined his head in a gesture of deepest respect, fully aware of the honor paid him, encased in human flesh as he was. The One did not often leave the heavens, leaving that for his army of angels.

"You are troubled," said the Voice, "but there is no need."

"I don't understand." Surely he wasn't meant to feel this burning need to press his lips against another's, to feel her skin beneath his fingertips, her breath upon his cheek? "The woman in the other room. She . . ." He found himself ashamed to say the words aloud, yet forced himself to do so, for there was nothing he knew that the One already didn't. "She tempts me."

"Yes," the Voice agreed, with a tinge of sorrow, "for you've wandered too long among my flawed, imperfect children, and become almost as flawed as they."

Gabe's heart began to pound. "I but seek to do as you would have me do, and protect the mortals from the Darkness."

"The Darkness is always among them," the Voice answered, "like a wolf among the sheep."

Deep within, Gabriel trembled.

"We've come to a time of parting, my son." The regret in the Voice was unmistakable.

"No!" Gabriel denied it, standing tall before whom he served. "I am your true and faithful servant! I've done nothing wrong!"

"Love is never wrong, my child."

"I don't love her," he protested. "No more than I love all mankind."

"It is not your love for a mortal woman that

weakens you, but your love for your brother Samael."

Struck dumb by these words, Gabriel remained silent.

"Your hopes for his redemption have left you vulnerable. Samael knows this, even if you do not, and he has set the wheels of fate in motion. You are but a pawn in his game, but now you must play it, or we risk losing all."

Confused, Gabriel shook his head.

"Mankind was created in my image, as were you. Within each man dwells a divine spark, and within each of my angels dwells a spark of humanity. Your humanity—your heart—has been touched, and your physical being has responded."

Gabe opened his mouth, but had no words, for he was unable to deny his body's response to Hope's kiss, her touch.

"The line between earthly and divine, for you—O Gabriel, Son of Mercy, Servant of Truth—has now become blurred. You will remain here, my servant in flesh only, and follow this experience where it may lead you."

There was a buzzing in his head, a tingle between his shoulder blades.

"You are still my instrument," stated the One, "who will now be honed on the sharp edge of humanity, your feet on the Earth and your head no longer in the clouds. Follow your heart, but leave your wings with me, my son."

The weight of the pronouncement brought Gabe to his knees. "No, I—"

"Fear not," said the One, "for I am with you always." The Light began to fade. Gabe, unable to help himself, cried out for it to stay, but it was gone, leaving him feeling heavier and—despite the One's final words—more alone than ever before in his long, long life.

"Gabriel?"

Hope stood in the doorway, a look of fear on her face. When she saw him on his knees, the look was replaced by one of concern. She rushed toward him, placing her hand on his shoulder, but he jerked away.

"Don't touch me."

Her sharp intake of breath told him he'd hurt her, but her pain could be nothing compared to his. Because of her, with her wide green eyes and her heart full of pain, he'd lost everything. Burying his face in his hands, he fought the urge to weep, to rail, to cry out again to the One who'd always been there for him. Never before had he felt the beat of his heart so strongly, heard the breath in his lungs leave his mouth in such gasps.

His body felt so heavy now, all of his strength
gone. Behind closed eyelids, mind spinning, he
saw the Darkness rushing toward him, and this
time, he had no defense. It washed over him like a
flood, and then there was nothing.

When Gabriel slumped to the floor, Hope cried
out, horrified. Despite his order not to touch him,
she fell to her knees beside him, both hands on
his back. He was limp, unconscious, his head
lolling on the carpet as she struggled to turn him
over.

"Gabriel! Gabe, please . . ." Panicky, she laid
an ear against his chest, and felt his heartbeat,
steady and strong, beneath her cheek. His mouth
was slightly open, and she felt his breath, warm
against her fingers. Relief flooded her, but she was
unsure of what to do, so for a moment she just
stayed with her head against his chest, closing her
eyes, listening to the steady beat of his heart.

He stirred, moving his head, his hand coming
up to rest itself on her hair. Tears came to her eyes,
unbidden, and she bit her lip to keep them from
falling, not wanting the moment to end. Somehow, someway, in the middle of this nightmare
she called a life, she'd fallen in love with the one
man she could never have. But for now—for just

this moment—she could remain still, and pretend that he loved her back.

Gabe stirred again, his body tensing beneath her, and the moment was gone. "What happened?" He pushed her away, and she tried not to let on how it hurt. "What are you doing?"

She sat back on her haunches, still biting her lip. "You passed out," she told him, meeting his confused gaze. "I was just checking to see if your heart was still beating."

A spasm of pain crossed his face.

"Are you all right?" she asked, alarmed. "Where does it hurt?"

He shook his head, looking away. "Nowhere," he said, "and everywhere." Rolling away from her, he put a hand on the floor and pushed himself into a sitting position, then rose to his feet. He moved stiffly, like an old man, and Hope could barely restrain herself from helping him as she rose, too.

"What happened?" she asked. "Can I get you anything? What do you want me to do?"

He looked at her, golden brown eyes clouded. "I want you to leave me alone," he answered hoarsely, and moved to the couch, where he sat.

Tears threatened again, but Hope was damned if she was going to let them fall. "Too bad," she told him flatly. "I'm not going anywhere, except to the kitchen to make us both some coffee."

And because she couldn't think of anything else to do, that's just what she did. Once there, she went through the familiar motions she made every day: filling the coffeepot with water, measuring the coffee, getting two mugs from the cabinet instead of one. Her hands shook, but she ignored their shaking, opening a can of food for Sherlock as he meowed his morning hunger in his usual way, getting him clean water, using the time to compose herself. By the time the coffee finished brewing, and Sherlock had emptied his bowl, she was almost able to pretend that everything was normal.

Except it wasn't, because she had a hostile angel on her couch and a broken living room window, caused by a demon who'd been out to get her.

"Here you go," she said, carrying both mugs into the living room. "Do you take milk, or sugar?"

Gabriel sat where she'd left him, a blank expression on his face. His eyes were red-rimmed, staring at nothing. He didn't move until Sherlock, refusing to be ignored, leapt into his lap, purring loudly.

"Take this," she ordered, finding his stillness unnerving. "You look like you need it."

With one hand on the cat, he reached out and took the mug, a faraway look still in his eyes.

"Drink."

Almost like an automaton, he did as she said, and took a sip, swallowing with a grimace.

"It's not *that* bad," she said defensively, referring to the coffee.

"No. It's far, far worse."

Worried, she perched on the edge of the couch next to him. "Tell me what happened."

He shook his head, allowing Sherlock to make himself comfortable in his lap. "You wouldn't understand."

"Not if you don't tell me, I won't," she answered tartly. The pressure of the last few days was definitely getting to her, because she found herself jealous of her own damn cat.

Gabe sighed, stroking the cat's fur, over and over. "I can no longer protect you," he said, in a hollow voice. "Everything's changed."

A cold knot of fear formed in her stomach, but strangely enough, it seemed to be on Gabe's behalf, not her own. "Gabriel," she said softly, "look at me. Tell me what's happened."

Finally he turned his head to look at her. For a moment he said nothing, merely searching her eyes for something she couldn't see, then letting them rove over her face, her hair, finally settling on her hands, cradling the coffee cup. "I'm no longer who I was," he told her hoarsely, "and I have no idea who I'll become."

The pain on his face made her want to reach out and give him comfort, but she didn't dare. "What are you saying?"

"I'm no longer an angel." His eyes hardened. "I'm now human, just like you."

Dumbstruck, she leaned back, unsure of what to say. A part of her was horrified, and a part of her—the secret, incredibly selfish part—was glad, for if he was no longer an angel, it meant he was no longer out of her reach.

It also meant that she was in deep shit again, demon-wise.

"How is that even *possible*?"

The look he gave her was a bit scornful, and it was then she realized that he was truly, deeply angry at her. "You, of all people, can ask me this?"

Flushing, she looked away. "Are you . . ." She licked her lips, not really wanting to know the answer to the question she was about to ask. "Are you saying this is my fault?"

There was a silence, broken only by the low rumble of Sherlock's purr. The stupid cat seemed oblivious to the tension in the room.

"No," Gabriel answered, so low she could barely hear him. "It's mine."

Her heart nearly broke at the pain in his voice, but he'd already made it clear he wanted neither her sympathy nor her pity. "It . . ." She hesitated. "It was only a kiss . . . surely God wouldn't punish you this harshly for something so simple?"

Except it hadn't been simple, not for her. It had been earth-shattering, devastating, life-changing.

A muscle ticked in his jaw. "It doesn't matter why He did it. It's not up to me to question the ways of the One. He deemed it so, and so it is."

The One. The One who'd never been there for her, and who'd now turned His back on yet another who didn't deserve it.

"There must be a way to fix it," she said staunchly, gripping her cup so tightly it hurt. "There has to be."

He shook his head, staring mutely down at the cat.

"So you're giving up?" She hated seeing him this way, couldn't even imagine what he must be going through: to have had the universe at his fingertips, and then have it snatched from his grasp. All those years, doing all that good, for countless people just like her, only to be cast off, with no purpose. It wasn't fair.

Looking at his bowed head, the silken hair she ached to touch, she couldn't help but think his posture was so innately, intrinsically *wrong*. And then suddenly, instinctively, she knew the only way to reach him. "You promised to protect me, but now you're just going to walk away with your tail between your legs?"

His head came up, a gathering frown between his brows.

"I guess all that talk about me being safe with you was just that . . . talk."

The frown turned into a glare. "I no longer have the ability to keep you safe."

She forced herself to get angry, hoping to make him that way, too. "Why, because you're just a puny mortal now, like me? Better not tell that to the army, or the navy, or a police officer on the street! Unlike you, they put themselves out there to serve and protect, and they don't need a pair of angel wings to do it!"

Gabriel put down his coffee cup and stood, dumping Sherlock from his lap. "Are you calling me a coward?"

Hope put her coffee cup down on the table, quite deliberately, and stood up, too. "If the shoe fits."

His brown eyes, usually filled with light and

kindness, darkened. His jaw clenched as his shoulders went back, emphasizing his height and the breadth of his chest.

Inwardly she quailed, well aware that what she was doing was the equivalent of poking a bear with a stick, but it was too late to back down now. "Maybe you think it's okay to cut and run, but I don't!"

"I'm not running away," he said, through gritted teeth. "I just don't have the tools I need to protect you."

"That's not true," she said, putting her hands on her hips. "We still have the Key . . . the *Ars Goetia*. I may not know how to use it, but you do."

He eyed her narrowly, shaking his head. "Foolish girl . . . the Howling Art is not something to be taken lightly. I would've thought you'd learned that lesson last night."

She flushed at the reminder of how she'd stupidly thought she could call the shots when it came to demons, and nearly died because of it. If Gabe hadn't come to her rescue . . .

"I *did* learn my lesson," she said, unwilling to give up just yet. The spark in Gabe's eyes was back, and she wanted to keep it there.

Selfishly she also wanted to live, and if she could manage both, then why not go for it?

"I don't plan on trying anything like that ever again, but surely someone like you, someone who knows what they're doing—"

"Do you have any idea what could be unleashed?" He hissed the words, growing angrier by the minute. "Or do you just not care about the rest of mankind, and what could happen if the doorway to the Darkness were opened?" Raking her with a scornful glare, he answered his own question. "Clearly not, since you were willing to transcribe the book and put it on the Internet."

"That's not fair!" she cried, stung. "I felt as though I had no choice!"

"You had a choice last night."

The image of him standing over her while she begged him to sleep with her made her cheeks burn. "I didn't know what would happen!"

"You seem to say that a lot. Tell me, would it have mattered?" He threw the words at her, clearly expecting an answer.

Hope bit her bottom lip to still its trembling. She could've lied to him easily, but lies had gotten her nowhere. He'd done nothing but try to help her, and everything that had happened since was her own damn fault. She owed him the truth.

"I wasn't thinking about the effect it might have on you."

Unable to meet his fiery golden gaze any longer, she looked away. "I was only thinking of myself." *And that I wanted you.* For pride's sake, she left those five words unsaid. "It was incredibly selfish, and more than stupid. I'm sorry."

Gabe said nothing, and after a moment, she gathered the courage to once again look him in the eye. "I've caused you nothing but trouble, and you have no reason at all to help me, but I hope you will. And someday, maybe, I hope you can forgive me."

He stared at her, his glare like a sword to her heart. Silence stretched between them, broken only by Sherlock's gentle meow as he twined his way between them, rubbing himself against Gabe's leg.

"Please," she whispered. "I never wanted any of this, I swear . . . all I wanted, in the beginning, was to find my sister."

There was no softening in Gabriel's expression, however. She was trembling when he finally said, "Go pack a bag. We have to go; it's not safe to stay here any longer."

Relief made her knees weak. "Where are we going?"

He turned away, ignoring both her and the cat as he moved toward the window. He stood there for a moment, staring out at the city.

"I may not be able to help you, in the end." The line of his jaw was grim. "You made a fool's bargain with the biggest fool who ever lived, and he's not known for his mercy. I can't allow you to put the words of power where evil can find them, and because of that, you may die."

Her lip trembled, but she stilled it, for he was only being honest.

"I can, however, help you do one thing, which may or may not make your burden easier to bear." His shoulders, already so straight, straightened even further. "We go to find your sister."

Chapter Fourteen

Las Vegas had never been one of Gabriel's favorite places, but after the experience of his first airplane flight, he was glad to be there. He'd no idea how mortals stood being cooped up for hours in such a cramped, stuffy environment, when beauty and freedom were just outside their windows. It had given him a whole new perspective on the human experience, and he hadn't cared for it at all.

Even less did he like the hotel Hope had chosen, for the lobby of the Venetian was a gaudy, noisy imitation the Sistine Chapel. Staring up at the frescoed ceiling while she checked in, he tried his best to be stoic, but his heart was heavy.

You are still my instrument, the One had said.

Remain here, and follow this experience where it may lead you.

Why, in the name of all that was holy, it had led him to Las Vegas, he'd never know, but it was not for him to question the ways of the One. *You are but a pawn in Samael's game, but now you must play it, or we risk losing all.*

Firming his chin, Gabriel swore to himself he wouldn't lose, even if he didn't know the rules of the game yet.

In order to remove the threat to Hope, he needed to remove the leverage Sammy had over her, and that meant finding her sister.

"Are you ready?" Hope had come up beside him, looking tired and strained. "We're all checked in."

"I'm ready," he told her, and meant it.

They'd said little to each other during the trip. A part of him knew that his physical attraction to her wasn't entirely her fault, but another part of him blamed her anyway. At any rate, it seemed better to keep his emotional distance, and she hadn't pressed him. He'd spent their travel time immersed in prayer and contemplation, while she'd been lost in thoughts of her own.

She led him down a long, ridiculously ornate corridor, the smell of cigarettes and the level of noise increasing as they went. The corridor came to an end at the casino, which they were forced to make their way through in order to reach the elevators. Bells rang and lights flashed, and people were everywhere, most of them with drinks in their hands, though it was yet midday. Young women in short skirts and too much makeup threaded their way among young men in sloppy, rumpled clothes, while middle-aged men and women slumped over slot machines like automatons, feeding in tokens and pulling handles as though hypnotized. His nose rebelled at the smell of cigarettes, his ears at the noise, and his heart at the wastefulness of humanity's time and money.

A particularly loud commotion at one of the roulette tables caught his attention; someone had apparently just won big. He glanced that way, but kept walking until an all-too-familiar voice caught his ear.

"Here you go, sweetheart. Take this and buy yourself something pretty with it." Ooohs and aaahs came from a crowd surrounding the table, and Gabe turned his head to see Sammy carelessly deposit a large stack of chips into the eager hands of a young Asian woman in a low-cut, pink-sequined dress. Sammy looked up, met his eyes, and told the woman, "Seems like today is my lucky day."

Anger rose in him like a tide. Gabe stopped dead, as Hope went on a few more steps without him.

Sammy, casually yet elegantly dressed in a white button-down shirt, black linen jacket, and jeans, rose from the roulette table to a chorus of disappointed female cooing. Almost all the people watching him play were women, and the few men sitting at the table looked glad to see him go.

"Gabriel, my old friend," said Sammy, as he walked toward him. "Come to try your luck in Sin City, have you?"

"I make my own luck," Gabe told him tersely. Unaware he'd stopped, Hope had kept walking and was now out of earshot, but any minute she'd turn and see whom he was talking to. "What are you doing here?"

Sammy shrugged, a diamond stud glinting in one ear. "The Underworld gets so boring this time of year. I needed a little fun, a little excitement."

"Yes," Gabriel said, keeping a rein on his temper. "I can imagine there are only so many lost souls you can torment before you need fresh ones. What an excellent place to harvest them."

"Exactly. I've made many a deal here, you know.

It's amazing what people will do when they're drunk, desperate, or just plain greedy."

"What do you want, Samael?"

Sammy looked away from him, a smile curling his lips. Gabriel followed his gaze, and saw Hope watching them, clutching her rolling suitcase, her face as white as a sheet. "You know what I want."

"You can't have her!" Gabe said fiercely, keeping his voice low. He couldn't help the surge of protectiveness that made him step closer, putting himself between the Horned One and Hope. "I may be grounded, but I'll take you on regardless."

Sammy's eyes snapped back to his, a frown forming between his perfect blond brows. "What?"

"You heard me." It never occurred to him that Samael would be in the dark about what had happened to him. Samael's preternatural abilities included the ability to read minds, and Gabe was certain he'd been under surveillance since they'd met on the rooftop, what seemed like a lifetime ago. "Come to gloat in person, have you?"

A strange expression crossed Sammy's face, one that Gabriel couldn't read. "Let's go someplace a bit more private, shall we?"

"Why? Don't want an audience? There's a first." He was furious in a way he'd never been before; he was a Protector unable to protect, and his body—the only weapon he had at his disposal—cried out to be used.

A blond brow rose. "Tsk, tsk, Gabriel. You seem eager for a fight. Violence is against your angelic oath, isn't it?"

"Thanks to you, I'm an angel no longer, and I'll do whatever the hell I want."

If Gabe didn't know better, he would've sworn there was a flicker of surprise in Sammy's blue eyes before they narrowed. "Succumbed to the lure of the flesh already, have you?" The Great Shaitan flicked a contemptuous look toward Hope. "She must be sluttier than I thought."

Unthinkingly, Gabe's hands shot out to grab his onetime brother by his oh-so-elegant linen lapels. Sammy didn't flinch, even when their faces were mere inches apart. "Do. Not. Speak of her that way," Gabriel ground out. "Or I'll rip your forked tongue right from your throat."

"My, my," Sammy answered coolly. "Jealousy *and* threats of violence. How the mighty have fallen."

"Is there a problem here?" A burly security guard appeared at Gabriel's elbow, and was quickly joined by a second, even burlier.

"Not at all, Officer," Sammy said mildly,

making no effort to free himself. "Just two old friends, catching up."

"Catch up somewhere else," the security guard growled. "Now."

Gabe forced his fingers to relax, releasing Sammy's jacket. His eyes never left those of his onetime brother, as clear and blue as the sky, and just as remote. "I apologize, Officers," he told the guards. "Just a bit of horseplay between friends."

Sammy took a step back, shrugging his jacket into place, and smoothing a wrinkle from his lapel. "We were just about to go for a drink, weren't we, Gabriel?"

Well aware that *he* was the one the two security guards considered a threat, and not wanting to send Hope into a panic, Gabe forced his lips to smile.

"We were," he agreed, slapping Sammy on the shoulder a bit harder than he needed to. "Sorry to trouble you two gentlemen." Keeping his hand on Sammy's shoulder, he started guiding him away.

Hope, very pale, was staring at him. He gave her a grim look, and jerked his head toward the elevators, but Sammy was having none of it. He slipped from Gabe's grasp like smoke, and took the few steps to where Hope stood. Gabe found himself oddly proud of the way she drew herself up and faced him. She had a death grip on the handle of her suitcase, the knuckles showing white, but she looked the Devil in the eye.

Behind him, the guards walked away, having no doubt seen their share of personal drama before.

"Hello, Hope." To his credit, Sammy didn't try to touch her. "Come for a romantic getaway with your new boyfriend, I take it?"

"No," she answered shortly. She shot Gabe a glance, color coming back to her cheeks. "He's not my boyfriend."

Sammy paused, dispassionately eyeing both of them in turn. "Well, well, well," he murmured, "it seems as though something's amiss. Trouble in paradise already?"

Hope looked to Gabe, but he merely shook his head impatiently. Let Samael think what he liked, especially if it was to his and Hope's advantage.

"None of your business," Gabriel said, "and enough with the small talk. Where's Hope's sister? Where's Charity?"

"And why would I tell you that?"

"Because if you don't, I'm going to mess up that pretty face of yours, security guards or no security guards."

The amusement left the Great Deceiver's eyes. They became cold, and flat.

"I'd suggest you watch what you say to me."

Furious at the knowledge of how far he and his onetime brother were now outmatched, Gabriel said boldly, "Make me."

A stare-down, different from those they'd had in the past, lasted both a moment and a lifetime. There was a look in Samael's eyes that Gabe didn't recognize, and he didn't know what it meant. On his part, he struggled not to show his desperation, his fear that his oldest friend—the personification of all that was evil—might take away the slender, golden-haired girl standing next to him, and put her someplace he could never, ever go.

"Gabe." Hope touched his arm, tentatively, which only increased his tension. "Don't."

"Listen to her, Gabriel." Sammy broke eye contact, glancing around the casino. "Many of these people will burn in Hell soon enough . . . you don't want any of them to end up there prematurely just because of your temper, now do you? I meant what I said about that drink, by the way. Come, let Hope go get settled in her room while we have a chat."

"You'll send one of your minions after her the moment she leaves my sight," Gabe growled, not trusting Sammy one bit.

"I'll do no such thing; she'll be perfectly safe. What's the matter, don't you trust me, *brother*?"

Gritting his teeth, Gabe was forced to acknowledge that he, on more than one occasion, had pulled the "brotherly trust" card.

"Fine. But I expect you to keep your word."

Sammy grinned, looking, for just an instant, as he had in those long-ago days when they were friends. "You're the only one who does, Gabriel, the only one." The Prince of Darkness inclined his head slightly. "She'll be safe while we talk, I swear it."

With a warning glare to Sammy, Gabe took Hope by the elbow and led her aside. Even angry and tense as he was, his fingers tingled as they touched her bare skin. "Go on up without me," he told her, "and make sure the door is locked. What's the room number?"

She handed him the small card that showed the room number, taking a key card for herself, then shot a glance toward Sammy before turning her green eyes back to his. "I'm scared."

He felt himself soften toward her, wishing he could reassure her and tell her everything was going to be all right. "I know you are," was all he could say.

She bit her lip, tucking her short hair behind

an ear. "Are you sure you'll be all right? I mean, without your powers . . ."

He shifted so that Sammy couldn't see her face, so pale and set, and murmured. "It'll be okay."

She stared up at him. "Be careful," she answered softly, then turned and walked away.

Gabe stood there, watching, until Hope was swallowed by the crowd, and he could see her no more.

"Now what's all this about you being grounded?" They were seated in a back booth in one of the casino's many bars. Sammy had ordered a Hennessy for himself and a soda for Gabe, knowing his old friend had no love for alcohol. He couldn't shake an odd feeling—which he suspected was guilt—but it had been so long since he'd felt anything like it that he wasn't sure.

Gabriel regarded him stonily. "Like you don't know. That's exactly what you wanted, isn't it?"

"In all honesty, no," Sammy replied, surprised to find it was so. "I merely wanted to teach you a lesson about forbidden fruit, and how hard it is to resist. I never expected you to actually pluck it."

"Liar."

"I am that," he acknowledged.

Gabriel gave him a disgusted look, leaning back

as a waitress in an incredibly short skirt brought them their drinks.

"Can I get you two gentlemen anything else?" She smiled at them both, lingering at the table as she slid their drinks in front of them.

Gabriel ignored her, while Sammy gave her an unabashed once-over. "Not at the moment, but keep them coming."

The woman—a girl, really, for she looked barely old enough to drink herself—answered him saucily, "Oh, I do, darlin'. I do," before walking away with a definite sway of her scantily clad hips.

Sammy took a sip of his cognac, not bothering to inhale the fragrance, as he usually did. The burn centered him, reminding him that guilt had no place in his world.

"I want to know where Hope's sister is," said Gabriel, not touching his soda. "And then I want you to go away and leave them both alone. You knocked me off my pedestal, and got what you came for. It's over."

"I'm not so sure about that, Gabriel. There's still the small matter of the Key." He put down his glass, running his finger along the rim. "Or did Hope neglect to inform you about that little detail?"

Gabriel's jaw flexed. "How did you get it?" he asked stonily.

"I inherited it, along with all the other treasures Solomon stored in his precious temple. The Eye of Caradoc, the Crystal of Khartoum . . . old King Sol was a bit of a collector, it seems."

"He wasn't a collector," Gabe ground out. "All those items were meant to be kept from the Darkness, not used for its benefit."

"Oh, the irony," Sammy stated calmly.

"I'm not going to allow Hope to put the words of power on the Internet," Gabe said grimly.

"Then she will die, and so will her sister." He shrugged, noting how his onetime brother's hand clenched atop the table. "That was the bargain we made."

"Then unmake it."

"That would set a very bad precedent," Sammy returned. "I have my reputation to consider, after all."

He half expected Gabriel to lunge for his throat at that point, but Gabriel merely glared, forcing Samael to meet his eyes.

"And what about you? You seem awfully calm for someone who's just been thrown out of Heaven . . . where's the ranting, the raving, the *angst*?" He took another sip, eyeing his onetime brother narrowly. "Can it be that you actually think Hope might be worth it?"

Gabe was silent for a moment, eyeing him narrowly in return. "My feelings for Hope are none of your business," he finally said. "As is my relationship to the One. If He chooses to punish me with the loss of my wings, then I accept the punishment."

"Oho," Sammy cried, "how noble of you, how strong." He raised his glass in a sour salute. "Ever the lapdog, aren't you? Our dear Father can do nothing wrong in your eyes, can he? If you think he's going to relent because of a show of long-suffering patience on your part, you'd best think again."

"Is that all you have to say to me?" Gabriel hissed. "This is your fault, all of it. You set these wheels in motion . . . you found her at a moment of weakness, put her in an impossible position, and then deliberately placed her in my path. How *dare* you blame it on the One?"

"You didn't have to take on the job of saving her soul," Sammy answered mildly, though inside, he felt a worm of guilt continuing to squirm.

"No, I didn't, but I did, so you must be very happy." Gabe looked away, but not before Sammy had seen the pain in his brown eyes, so familiar, and yet so different. "Now tell me where her sister is so we can all live happily ever after, you sorry-ass son of a bitch."

In all the years they'd known each other, Sammy had never known Gabriel to use anything but the mildest of profanities, and it was this that convinced him that Gabe was telling him the truth about his fall from grace. Why he hadn't known about it was another matter; his spies rarely let him down.

"Gabe." He leaned in, keeping his voice low. "I can see you're upset. I understand how you feel—"

"Do you? I find that hard to believe." Bitterness and scorn dripped from Gabe's voice. "You saw Eve in the Garden and you took her, uncaring of the consequences." He gave a snap of his fingers to emphasize the point. "*I* saw a woman I thought was in need and tried to save her, only to find she was just a tool in my oldest friend's nasty little bag of tricks. Why did you do it, Samael? I tried to help you, I gave you an opportunity to prove yourself to the One in the hopes He would forgive you—"

"But He didn't, did He? Instead He just sent you to lord it over me with your goodness and your mercy—"

"He didn't send me," Gabe said fiercely. "Every time I've come to you I've done it of my own free will!"

"More fool you, then," snapped Sammy bitterly. "What did you expect me to do, Gabriel? You know my faults, you know my nature!"

Their voices had risen. A couple at a nearby table shot them curious glances, as did the waitress who'd brought them their drinks earlier.

"Yes," Gabe said, in a lower tone. "I know your nature. You're selfish, and childish, and spiteful, and in all these centuries you've never learned how to be otherwise. I pity you."

Sammy felt the cognac turn to acid in his belly. The glass in his hand shattered, spilling dark brown liquid, like old blood, across the tablecloth.

"I don't need your pity," he ground out. "Save it for your girlfriend."

Alarm, quickly banked, flared in Gabriel's eyes. "She isn't my girlfriend, and besides, you said she was safe."

"Do you love her?" he demanded.

"What does that have to do with anything?"

Everything, Sammy thought, and then banished the thought from his mind.

"It isn't over, Gabriel." He picked up his napkin, deliberately wiping his fingers clean. "I gave her a job to do, and she's yet to do it. It's not my fault if she's somehow managed to touch your heart in the meantime. Be warned, my friend: there's a difference between sex and love, and you have yet to learn it."

"Like you'd know the difference," Gabriel sneered, his rage plainly overcoming his common sense.

"Oh, I know all about love," said Samael the Black, Son of Perdition. "And I particularly know what it means to lose it." He tossed his napkin on the table like a gauntlet. "Soon, you'll know it, too."

And then, like the shadows over which he ruled, he faded away before Gabriel could say another word.

Gabe sat there in the booth for some minutes, pondering the conversation.

Do you love her? Samael had asked, as though love were an option.

Did he care about Hope? Certainly, as he cared for all humankind.

Did he want to protect her? Absolutely, for he was a Guardian; the loss of his wings hadn't changed that.

It was still unbelievable to him, the idea that he was now earthbound, unable to shed himself of skin, bone, and sinew—unable to rise above this mortal coil and soar, weightless, to places where only wind and silence reigned.

It would've been easy to become angry at the loss of his wings, but anger was a luxury he couldn't allow himself, for it smacked of self-indulgence and self-pity. The One had willed it so, and treated him kindly even in the doing; separation from the heights didn't mean separation from Heaven itself. The initial shock had worn off during the interminable plane ride to Las Vegas, and while it had been tempting to blame Hope for what happened to cause his current state of powerlessness, he knew there was more than enough blame to go around.

Sammy, first and foremost, for tampering with the life of such a fragile, tragic soul, and using her to strike out at the only friend he'd ever really had. Himself, secondly, for allowing himself to envision—nay, perhaps even long for—a bit of the humanity he'd so long observed and protected. He saw again Hope's face, lit only by the light from the hallway, lashes like feathers on her cheeks, and knew he had only himself to blame for that kiss; that soul-searing kiss that had stolen the breath from his lungs, and perhaps—just perhaps—his heart along with it.

"Can I get you anything else, handsome?" The young waitress was back, giving him an arch smile above the tray she balanced on her hip. A flicker of surprise touched her overly made-up face as she caught sight of the broken glass and cognac-soaked napkin on Sammy's side of the table, but she made no comment as she leaned over to clean it up, giving Gabe a clear view of her cleavage, and the line of her hip in her too-short skirt.

"Your friend coming back?" she asked lightly, shooting him a flirtatious glance.

"He'll be back," said Gabriel darkly, though he wasn't referring to the booth or the bar.

The waitress straightened, placing the broken glass and napkin on her tray. "That's too bad." She shrugged. "I get off in an hour, and wouldn't mind a little company."

He looked at her, knowing objectively that she was pretty—very pretty—and finding himself not the least bit tempted to take her up on her offer. He was human now, but he felt as he always did; detached, finding it slightly sad that such an attractive woman didn't see her own value, and thought so little of herself that she would offer herself to a stranger.

There was someone else whose company he preferred, and the knowledge slipped into his mind like a shadow, seeking its day in the sun. This gaudy, noisy bar with its tinkle of glass and forced laughter, reeking of cigarettes from the nearby casino, was not where he wanted to be.

He wanted to be with Hope, in a quiet apartment with hardwood floors and buttery yellow walls, the smell of banana pudding in the air, and Sherlock stretched out upon the floor, yellow eyes gleaming.

"Sorry," he told the waitress, "but I'm with someone."

The waitress shrugged again, arching a perfectly plucked brow. "Lucky her," she said, and walked away, swinging her hips.

He sat there a moment more, absorbing what he'd just learned about himself. *You are still my instrument*, the One had stated. *Follow your heart, but leave your wings with me.*

Was it possible? Was he allowed to now follow the yearnings of his beating, racing, all-too-human heart?

She'll die, Samael had said, and Gabriel knew that to be truth, whether Hope met the terms of his bargain or not, for she was mortal.

But now, so was he, and he would be foolish to waste the time they had left, whether it be two weeks, two years, or two decades.

He rose from the table, resolved to do everything in his power to make sure she lived as long as possible, even if he had no clear idea—as yet—how to make it so.

Chapter Fifteen

Hope paced the floor of her hotel room, waiting anxiously for Gabe. This was all her fault, all of it, and he'd been stripped of his wings because of her. Yet he'd still come here to Vegas with her to find Charity, and he was still protecting her, even though he'd lost his powers.

What would the Devil do to him?

Bowing her head, Hope sat down on the edge of the bed and closed her eyes, searching for strength. It wasn't fair to expect Gabe to save her every time she turned around. He wasn't a knight on a white horse, and she wasn't a damsel in distress. She was an idiot who'd gotten herself into some deep shit, and he was an angel whose heart was too big for his own good. He was downstairs squaring off with Satan himself, while she was locked in a hotel room, tilting at shadows, many of them in her own mind.

Her thoughts were interrupted by the sound of a key card in the door. She stood up just as the doorknob turned and the door opened, stopping short with a *thunk* as the swing lock engaged.

"Hope?" It was Gabe's voice. "Let me in."

She peeked through the keyhole again, just to be sure it was he before doing as he asked. He met her eyes briefly, then brushed past her into the room. His face looked drawn, his movements quick and tense.

"What happened?" she asked. "What did he say?"

He went straight to the window. "We should keep the curtains closed," he said tersely, but took a moment himself to stare out at the sky, and the crowded, urban landscape below.

Her heart sank, for the message he conveyed by what he *hadn't* said wasn't good. She watched as he ran a hand through his hair, the muscles in his back and shoulders clearly delineated through the navy cotton tee he wore. Broad shoulders, lean hips, faded Levi's. He could've stepped from the pages of a magazine advertising men's casual wear, complete with the brooding look that models seemed to aspire to.

She sighed, knowing herself both helpless and hopeless when it came to brooding, brown-haired angels. "Gabriel, tell me what happened."

He drew the curtains shut, enclosing the room in dimness. "Not yet," he told her. "Do you have the *Ars Goetia*?"

"In my bag."

"Give it to me."

Hope did as he asked, fingers shaking. Once she turned over the book, she pretty much sealed her own death warrant, but there was no longer any thought of her doing otherwise; she owed him that much, and more.

Gabe, still by the window, lifted his hands, gripping the small book, and began to speak. His voice, rich and deep, sent chills down her spine.

"Powers of the kingdom, be beneath my left foot, and within my right hand. Glory and eternity touch my shoulders, and guide me in the paths of victory. Mercy and justice be the equilibrium and splendor of my life. Understanding and wisdom give unto me the triumph."

There was more, spoken in a language Hope didn't understand, the cadence and beauty of the words leaving her dazzled.

"Be that which Thou art, and that which thou

willest to be. Ishim, assist me. Cherubim, be my strength. Elohim, be my brethren. Malachim, protect me, Seraphim, purify me. Chachmalim, enlighten me. Alleluia, alleluia, amen."

In the darkened room, Gabe's outline seemed to glow, faintly, light seeming to dance along the edges of the book. Scarcely daring to breathe, Hope waited until the light faded, and Gabriel lowered his hands.

"Wow," she breathed. "What was that?"

With a sigh, Gabe moved to her side, drawing her down to sit beside him on the edge of the bed. "It's a simple preparation spell," he said. "I need you to be brave, now, very brave."

A chill went down her spine. "What are you going to do?"

"I'm going to find out where your sister is, but I doubt you're going to like the way I'm going to do it."

She looked down at the book, and her heart sank. "But . . . why—" Her lips were dry, and she licked them. "Why this way?"

"It's the quickest," he told her gravely, "and we're running out of time."

Her heart sank to her toes. "He's still holding me to the bargain, isn't he?"

"He is," Gabe answered, not bothering to sugarcoat the facts. "If you want to find your sister, we need to do it now."

His hand, big and warm, was on her elbow. Slowly it slipped down to encircle her wrist, his fingers grazing gently over the bandage, his palm coming to rest atop her hand, which he squeezed, as though imparting his strength.

She felt it, that strength, and met his eyes, even though she didn't want to. "Trust me," he told her gently, "and don't be afraid. I won't let it hurt you."

It.

The word conjured up a vivid reminder of the day she'd awakened in a strange bed, Sammy Divine's unholy familiar looming over his shoulder, red eyes gleaming.

"It will most likely be a Vulturi, and it will do its best to frighten you into leaving the circle of protection I'm about to cast," he said gravely. "There's no telling what it will say, or what it will do, but you must—at all costs—remain still and silent, here upon the bed. Do you understand?"

Hope began to shake, terrified at the thought of coming face-to-face, yet again, with a demon. "What if it doesn't know where Charity is?" she cried, not happy with the turn of events. "What if it won't tell you?"

"It will tell me," Gabe said grimly, "and it will know, because *he* knows."

"But you're not an angel anymore." She hated the cowardly urge to argue, but couldn't seem to help herself. "What if you can't control it?"

Gabe looked down. "Hope, sweetheart . . ."

Her heart stuttered at the endearment, and she nearly missed the significance of what he said next.

"I wrote the book on controlling demons," he murmured, and held up the *Ars Goetia*.

"You—"

He nodded. "It was intended for good, a way to keep the forces of Darkness in their place, subject to and beneath the heel of the One. Solomon used it to force the most rebellious of demons, the ones who openly rebelled against the One, to build a temple to His Glory." He bowed his head, running his thumb over the soft leather. "The words were originally inscribed on stone tablets, of course—I don't know how they came to be transcribed into book form. They were never meant for eyes other than Solomon's, but somehow they survived, all these years, in the care of him whom they'd been used against."

"Sammy Divine," she said faintly. "The Devil."

"Samael the Fallen," he corrected heavily. "Now forever known as Samael the Black."

He straightened, giving her hand another squeeze. "I'll tell you all about it once this is over, but now I must begin, before the preparation spell wears off." The air of heaviness about him lifted, as though he'd removed a cloak. "You'll do as I say, and remain here on the bed?"

Numbly she nodded, not wanting to let go of his hand.

Unexpectedly he smiled, teeth gleaming white in the dimness. "You're braver than you think, Hope. Don't forget that."

Then, giving her hand a final squeeze, he rose from the bed. "Move into the middle," he told her, "and stay there."

Going to the window, he opened the curtains a mere crack, allowing a beam of light into the room. It fell across the foot of the bed, neatly cutting the room in half: he on one side, she on the other.

Without speaking, Hope reached behind her and grabbed a pillow, clasping it tightly to her stomach as she scooched backward to sit cross-legged on the bed.

Gabe still held the book, which he brought up to hold between both palms. He bent his head and closed his eyes.

There was a silence, which Hope didn't dare interrupt.

Then he began to speak, in a language that made no sense to her, but was nonetheless beautiful. An unexpected peace filled her, and though she wished she could understand what he was saying, it didn't matter, because she could see him, and she could hear him, and those things—suddenly—became the two most important things in her world. Everything else—her missing sister, her depression, her suicide attempt, and her subsequent deal with the Devil—it all faded away in the knowledge that Gabriel was here, with her, and as long as he was, everything was as it should be.

"Obey ye, obey ye, the names of the Creator, and come forth in all ways gentle and peaceable, and do in all things as I shall command you."

She understood him now, and didn't know whether it was because he was speaking English or because she could just finally, truly *hear* him.

Gabe opened his arms wide, keeping his eyes closed as he spoke. "By the holy words written in this book, and by the other holy names that are written only in the Book of Life, I conjure you to come before me promptly and without malice. By the One whose virtues and potencies rule over all, who dwelleth in the Heavens and moves upon the wings of the wind, who commanded the universe to be created, I conjure you, O evil and rebellious spirit, abiding in the Abyss of Darkness, to come forth."

A bad smell reached Hope's noise, growing stronger and stronger until she wanted to gag. She buried her mouth and nose in the pillow, and stayed quiet.

"Come, by the name of the One who formed the vault of the heavens and laid the foundation of the Earth beneath, I command you come, so that you may execute and accomplish my demands with all mildness and courtesy."

A figure was taking shape in a far corner, the point in the room that was farthest from the beam of light from the window.

Hope watched, unable to turn away, as it became a face: a twisted, misshapen face the color of moldy bread, with two holes for nostrils, and protruding teeth that were filled with—judging by the smell—rotting flesh.

"Who summons me?" the face rasped, the stench of its breath making her want to vomit.

Gabriel's eyes opened, though he didn't move.

"Gabriel, Bringer of Light, Servant of Truth," he replied, in a voice that rang with conviction. "*I* summon you, demon, and you will do as I say."

The Vulturi laughed, a sound that made Hope's flesh crawl. "You and who else, stripling? Where's a flaming Sword of Righteousness when you need it, eh?"

In a flash, the face of the Vulturi zoomed toward Hope where she sat on the bed, growing so large it nearly blotted out her vision. She bit the pillow, closing her eyes, feeling its hot breath on her hair, mentally screaming her terror though her throat was locked tight.

"Back," said Gabriel, never raising his voice. "Get back, you piece of filth, or I shall burn you where you stand. The Light obeys me, and you cannot stand against it."

There was a sound like air leaving a balloon, rude and vulgar, but even with her eyes closed, Hope could feel the demon recede to its corner.

"What do you want?" it hissed grudgingly. "I have work to do among the damned."

"Where is Charity Henderson?" Gabriel's voice was closer now, letting Hope know that he'd moved to stand at the foot of the bed. She almost opened her eyes, but decided it was wiser not to. "Where is this woman's sister?"

The demon laughed, sending tendrils of terror down her spine. She squeezed her lids shut even tighter, burying her face deeper into the pillow.

"The same place her parents are," the Vulturi

rasped. "Burned to a crisp, just like her mommy and daddy."

The words struck Hope with the force of a blow—she cried out, unable to help herself.

"Mmmmm . . ." crooned the demon, "the smell of their flesh as it roasted was sweet, so sweet. A few moments more and the flames would've had you, too, my little precious."

"Leave her alone," Gabe said sharply. "Pay attention to *me*, as I command you."

"Shouldn't have been playing with Daddy's lighter, now should you?" the demon went on maliciously. "Didn't you take a fire safety course in school just the week before? Why yes, I believe you did."

Hope tried not to listen, but it was hard, so hard . . .

"Silence!" ordered Gabriel, in a voice so terrible even Hope flinched.

A growl came from the corner, low and vicious.

"Where is Charity Henderson?" Gabriel repeated. "Tell me, by the name given to Moses as he stood before the burning bush, by the name of the eternal and everlasting One."

"Charity is dead . . . haven't you heard?" the Vulturi rasped with a chuckle, but Gabriel would have none of it.

"Liar," he shouted. "I command you to tell me the truth! In the name of the One, I command you!"

Another hiss, like that of someone in pain.

"She lives," said the demon slowly, "if you can call it living."

"Where?"

There was a silence, while the smell in the room grew to a level that left Hope gasping, despite the pillow.

"4218 South Third Street," said the demon, ending on a screech that made her ears hurt. "May you meet death there, Lightbringer." It made another noise, like the howling of a thousand voices, lost and hungry. "We'll be waiting for you when you do."

"Wait as long as you like," Gabriel replied, his voice unruffled. "But for now, be gone."

Hope began to rock back and forth, wanting only for the moment to be over, the smell to be gone, the nightmare to end.

"I exorcise thee," intoned Gabriel, his voice getting louder, "by the virtue of these names . . ."—a string of which ensued, none of which Hope could begin to remember or pronounce. "Return to your place, in the name of the One."

Then, to her surprise, Gabriel recited what

seemed to be the entire first chapter of Genesis, starting with, "In the beginning . . ."

Tears squeezed from behind her lids, for Hope was certain that she'd forgotten it, yet the story was familiar, so familiar. As she listened, she remembered her mother and father, dressed in their Sunday best, dropping her and Charity off in Sunday school before going into the sanctuary of Bethlehem Baptist Church. She remembered her Sunday school teacher, Mrs. Webster, beaming at her, handing out bits of candy when she memorized the weekly verses correctly. The smell of the building—old wood and beeswax—the color of the carpet, the big white cross on the wall.

So many things she'd thought she'd forgotten, until Gabriel recited one of the earliest stories ever told, and she remembered.

She clung to those memories, along with the pillow, until Gabe finished, and the silence in the room was absolute.

"Hope." The bed dipped as Gabriel came to sit beside her. "Are you all right?"

Without thinking, without hesitation, she turned her face into his chest, and wrapped her arms around him. He did the same, pulling her close.

Beneath her cheek, his heart—his human, beating heart—was pounding, as was hers.

She wanted to cry, but didn't, for she'd had enough of tears. He'd been strong for her, and kept her safe, just as he'd promised, and she wouldn't repay him by falling apart as soon as the worst was over. Let him draw strength from her for a change, if at all possible.

They sat there for a few moments, his breath on her hair, the broad planes of his back beneath her palms. "Thank you," she whispered. "Thank you."

He drew away, and she let him go, wishing she didn't have to. In the dimness of the hotel room, his face looked drawn, and tight.

"That must've been so hard," she murmured. "I don't know how you did it."

He gave her a tired half smile. "To be quite honest, I'm not quite sure how I did it, either. Before, I've always had my flaming Sword of Righteousness as a backup."

Hope gave a nervous laugh at the joke, then let it die when she realized that he was serious.

"I'm pretty sure it took the last drop of residual power I had," he told her. "From here on out, it's hand-to-hand combat. No more ethereals if I can help it."

She shuddered, unable to help herself. "Ethereals?" The memory of that face, that horrible, moldy face . . . She thrust the image away.

"Some demons are ethereal, some are corporeal, like the Dronai in your apartment." He put out a hand, as though about to smooth her hair, then let it drop. "But that's enough about them . . . to speak of them gives them power."

"Then let's never speak of them again," she said decisively.

There was a silence, then "You never told me about your parents."

She looked away, staring at the beam of sunlight that cut across the bed. "It's not something I like to talk about."

"I'm a good listener," he said softly, and so, because the room was quiet and the wounds were already bare, she told him.

"I was twelve," she said. "Mom and Dad were romantics, I guess, because we always had candles on the dining room table. One night, I couldn't sleep, and I wanted to read, but I was afraid to turn on the light, because they'd catch me. So I went downstairs, lit one of the candles, and took it into the living room. I curled up on the couch and read for a while, but then I got sleepy." She smiled a little, remembering how warm and cozy and *smug* she'd felt that night, thinking she'd outsmarted her parents. "Sometime later I apparently woke up and stumbled off to bed, but I forgot all about the candle. I woke up in the hospital, being treated for smoke inhalation. It was the next day before they told me that both my parents were dead."

Gabe reached out and took her hand, saying nothing, and it was his silence that enabled her to continue. "Charity was only eight at the time. We were separated, put into different foster homes, and it wasn't until I was twenty and could prove I could support her that I got her back."

"That must've been tough," he murmured. "Quite a responsibility for one so young."

Hope shrugged. "I wanted it. I'd torn our family apart, and I wanted to put it back together. It just didn't work out the way I planned, that's all. Charity didn't need me to be her mother, she needed me to be her friend, and I failed at that. She was always out, always going, always partying . . . and then one night, she just didn't come home."

Gabriel sighed, lacing his fingers through hers, almost as though he didn't realize what he was doing. "I, too, know the pain of an errant sibling." His broad shoulders seem to slump a bit. "Samael and I were brothers once, you know."

She didn't, but kept quiet, letting him have his turn to talk.

"Eons ago, before the age of mankind." He looked away, remembering. "The universe was our playground. Samael was always a bit wild, more daring than most of our angelic brothers, but never cruel."

The image Gabriel painted didn't match the monster she'd come to know, but Hope didn't doubt his word. He was clearly pained by the memories.

"Everything changed when the One decided to create mankind in His own image. Some of the angels were jealous, some merely curious. Samael was unable to resist spying on them, and it was then that he saw Eve, alone in the garden."

Hope's eyes widened when she realized what he was saying. "But . . . but I thought it was a serpent who . . ."

Gabe uttered a low laugh, completely devoid of humor. "Think about it, Hope. Early civilizations were very big on imagery."

"Oh my God," she breathed.

"Exactly," he answered grimly. "Angels mating with humans is strictly forbidden, so when Samael did it, he was punished, severely."

Hope lowered her head, feeling her cheeks burn with shame. No wonder Gabriel had turned her down, and yet she'd still tried to seduce him. Even without his participation, she'd managed to ruin his life through her own selfishness.

"Samael was cast down, and instead of accepting his punishment as just, he incited a war, an uprising against the One, causing many of our brothers to be cast down as well. Everything he's done since has been done in an effort to prove that if mankind can be forgiven for being unable to resist temptation, he should be also."

"That's pretty twisted," Hope murmured, doing her best to follow.

"It is," Gabe agreed heavily. "Samael is nothing if not complicated."

"You still care about him, don't you?"

He pulled his hand from hers, using both of them to scrub his face, and didn't answer.

The urge to comfort him became overwhelming, and greatly daring, Hope put her hand on his shoulder. He froze, but didn't move away. "I'm so sorry," she murmured, "I'm so sorry for all of it, including my part in it."

Gabe turned his head and looked at her, but she couldn't read his eyes in the dimness. His hand moved to cover the one she'd placed on his shoulder, and her heart skipped a beat.

"He's not going to stop," he told her, in a low voice. "He'll come after us again."

Instead of being frightened, her heart soared at his use of the word "us."

"I'm afraid of what he might do to you, Hope, and without my full powers, I'm not sure I can prevent it. The incantations within the Key of Solomon can only hold him back for so long . . . he's grown stronger through the ages."

For the life of her, she couldn't bring herself to say anything more than "You're stronger than he is, and you always will be."

"When it comes to you, I'm not strong at all," he murmured huskily. He leaned toward her, his lips drawing hers like a magnet. Warm, firm, and oh so tender . . . just a brush at first, and then deeper, longer. The next thing she knew she was in his arms, his body hard against hers, and nothing else mattered, on Earth or in Heaven.

At the touch of Hope's lips, so soft against his own, Gabriel was lost. He wanted more of her, more, and before he knew it, he'd wrapped his arms around her and dragged her hard against him. Her mouth opened to his kiss, her breath mingling with his, the heat of it drawing him in like a fire on a cold day. She made a noise, low in her throat, but he barely heard it as he turned, the better to hold her, and pressed her back upon the bed, never taking his lips from hers.

Her arms were tight around his shoulders, yet

he wanted them tighter still. The soft globes of her breasts were against his chest, drawing a groan from deep within him. His manhood stirred, pressing against the curve of her hip, and he could no more control it than he could stop the rising of the tide.

For it was the tide that had him now, a tide of desire like nothing he'd ever known, and he would happily, gladly drown in it.

Follow this experience where it may lead you, the One had said, and his heart filled with gratitude, for once again, the Almighty had shown him grace and wisdom. As an angel, this flood of heat and pleasure was forbidden, but as a man . . .

Gabe ceased to think as Hope's lips slanted over his, and her tongue touched his lips. Instinctively he seemed to know what she wanted, and opened his mouth so that she could taste him more fully. His heart began to pound as her tongue slipped inside to twine with his, tasting of sweetness and heat, and glorious, decadent deliciousness. Time ceased to exist, for there was only now, only Hope, warm and alive in his arms. Her fingers were in his hair, the scent of her, as sweetly feminine as a rose in a garden, in his nose.

He felt her hands, tugging and pulling at his shirt, and broke contact only long enough to let her drag it over his head before plunging once again into an exploration of her luscious mouth. She arched against his bare chest, running soft hands over his back and hips, and he sensed her frustration at the layers of clothes that separated them, for he felt it, too.

Regretfully, he pulled his lips from hers and rose from the bed, unbuckling his belt as he went. He had no patience with modern fastenings, his fingers tearing at both the button and the zipper on his jeans as he kicked off his shoes. In mere moments he'd stripped them from his body, leaving him naked, his manhood hot and hard in the cool air of the hotel room.

Hope had risen to her elbow on the bed, and gasped as he straightened, her eyes going from his groin to his face, and back again. Modesty had never been a problem for him, and it wasn't a problem now—he felt himself swell even further with the knowledge that what she saw pleased her.

Offering her his hand, he helped her stand, but as her fingers went to the buttons on her blouse, he stopped her.

"Let me," he murmured, and proceeded to do what he'd never before done, and disrobe a woman.

Button by button, he opened her shirt, then slipped it from her shoulders. Another button at her waist, a zipper, then he knelt to help her step from her shoes. Still on one knee, he put his hands to her hips and drew down her pants, leaving her clad in lacy undergarments of pink and white. As she stepped free of her jeans, he caught a glimpse of her inner thigh and smelled, for the first time, the scent of a woman's arousal. It was dizzying, intoxicating, causing him to momentarily close his eyes before hooking two fingers in the scrap of lace that hid her femininity from his eyes, and draw that down, too.

He stared, transfixed, at the golden curls that covered her mound, scarcely noticing as Hope's hands left his shoulders to remove her bra, letting it fall atop the pile of clothes at her feet. He looked upward then, at the rounded curve of her breasts, twin mounds tipped with pink, and above that, to her face.

"You're so beautiful," he whispered, and even in the dimness he could see how her lower lip trembled. He put his hand to the soft curve of her belly, and she caught her breath, holding it, as he passed his palm over her warm skin, letting it coming to rest at her waist. He rose, naked and yearning, and caught her against him for another kiss, even more passionate than the ones that had come before.

Then they were on the bed, and he groaned aloud

at the feel of her bare skin against his: her leg, hooked over his thigh, her breasts, crushed to his chest. Unable to stop, unwilling to hold back, he dipped his head and drew one of them into his mouth, thinking no fruit could possibly taste sweeter.

Hope gasped, arching her back, offering herself to his lips and tongue, and Gabe took all she offered, and more. His hands stroked and squeezed, his cock surged and throbbed, and everywhere she touched him he felt fire dance along his nerve endings like electricity in a storm. The noises she made inflamed him, and when his fingers slipped down to touch the damp curls at her center, so wet and hot, he shuddered and gasped as much as she. Not content to just touch, however, he slid down and kissed her there, her scent driving him beyond the point of rational thought.

"Gabriel," she whispered, and the sound of his name on her lips drove a shaft of heat from his lips to his groin. He wanted to devour her, to plunge his tongue within her heated depths as he'd done with her mouth, but she wound her fingers in his hair and dragged him up for another scorching kiss. He gave it to her gladly, feeling her heart pound beneath his hand as he cupped her breast, learning the contours of her body with his fingers and palm, roving over her hip and buttocks.

She threw her leg over his thigh again, bringing his manhood close—oh, so close—to her heated femininity, and he surged, unable to help himself, into warm, honeyed bliss.

He cried out, as did she, his neck arching as he raised his face toward Heaven. Nothing could've prepared him for this, for as his flesh joined with hers, it was as though he'd found a part of himself he'd never known was missing. As her body received him, his soul soared, much as it had when he'd soared above the clouds, weightless and filled with glory, yet this was glory of an entirely different kind.

Hope's arms were around him, her lips against his chest, her breath warm on her skin as she moaned and gasped in time with the movements of his body. His hips had a mind of their own, pressing his hardness forward into her softness, over and over again. It seemed to go on forever, yet was over all too soon, for he felt her tighten and shudder, crying out against his throat. Her inner passage rippled and throbbed, squeezing his cock to near-bursting, and then burst he did, in a flood of ecstasy that shook him to his core, flinging him into the cosmos with a showering of sparks and holding him there, suspended, before letting him fall, her name on his lips.

Chapter Sixteen

"It's a bit cliché, don't you think?"

Samael the Fallen, onetime angel and full-time devil, studied his reflection in the mirror, adjusting the hooded cowl of the black robe that covered him from head to foot. "Every year, year after year, brought forth by bell, book, and candle for a bit of bloody theater and a night of shameful abandon." He gave a small snort of disgust. "As if humans needed my permission *or* my presence to engage in their depravities."

"Traditions are important to your followers, Master." Nyx answered him a bit stiffly. "Particularly when it comes to the Black Mass." He twitched a fold of the black robe into place on his master's shoulder, always a bit fussy during Sammy's fittings. "Humans are easily confused by anything that doesn't fit their conception of evil."

Samael sighed. "Evil has its limitations," he said cryptically. "Take that stupid goat mask, for instance—how ridiculous that *I* should be the one portrayed as a beast, when humans are the ones so mindlessly eager to offer their necks to the sword."

Nyx said nothing.

The Great Shaitan, High Lord of the Abyss, turned to regard his right-hand man. The fire that crackled in the bedroom grate cast no light over the still, dark figure, but Sammy knew his servant well, and noted how the tips of his black-feathered wings quivered slightly, a sure sign of disquiet.

"Is there a problem?" Samael asked, his voice deceptively smooth.

Nyx hesitated, keeping his gaze downward, toward the gleaming hardwood floor.

Throwing back the hood of his cowl, Sammy cocked his head, regarding his minion questioningly. "Well?"

"This sudden aversion to the Mass . . . surely you're not considering canceling it?"

"What I do or don't do is none of your concern," he told the demon sharply. "How dare you question me?"

"I'm worried about you, my lord," Nyx replied in hushed tones. "You're not yourself these days."

His Satanic Majesty suppressed an urge to snarl like the beast he'd just denied being. Turning his blond head to once again regard his reflection in the mirror, he answered calmly enough, "You think you know me so well, do you?"

Despite his eight-foot wingspan and menacing aspect, Nyx was the one who seemed to cringe, becoming smaller at his master's cool tone. "I speak only out of love and devotion, O Dark One."

"Love," Sammy sneered. The black-robed man in the mirror—blue-eyed, blond, and impossibly handsome—sneered right back at him. "I'm sick of the word. I gave you no emotion save that of loyalty when I created you. Love should be anathema to you, as it is to me."

"Perhaps emotions can grow over time." Nyx kept his gaze on the floor, but Sammy was not fooled by the diffidence in his voice. "Perhaps the created can take on aspects of the Creator, without ever meaning to."

Samael's hand lashed out, and the demon found himself gasping for breath, the long, pale fingers of his master like steel around his neck.

"What are you implying?" growled Satan. "I have no loving aspect for you to possibly emulate."

Unresisting, unable to voice his dismay, Nyx opened wider his red eyes, two burning coals of fear that seemed only to feed his liege's fury.

"Perhaps you merely repeat what you hear," Samael said between his teeth, never raising his voice. "Like a black-winged parrot with no mind of his own." He shoved Nyx backward, releasing him.

Nyx stumbled back, steadying himself against the wall of the bedchamber. "Your pardon, Master," he rasped, raising a taloned hand to his abused throat. "I spoke out of turn."

"Oh, don't stop now," Sammy snarled, feeling his rage and frustration build. Despite his rough treatment of Nyx, his anger was actually directed at himself; his confrontation with Gabriel had shaken him more than he cared to admit. "Do tell me what the great unwashed masses of the Underworld have to say."

Cautiously regaining his feet, Nyx stayed against the wall, out of his master's immediate reach. "I don't listen to the rabble, O Great One. I know only that they, like the humans, are easily confused by anything out of the ordinary and are quick to seize advantage. The Black Mass is a reminder of how you are still revered and honored among the humans, and may help lay their cursed mutterings to rest. Blood sacrifice is always a morale booster for the troops."

With a sigh, Sammy turned away. "There's not enough blood on Earth to satisfy them."

"Someone's in a mood today." Pandora strolled into his bedchamber, dripping with jewels, trailing exotic scent. Her choice of gown was a vibrant shade of rose, diaphanous with veils, yet clinging to her lushness everywhere it counted. "I could hear you growling and snapping all the way down the corridor."

Nyx gave a growl of his own, clearly frustrated that Pandora managed to come and go as she pleased, much less dare criticize his master.

"Your pet needs a leash," she said to Sammy, flicking her hand at the demon as she would a gnat.

For once, Sammy found himself unamused by her cheek. "What do you want, Pandora?"

Her lower lip, rouged to the same shade as her gown, thrust forward in a pout. Being no fool, however, she noted the dangerous gleam in his eye, and withdrew it. "I came to take Cain for a little field trip." She shrugged a plump shoulder. "He's been cooped up here too long. The fireflies are swarming in the Elysian Fields; I thought it might amuse him."

"Master," Nyx spoke up, gesturing toward the black robe Sammy still wore. "Perhaps it's time to present the Dark Princeling formally as your heir, and initiate him into the mysteries."

"Don't call him a princeling," Sammy snapped, "and absolutely not." The boy was far too young to be present during a cold-blooded murder, unless it happened to be his *own*. During Cain's stay in the Underworld, Sammy had certainly been driven to the brink of murder several times over. "Where is he?"

Pandora looked at Nyx, while Nyx looked at Pandora.

"I haven't seen him since yesterday," Pandora said, with another shrug. "I agreed to teach him some polish, not be his nursemaid. I believe that's Tall, Dark, and Ugly's job."

"I'm no one's nursemaid," Nyx said hotly, but Sammy interrupted them both with a word.

"Enough!" Casting them both a disgusted glare, he tore open the black robe and tossed it over a chair. "You bicker like children."

A screeching arose from the corridor outside, drawing their instant attention. Sammy sighed and rubbed the bridge of his nose, wondering exactly what kind of trouble his son had gotten himself into this time.

Nyx moved toward the door, but hadn't reached it before a small gray whirling dervish swept into the room, hotly pursued by two winged Dronai guards, who stopped short on the threshold, flapping their wings and gnashing their teeth.

"Master," screeched the dervish, "Master, you must come!"

To Sammy's utter shock and surprise, the creature attached itself to his leg, evading Nyx's lightning attempt to grab it. He looked down and saw a very damp, very agitated little fire imp, whose already bulging eyes were about to start from its very ugly head. "It's Cain, Master," the fire imp gabbled. It was his son's now ever-present shadow, Tesla. "She took him!"

He went cold, raising a hand to prevent Nyx from touching the imp. "Who took him?"

"Galene," babbled Tesla, "she pulled him down into the Sea of Sorrows."

Pandora gave a gasp of horror, her hand going to her mouth.

"Show me," Sammy said flatly, not wasting any time on questions, and took the imp with him into nothingness. An instant later they were on the seashore, gray and stormy, in the cove where'd he'd first seen the Nereid.

"There," pointed Tesla, toward the outcropping

of rock where he himself had sat to listen to Galene's song. "We were just playing," the imp gabbled, "picking up shells while she sang to us. She wanted Cain to swim with her, like he does with the water nymphs."

Sammy felt the imp's shudder, for he had yet to let go of Sammy's leg.

"The two of you followed me here," Samael said hollowly, not needing or expecting confirmation, and the imp didn't bother to give it.

"I told him not to listen to her, I swear I did!" Tesla's voice cracked, and he buried his face against Sammy's knee like a child. "But he did, and then . . ."

The sea was stormy, gray tipped with whitecaps, mirroring the gloomy clouds overhead and the unspoken despair Sammy felt within his chest. Prying the imp's long-fingered hands from his legs more gently than even he realized, he said, "Stay here, away from the water."

And then he waded in, letting the waves crash against him, buffeting him with their force as he cut a swath toward the deep, on his way to the lair of the Leviathan.

Chapter Seventeen

Hope lay in the darkened hotel room, her cheek on Gabriel's chest and his arm warm on her back, his hand resting on her shoulder. Everywhere their bodies touched it felt so *right*, so magical, and it was a magic she never wanted to end. She was boneless and exhausted, but sleep was out of the question, for if she slept she might wake to find it had all been a dream.

Gabe was awake, too, for his fingers traced small circles on the skin of her shoulder, leaving tingles in their wake. "Are you all right?" he murmured. "Did I hurt you?"

Unable to help herself, Hope smiled. "I should ask you the same thing. It was your first time, after all."

He chuckled, stretching. "Yeah, but I was pretty darn good at it anyway, wasn't I?"

She laughed, and it felt so good that she laughed some more, tickling his ribs until he caught her hand and pressed her on her back. His hair, wildly mussed from her fingers, fell over his cheek, and she caught her breath at how beautiful he looked when he laughed, masculine grace in his every move. She thought about how wonderful it would be to see him like that every day, carefree and smiling, instead of carrying the weight of the world on his shoulders.

"You're outmatched, Miss Henderson," he teased. "Better give up while you can."

"I already have," she told him softly, tucking his hair behind his ear, the better to see his face.

His smile faded as he stared down into her eyes. "I don't know what the future holds," he said, recognizing how her mood had changed. "I can't promise you anything, can't offer you anything, except my best efforts to keep you safe, and help you find your sister. Beyond that . . ."

The mention of Charity gave her a pang, for she hadn't been thinking of her sister, despite what they'd gone through to find out where she was. Shoving guilt aside, Hope let her fingers trace the line of Gabe's jaw, the curve of his lips. "That's more than I ever hoped for," she whispered, doing her best to memorize this man, this moment. "*You're* more than I ever hoped for."

He bent his head and kissed her, and she savored every second of it, wishing it would go on and on. He stirred against her thigh, and she couldn't help but slide her hand down his lean hip and pull him closer, pressing against him as he grew and lengthened, then cupping him in her hand. He made a noise deep in his throat, half groaning and half pleading, but the thought was in her head that these stolen moments might be the only ones they ever had, and she didn't want to waste them. So she squeezed and stroked and kissed him with all the unspoken love in her heart, until any thoughts of stopping were as far away as the moon.

This time, when she opened her thighs and took him inside, he slid into her gently, slowly, as though they had all the time in the world, worshipping her body with his lips and tongue as his maleness nudged and probed her very core. With a tenderness that stole her heart all over again, he made love to her the way she'd only imagined it could be done.

And when it was over, and they lay spent and gasping in each other's arms, she bit her lip to keep from saying what she truly wanted to say, merely holding him close until he finally, reluctantly rolled away.

"We have to go," he murmured. "It's dangerous to stay too long in one place, and we have to start looking for your sister."

"I know."

She took his hand as he lay next to her, threading her fingers through his.

He held it for a long moment before he rose from the bed and started pulling on his clothes.

"Gabe?" She lay unmoving, watching him dress.

He paused, wearing only unzipped jeans, and gave her his full attention. "Yes?"

"Are you sorry?"

Without hesitation, he leaned in one more time and kissed her lightly, saying only "No."

And with that she had to be content. She got up and went into the bathroom, scooping her clothes from the floor as she went.

Forty-five minutes later they exited a cab in front of Straight Up, a divey little bar in an apparently dicey part of town—so dicey, in fact, that the cabbie had seemed reluctant to take them there. "There's lots better bars on the strip, man," he'd told Gabriel, but Hope had just repeated the address and he'd shut up. He hadn't lingered dropping them off, either, taking his fare and driving off before the door to the cab had barely closed.

It was midafternoon, and Hope was glad, because she wouldn't want to be there after dark; the buildings were old and run-down, trash littered the streets. Used cigarette butts were all over sidewalk in front of the club, which had a neon sign of a martini glass in the window, the base of which was burned out.

"I don't like this," she muttered, but Gabe didn't answer, keeping an eye on two men who were loitering down the block, watching them. He held the door open for her, and they went in.

The smell of stale cigarettes nearly knocked Hope over. Dimly lit, the place was bigger than it looked from the outside, with a stage to the right and lots of small, two-person tables, all of which were empty. Bad eighties music blared from the speakers surrounding the stage, and a long bar, studded with bar stools, dominated the left side of the room. The bartender, a beefy black man who could've been any age between thirty and fifty, eyed them briefly as they came in, then went back to reading the newspaper he'd spread out on the bar.

"Stay close," Gabe murmured, and Hope was happy to do just that. The bar's only patron was slumped on one of the stools, looking rumpled, drunk, and none too clean.

"What can I do for you?" asked the bartender, barely glancing up from his paper.

"We're looking for a girl," said Gabe.

"You and everybody else who comes here, man. You and the little lady want a drink, or what?"

It was then that Hope, glancing nervously around, noticed the steel pole in the middle of the stage, and was horrified to realize that she'd just brought an angel to a strip club.

"Not just any girl," Gabriel told the bartender. "A specific girl, named Charity Henderson."

"Never heard of her."

Undeterred, Gabe pulled a picture from his back pocket and held it out. Surprised, Hope realized it was the picture of her and Charity by the fountain in Little Five Points; he'd obviously taken it from her apartment without telling her.

The man behind the bar gave it a cursory glance, then flicked his eyes toward Hope. "Quite a resemblance," he said briefly, but offered nothing further.

Gabriel sighed, and pulled Hope aside. "He wants money," he murmured, "and I don't have any."

Hope glanced around at the bar again. "I really don't think Charity would ever set foot in a place like this, Gabe. We're wasting our time."

Gabe shot another glance at the bartender, who was studiously ignoring them in favor of his newspaper. "I didn't spend all that time on the streets without learning a thing or two, Hope. He knows something."

With a sigh of her own, she opened her purse, fished around in her wallet, and handed him several twenties, leaving the distribution of them up to him. It was only money, after all, and her computer business more than paid the bills.

"Maybe you could take another look," Gabe said to the bartender, handing him both cash *and* the picture this time.

The money disappeared in one smooth motion, as the guy pretended to check out the picture again. "Your sister, huh?" he asked Hope, and she nodded. "Yeah, I've seen her around. Come back tonight, around eleven. You might see her then."

"We don't have until tonight," Gabe told him tersely. "Where can we find her?"

The bartender shook his head, handing the photo back. "Hey, man, I just work here. I don't know where these girls live, and I don't care."

"'These girls'?" Hope picked up on the inference, and didn't like it. "Are you trying to say she *works* here?"

The guy gave her smirk. "If you call shaking your tail working, then yeah, she works here."

Momentarily speechless, Hope looked him in the eye. "You're lying," she said, beginning to tremble.

He shrugged. "Got no cause to lie, baby. You come back here at eleven, you'll see for yourself."

Gabriel leaned in, addressing the bartender. "If she works here, then I'm willing to bet you can find her address somewhere in the back office." He held up two more twenties, then added a third. "How much?"

The guy shot a nervous look toward the drunk who was slumped on his stool at the end of the bar. "Cain't do that, man," he murmured. "Not for no sixty fuckin' bucks. Man got to work, and the owner of this here place likes his privacy, if you know what I mean. Besides"—he shook his head—"none of these bitches use their real names or addresses."

Hope, listening to their conversation in a disbelieving daze, came to attention. "Don't call my sister a bitch," she snapped.

The man gave a short huff of laughter, looking her up and down. "Yeah, you her sister, all right. She a spitfire, too."

"That's it," said Gabe grimly. "You tell us what we want to know or—"

"Or what, man?" The bartender stepped back, pulling up his shirt to reveal the butt of a gun, tucked into his waistband. "You and the little lady are outta your league here. Best get your asses out the door while you still can."

"Now, Larry, is that any way to talk to paying guests?" A man stepped from a shadowy corridor to the left of the bar. He was dark-haired and muscular, too well-dressed for the dinginess of their surroundings, wearing gray dress slacks, a dark red Polo, and a black suit jacket.

Hope disliked him on sight, for his air of smug self-assurance reminded her too much of a certain blond-haired devil, though this guy was nowhere near as good-looking.

"Looking for Charity, are you?" the man asked. "Normally I'd tell you that charity is hard to find in a place like this, but you two happen to be in luck." He smirked at his own joke, while the bartender gave a chuckle.

"Where is she?" Gabe took a step forward, semi-shielding Hope with his body.

The man eyed him up and down, making it clear he was unimpressed with Gabe's bravado. "I don't air my business in front of the help," he said, "but if you'd like to step into my office . . ." He lifted his hand toward the shadowy corridor he'd just exited.

Hope became aware that the drunk on the bar stool at the end of the bar had straightened, and glanced that way to see that he was clearly not as inebriated as he'd seemed. He was watching them intently, one hand beneath his shirt, and she realized that he, too, had a gun hidden in his waistband.

Gabe saw him, too, but said nothing. He stepped aside to let her pass, placing a hand lightly on the small of her back to usher her wordlessly toward the corridor and the man who waited for them to enter his office.

She caught a whiff of cologne as she walked past the bar owner, keeping her head high and doing her best not to show the panic she felt. No one knew where they were; they could disappear from the face of the Earth with no one the wiser. Gabe's presence was all that kept her from bolting toward the door—that, and the teensiest hope that if she just kept walking, she might find Charity waiting in the guy's office.

When she reached a door at the end of the corridor marked PRIVATE, she paused. It was opened from the inside, the door handle being held by yet another muscle-bound guy in a jacket, who gave them an expressionless stare in lieu of a welcome.

"Go keep an eye on the front," the bar owner told the goon. "I'll call you if I need you."

Once in the office, he shut the door and went to the other side of spotlessly clean desk, gesturing for Hope and Gabe to sit. Thankfully, once the door was shut, the horrible eighties music was cut off as though the room was soundproofed, which it clearly was. *Nobody would hear the gunshots*, she thought nervously.

On one wall was a row of security monitors, each with a view of a different part of the bar. In one of them, Hope could see the bartender, who'd gone back to reading his paper. Others showed the varying views of the stage, the front door, and the corridor outside.

"You look a lot like your sister," the bar owner told Hope, by way of a preamble. "Ever do any dancing?"

Hope stiffened, her mouth dry.

"We're just here to find Charity Henderson," Gabe told the guy flatly. "Do you know where she is?"

"And you are?"

"My name is Gabriel."

"Pleased to meet you, Gabriel. My name is

Tony. Tony Menendez. Your girlfriend know how to speak, or do you plan on doing all the talking?"

"I can speak," Hope said hastily, not wanting Gabe and the guy to get into it. "We're not looking for any trouble, I swear. I'm just looking for my sister."

Tony leaned back in his chair, eyeing her assessingly. "She told me about you, you know."

Hope, still reeling from the idea that Charity could voluntarily be working in a place or for a guy as sleazy as this, swallowed hard.

"Says you're the smart one, a real computer nerd or something like that, right?"

She nodded, heart sinking.

"I can always use smart people," he said, picking up a pen and toying with it. "Particularly if they know how to cover their tracks, capische?"

She didn't "capische," and had no intention of being used. "I do Web site design," she told him. "I'll leave you my card."

Tony gave a short bark of laughter, flicking his eyes toward Gabe. "Bet she's a handful, man. It's always the 'sweet and innocent' types who give you the most trouble, you know what I mean?"

"No, I don't," Gabe answered grimly.

"Your sister was never the sweet and innocent

type, now was she?" Tony seemed to enjoy toying with her, and Hope disliked him more with every second that passed. "In and out of foster homes, shoplifting, time in juvie. Lots of boyfriends, real party girl." He gave her a leer. "It's one of the things I like about her."

Hope bit her lip to keep from telling Tony to go fuck himself.

"Is she all right? Why hasn't she called me?"

Tony shrugged, putting down his pen. "She's fine. As to why she hasn't called you, I guess you'll have to ask her that yourself."

"When can I see her? Where is she?"

"What's it worth to you?" All the amusement was gone from his eyes.

"I—" Hope faltered a little. "I don't have much, but . . ."

"Oh, you got plenty, baby." The tone of his voice left no doubt of his meaning.

Gabe gripped the arms of his chair, leaning forward, but Hope put a hand on his arm, knowing he was outnumbered at least three to one by guys with guns.

Tony let the tension build, then, to her surprise, burst out laughing. "I'm just fuckin' with you guys. You're wound way too tight to be in this business, baby doll."

Oddly enough, Hope found herself offended, but refused to show it other than a lift of her chin.

"Although," he said lingeringly, "some guys like the smart ones."

"Yeah," Gabe ground out, clearly unamused. "We do."

Tony gave him a flat stare, perhaps becoming bored with his game of baiting Hope, and willing to go for bigger game.

A short beep sounded, and Tony's eyes went to the monitors. A slow smile spread across his face.

"I guess today's your lucky day," he said.

Hope turned her head, and there, walking into the bar, was her sister, Charity, wearing high heels, short shorts, and a fake fur jacket. Hope watched in the monitor as she smiled and waved at the bartender, clearly at home, and started walking toward the office with a sway in her hips and a smile on her lips.

Shockingly, the relief Hope thought she'd feel at seeing her sister again was transformed into nothing more than an urge to slap her silly. Unconsciously digging her nails into Gabe's arm, she found she couldn't wait to do just that.

Chapter Eighteen

Down Sammy dived, deeper and deeper into murky grayness that went on and on and on. There was life of a sort in the Sea of Sorrows, ghostly creatures with blind, unseeing eyes, drifting to and fro without purpose on unseen currents. He ignored them, forced to use his body instead of his mind, for the depths of these waters were unknown, leaving him no focal point for transport. His immortality left him no need to breathe, no worries of being crushed by the weight of the water, but his movements seemed torturously slow. What kept him going was the image of a blond-haired child, dragged to his doom by Galene the Nereid, and the knowledge that he—and he alone—had failed to keep him safe.

Cain wouldn't die alone in these murky depths, for by all that was unholy, Galene was going to die, too, or his name was not Samael the Black, Ruler of the Abyss.

Far below, a flicker of movement caught his eye, and there she was, taunting him with the languid wave of her tentacles and an upward, sloe-eyed look. She bore a lantern, glowing green with phosphorescence, and as he watched she turned, swimming even deeper into the depths, leaving him a clear trail to follow.

Follow he did, though he knew she lured him into a trap, for traps could not contain him, and his fury knew no bounds.

Staying well out of his reach, lantern bobbing as she swam, Galene led him to a crevasse, deep within the Sea of Sorrows, and slipped within it.

Fearlessly he followed, using the ancient stone on either side of the crevasse to propel himself along, making better time that way. Soon, her light disappeared, leaving him in inky blackness, but a few feet farther the crevasse angled up, and he saw yet another, stronger, gleam above him. A few feet after that, Sammy's head broke the surface of the water, and he found himself in an underground cavern, filled with ghostly, greenish light.

"Father!" Cain's voice echoed throughout the cavern, filling him with an exultation so fierce he could scarce contain it. His son still lived, and for that he would merely kill Galene with a quick snap of her neck, instead of rending her limb from eight-legged limb while she still lived, as he'd planned.

It was not to be so easy, however, for as Sammy pulled himself from the water, he saw that Cain was lashed to a large rock by chains, and beside him lay the monstrous, scaly head of the Leviathan, its reptilian eyes wide and unblinking. The creature had clearly been roused from its long, legendary sleep. Its body, long and thick, was mostly hidden in shadow, for the cavern was vast, but all around it lay piles of treasure: caskets overflowing with coins, jeweled cups, strands of pearls, and fantastic jewelry gleaming with gems, everything glowing greenish silver in the eerie phosphorescent light. On a rock to one side of the cavern sat Galene, surrounded by five other Nereids, their onyx eyes shining, inky tresses trailing over their bare breasts. Their many-legged lower halves seemed unable to stay still, coiling and twisting over the stones upon which they perched.

Slowly, very slowly, the Leviathan stirred, the

ripple of its scales like the hiss of waves against the sand.

"Welcome," it said, in a deep voice that Sammy heard only within his mind. "I am honored."

With uncharacteristic caution, Sammy debated how best to answer. The creature was ancient, and he had no power over it. For eons, it had been content to stay quiescent in its slumbers below the Earth, and he had been content to let it remain that way.

"I've come for my son," he told it, deciding on the direct approach.

"Of course you did," said the Leviathan, with a slow blink. "That is why I took him."

Sammy's eyes went to Cain, chained to the rock. The boy was wet, and clearly frightened, but appeared unharmed. "What is it you want?" he asked.

"Be at peace, O Lucifer, Son of Morning. I have no quarrel with you," returned the Leviathan, keeping its slitted yellow eyes on his. "I wish merely to talk."

"There are better ways to get my attention." Sammy's anger, still close to the surface, made him add grimly, "Your methods leave much to be desired."

"Would you have come otherwise?"

Behind those yellow eyes, surrounded by scales, lurked an intelligence that Sammy decided best not to underestimate.

"No," he answered honestly, "for you appear a formidable foe. I've had no reason to disturb your sleep, nor any desire for your treasures. I want only my son."

"And you shall have him," returned the Leviathan, "as soon as I get what I want in return."

"Which is?"

The Leviathan raised its massive head as Sammy tensed, shooting another glance toward Cain, who appeared tiny and helpless in comparison.

"I want the Lightbringer," said the Leviathan. "The one known as Gabriel."

Inwardly he froze, though he schooled his face to betray nothing. "I have no control over Gabriel—he is both my equal, and my opposite. We are evenly matched, the Lightbringer and I."

"Not so," said the Leviathan silkily. "You have brought him low, and would bring him lower still, for I have seen it in my dreams. Strike now, while he is weak, and bring him to me. Only then will I let the child go free."

Rage, impotent and burning, rose like a wall in Samael's mind. He forced it down, tamping it back with reason and control.

"What do you want with Gabriel?"

"He holds the key to the magic which binds me here, beneath the deep. I would see the sun again, feel the wind upon my face. The cry of the gulls has long been lost to me, and though my friends the Nereids keep me company, their songs merely lull me into slumber, when it is wakefulness I seek."

Sammy shot a hostile glance toward the Nereids, Galene in particular. Cocking her blue-green head, she gave him a small smile that he couldn't read. She knew herself safe here, or she would never have dared to taunt him so.

"There is one more condition, O Son of Morning." The Leviathan gave a slow blink. "The Lightbringer must come willingly."

"What you ask is impossible," Sammy snapped. "Why would Gabriel do such a thing?"

"No greater love than this, that a man lay down his life for his brother. How much love does Gabriel, Servant of Truth, bear you?"

"None, now," was his brutally honest answer, for surely he'd killed any remnant of brotherly love when he'd tricked Gabriel into losing his wings.

"Then your son will die."

Unable to help himself, Samael looked again

toward Cain, bound with chains and totally, utterly dependent upon him. To the boy's credit, he said nothing, merely waiting for his fate to be decided. Pale with fear, blond curls dripping, he raised his chin and looked his father in the eye.

In that look, Sammy saw complete faith, and complete trust, and in that moment, he was so painfully proud of his child that he thought his heart would burst.

"How do I know you'll keep your word?" Within him were the first stirrings of defeat, for he could not—would not—betray the trust in those nine-year-old eyes. "How do I know you'll let him go once I've done as you asked?"

The Leviathan stirred again, a mere whisper of scales against rock. "I am not like you, O Prince of Darkness, for when I give my word, I keep it." The monstrous creature lowered its head, its huge yellow eyes giving a slow blink. "The child will be safe here, until you come again. Whether you come empty-handed or not is up to you. Go now, and do as I ask."

"Cain . . ." Sammy murmured his son's name one final time, whether in blessing or apology, he knew not.

"I'll be all right, Father." The boy's chin quivered, then firmed. "I'll wait for you."

Swallowing his pride along with his rage, he ignored the watching eyes of the Nereids and the hulking presence of the Leviathan to say, "I'll be back for you, my son, I promise."

"I know," Cain returned simply.

He turned to go, but stopped short as Cain asked, "Father?"

"Yes?" His heart, so long dormant, was near to breaking.

"Tesla . . . is he . . ."

With a grim smile at his son's concern for his friend, even at such a critical time, he answered. "Tesla is fine. No need to worry about him."

Cain swallowed and gave a short nod, apparently no longer trusting himself to speak.

Behind him, Galene began to sing a song about love and hate being two sides of the same coin—a song that Sammy had no desire to hear. She was joined by her sisters, their voices rising and blending in strange harmonies within the vastness of the cavern.

He watched as the Leviathan blinked again, his giant lids drooping as he listened.

It was to this eerie soundtrack that Sammy turned and dived back into the water, beginning his long, long swim to the surface.

When he reached it, he waded ashore in the

cove to see that Nyx awaited him, a hulking black shadow pacing anxiously along the shoreline, arms crossed. Tesla was there as well, huddled in a miserable heap on the sand. When the imp saw that Sammy was alone, he covered his ugly face with long-fingered hands, and set up a wail of grief that carried far out to sea.

"Silence," snapped Nyx, and kicked the imp to emphasize his point.

Tesla scuttled away from him like a crab, but continued his wailing. A few feet away he stopped, rocking to and fro in his sorrow.

"Master," said Nyx anxiously, as Sammy left the water. "What happened? Where is our Prince?"

Scrubbing the water from his face and hair, Sammy said tiredly, "He's alive. The Leviathan has him."

The imp's wailing stopped, subsiding into whimpers. Nyx's eyes flared red with rage, his hands curling into fists. "How do we get him back?"

Tesla, clearly unable to be still, wrung his hands and moaned softly as he listened for his master's reply.

Sammy shook his head, speaking his thoughts aloud. "At the moment, I'm not sure."

"But Your Majesty . . ." Nyx looked him askance,

clearly baffled at his master's indecision. "What should we do?"

Wearier than he'd ever felt in his long, long life, Sammy didn't answer. He stared out over the cold, gray ocean, remembering his son's courage, and the look of utter faith in his blue eyes.

Behind him, Tesla sniffled. Turning to the imp, uncaring of Nyx's opinion of his actions, he reached out a hand.

"Come, Tesla. Let's go home."

Chapter Nineteen

"Hey, babe, how's it—"

Charity, looking every inch a Vegas stripper in her high heels and short shorts, froze with her hand on the door handle when she saw Hope sitting in Tony's office.

Hope, not trusting herself to speak, felt her face crumple. Her eyes filled with tears.

Charity's did, too, and as Hope rose from her seat, shaking, she threw herself into her sister's arms.

"Hope," she cried, her voice breaking. "Oh, Hope, I'm so sorry."

Unable to sustain the anger she'd felt when she'd seen Charity in the monitor, waltzing in like she owned the place, Hope hugged her tight, burying her face in her sister's hair. Charity felt thin, too thin, and all she could do was hold on and cry. The next few moments were a wild mixture of relief, gladness, frustration, and confusion, punctuated by "sorrys" from Charity and sobs on both their parts.

"Hope and Charity," Tony said sourly, "ain't that sweet. What's the matter, ain't you got no Faith?" He chuckled at his own joke, while Charity stiffened.

Hope, feeling her sister's sudden tension, reluctantly loosened her hold enough to look Charity in the face. It was the face she remembered, but different somehow, older, yet still so beautiful. "Where've you been all this time? What's going on?"

Charity, fresh tears welling, bit her lip. Her eye makeup, of which there was far too much, had gotten smeared, her lipstick smudged.

"Enough with the waterworks," Tony ordered, "me and Galahad here are gonna need our own Kleenex in a minute."

"Gabriel." The sound of Gabe's voice, calm and even, reminded Hope to take a deep breath. "The name is Gabriel."

"Whatever," said Tony, making it clear the malapropism was deliberate.

Charity slanted her eyes toward Gabe, giving him a quick look, and used the interruption to swipe at her cheeks, pulling away from Hope.

"Sorry, babe," she said to Tony, not yet looking at him. "I'm just, y'know . . . surprised and all."

"Yeah, yeah." Tony was obviously getting bored with the show. "You and your guests take this outside to the bar; I got work to do. Go have Larry pour the three of you a drink, do some catching up."

Charity nodded, still not looking at him, and Hope realized it was because she didn't want Tony to see her face all tear-stained. That, along with his wise-guy attitude and lack of empathy over their reunion, told her pretty much everything she needed to know.

"Thanks, hon," Charity told him. "We'll do that."

Gabriel didn't waste any time, holding the door open and motioning for the two women to precede him into the hall.

With the sound of horrible eighties music reverberating in her ears, Hope followed Charity back into the bar area.

She led them to a table in the corner, digging in her silver sequined purse as she walked, her heels so high it almost appeared as though she were tiptoeing. Her hand came out clutching a small pack of tissues, one of which she offered to Hope.

Gabriel, being a gentleman, waited until both sisters were seated before taking his own seat.

Charity glanced at him curiously, but gave her attention to Hope. In between swipes and sniffles, she said again, "I'm so sorry. I never wanted you to see me this way."

"Tell me what's going on," Hope urged, doing her own swiping and sniffling. "What are you *doing* here?"

"It's a long story."

"We've got time," Hope said grimly, determined to get an explanation.

Charity shook her head, glancing toward the bar. The bartender was eyeing them curiously, as were Tony's two goons. "This isn't the best place to talk about it, Hope."

"Then let's go someplace else."

Charity started digging in her purse again, this time to pull out a small mirror. "I can't," she said, keeping her voice low. Using it to see the damage to her face, she started dabbing at a smear of eye makeup on her temple. "I have to work tonight."

"Work?" Hope found herself getting angry again. "You've been gone for two years!" She reached out and grabbed her sister by the wrist, forcing her to stop fixing her makeup. "I thought you were dead, Charity!"

Charity wouldn't look at her, just stared at herself in the mirror. "It was better that way," she said hollowly.

"Better for *who*?"

All those nights, worrying . . . all that guilt, smothering her until she'd done the unthinkable . . .

"You don't understand." Charity pulled her wrist away.

"You're right, I don't!"

"Hope." Gabriel's hand reached out to take hers. "Give her a chance to explain."

Charity shot him a grateful look. "I'm sorry we had to meet like this," she told him, "but I'm glad my sister finally met a nice guy."

"She's been worried sick over you," Gabe said. "Come with us to the hotel, where you two can talk in private."

Hope appreciated Gabriel's support more than he knew, and squeezed his hand.

Charity appeared extremely uncomfortable. "I can't," she repeated.

"Just tell me what's going on, Charity." Hope leaned in, keeping her voice down, though she doubted the three men over the bar could hear them over the strains of "Imaginary Lover." "I've been looking for you for two years, ever since you disappeared. Why didn't you call me? Why haven't you come home?"

Just then, the door to Tony's office slammed, and the man himself came strolling into the bar area. He glanced at Hope and Charity, adjusting his suit jacket, though it needed no adjusting, and went over to his men at the bar.

Charity, who'd been leaning in to talk to Hope, straightened and took one quick look at herself in the mirror again before tucking it away.

"Home?" she asked loudly, arching a brow. "You call that cracker box little apartment of yours *home*? I had to sleep on a pull-out couch."

Bewildered by the sudden change in attitude, Hope blinked. "We were going to get a bigger place, remember?"

Charity shrugged, rolling her eyes. "Whatever. I've got my own place now."

Gabriel leaned back in his seat, eyeing Charity narrowly.

"So you just ran off on purpose and let me think you were dead?"

"I didn't want to listen to your nagging," Charity said. "Just like I don't want to listen to it now."

Dumbfounded, Hope literally felt her jaw drop.

Gabe squeezed her hand again, and she looked

to him in disbelief, seeking some vague reassur-
ance that she hadn't heard what she just thought
she had.

To her surprise, Gabe skewed his eyes quickly
toward the bar, and said nothing. It was then that
she realized what was going on; Charity's words
were for Tony's benefit.

"I'm sorry if you don't approve of my lifestyle,"
Charity said loudly, "but not everyone is a dried-
up stick-in-the-mud like you." She gestured neg-
ligently toward Gabriel. "You and your boyfriend
need to get the hell out of here."

Unlike everything Charity had said in the last
few moments, it was clear that she meant the last
part. Deep in her sister's eyes was a look of pleading.

The door to the bar opened, admitting light
into the dimness.

"Yeah," Gabriel agreed grimly, surprising her.
"We need to get out of here."

She looked at him again to see that he was staring toward the door, and the men who had just
entered. There were two of them, dark figures sil-
houetted by the daylight.

Gabe stood up, moving fast, but the men moved
faster still. They rushed him, ignoring everyone
and everything else in the room, including Tony's
shouted "Hey!"

In one smooth motion, Gabe picked up a chair and swung it at the two strangers. It broke like kindling over the first man's arm, doing nothing to deflect him. He just batted it away and kept coming, grabbing for Gabe's throat. To Hope's horror, she saw that his eyes gleamed red, as did the second man's, who was right behind him.

"Hey!" Tony shouted again, "take it outside!"

Pandemonium ensued, during which Hope grabbed Charity by the wrist and dragged her away from the three men who were now grappling on the floor. It didn't look like Gabe stood a chance against them, and Hope was almost relieved when Tony's two goons jumped into the fray. One of the strangers—a demon, Hope now realized—turned on the interlopers, snarling, and sank his teeth into an arm. Hope saw his teeth, razor-sharp and inhuman, and heard the crunch of bone a split second before she heard the man's cry of agony.

More dark figures swarmed through the open door, some of them heading toward the knot of men on the floor, others heading toward Tony and Larry at the bar.

Charity was screaming, but Hope was silent in her shock, dragging her sister as far away from the fighting as she could while doing her best to keep an eye on Gabriel, who fought like a demon himself. The wall was at their backs, so she dragged Charity down on the other side of the stage and crouched there with her, an arm around her shoulders.

There was a gunshot, more shouting, the crash of furniture and the snarls of the demons as they made short work of Tony's men. Blood splattered, and bone crunched, and through it all Gabriel fought grimly for his life while Hope watched, helpless and terrified. From the corner of her eye she saw the bartender go down under the weight of two demons, while Tony stood motionless, hands in the air, as chaos went on around him.

It was all over in just a few moments. A third demon joined the two attacking Gabe, and held him, pinned but still thrashing. Three men, all Tony's, lay dead on the floor.

Charity had stopped screaming, but Hope could feel her shuddering as they clutched each other. To her relief, it appeared the demons wanted Gabriel alive, for while blood ran down the side of his face, and they were none too gentle with him, they didn't immediately kill him.

They hadn't killed Tony, either, who stood like a statue as one of the demons approached.

"You did well to stay out of it, human," the

demon rasped, in a grisly parody of a man's voice, "for you will live to see another day." It gave a chuckle, one that chilled Hope's blood. "Your time will come soon enough, however. When next you see us, I have a feeling you won't be so lucky."

Tony blinked rapidly, eyes huge in his face. He didn't look quite the tough guy anymore, Hope noted. Whatever skin these demons were in, they were still demons, and he obviously knew it.

"A trade," he blurted, keeping his hands in the air. "I offer the master a trade." Tony jerked his head toward where she and Charity crouched, afraid to move. "Take the girl . . . hell, take both of them."

Charity gasped, but Hope said nothing, her attention focused on Gabriel, who struggled uselessly against the inhuman creatures in human bodies who held him pinned to the floor.

"We do not make deals on the master's behalf," the head demon rasped. "If you wish to make a trade, you must offer the girl yourself, on the altar." It turned its head to look at Hope and Charity, eyes flaring red in the dimness. "Whether or not the Dark Master takes your offering is up to him."

Wherever they were, it was pitch black. Hope could hear Charity's breathing, rapid and shallow, and squeezed her hand. After Tony had expressed his willingness to slit their throats if it meant saving his own, they'd been taken by the demons who looked like men and dragged, kicking and screaming, out into the sunshine, then thrust into the trunk of a car. Despite the broad daylight, no one had seen them being abducted, or if they had, no one had cared.

She'd had to leave Gabriel behind, and Hope was worried sick about him. He'd fought like a mad thing as they were taken, and the last she'd seen of him, he'd been bleeding profusely, shouting her name. They'd driven for what seemed like hours, and by the time they'd been released from the trunk into the extremely dubious care of yet another guy with a gun, it had been full dark. The guy hadn't said a word to them, and she had no idea if he was human or not. He'd merely motioned them with his gun into a darkened building in the middle of nowhere, thrust them into a room, and locked the door behind them.

"Hope," Charity whispered. "I can't tell you how sorry I am to have gotten you into this mess."

Hope let go of her sister's hand to wrap an arm around her too-thin shoulders. "I got myself into it, Char." If she had any tears left, she would've shed them, but she was saving them all for Gabriel. "I'm just glad you're alive."

"This is my fault, all of it," Charity insisted stubbornly. "I should've listened to you, and never come to Vegas. I can't believe I was so *stupid*."

Talking took her mind off Gabe, and what those inhuman monsters might be doing to him. "What happened, Charity? What are you doing with a creep like Tony?"

Her sister leaned against her in the dark, reminding her of the times when they were both small, and one of them had had a nightmare. This time, it was a joint nightmare, and neither one of them was going to wake up to cartoons and cereal.

"I met him in the casino," Charity said softly, "playing blackjack. I'd lost all my chips and was about to leave the table when he asked me to stick around, be his good luck charm. He was winning, and I"—she gave a soft huff of disgust—"I was actually flattered by his attention. One drink led to another, and eventually . . ." Her hair brushed Hope's nose as she shook her head. "I don't have any memory of how I got there, but the next day I woke up in a place a lot like this."

"He kidnapped you?"

"Only because I was stupid enough to let him," Charity answered sourly. "I think he might've put something in my drink, though he never admitted to it. After two or three days of sitting by myself in the dark, no food or water, thinking I was going to die, he came and let me out."

She fell silent, while Hope waited, letting her sister find the words for what happened next.

"He had four guys with him," Charity said softly, "and I didn't have the strength to fight them. Tony let me shower, gave me something to eat, and then gave me some pills, to make it easier, he said."

That bastard. Rage, cold and hard, lodged itself in Hope's throat, making her want to vomit.

"When it was over, I didn't really care what happened to me," Charity said simply. "He kept giving me the pills, and I kept taking them, because he was right, it really *was* easier that way. He kept me in a locked room with no windows. The guys kept coming, and Tony would show up every night and make me feel better, help me get through the next day. I can't really explain it, but after a week, maybe two—I don't know—it felt like Tony was the only friend I had in the whole world."

What about me? her heart cried, but she left the words unsaid, for she couldn't imagine the horrors her sister must've gone through.

"I thought I was going to die, but I didn't," she said simply. "I begged him to let me call you, but he wouldn't let me. He told me I was used goods, and that nobody would ever love me except him." Charity shrugged. "In some crazy, insane way, I believed him, and after a while I just stopped asking."

"What a scumbag," Hope murmured, giving her sister a squeeze. "He's going to burn in Hell for what he's done."

"Yeah," Charity said softly. "He is."

"What about now? I mean, are you still . . ."

"Still what? Taking the drugs? Seeing the guys?" It was hard to ignore the sense of hopelessness in Charity's voice. "No. Once Tony had me where he wanted me, he stopped giving me the pills. Took me out of that hellhole and put me up in an apartment, made me get clean, even when I didn't want to. Told me it was ruining my looks, and that I had to earn my keep working at Straight Up." The pitch black surrounding them seemed to make it easier for her to talk about it. "I dance, I make a ton of money in tips, but all of it goes to Tony, and in return, he puts a roof over my head, buys my food, my clothes . . ."

Hope closed her eyes, fighting back the old, familiar sense of guilt. The thoughts that if she'd just fought harder to keep Charity with her when they'd gone into foster care, just been more understanding of a teenage Charity when they'd been reunited, even though she'd been barely out of her teens herself . . .

"Hope?" Charity seemed to have run out of steam, slumping against her. "Can you ever forgive me?"

"Of course I can," she murmured, wondering if she could ever forgive herself.

They sat there for a while in silence, taking what comfort they could in just being together. Hope's mind was racing, worrying about Gabriel, about what was going to happen to them, where they were, if anyone would ever find them. Maybe they'd just be left to rot, or maybe Tony would do to her what he'd done to Charity. Either way, she was pretty sure she'd never see Gabriel again, and it was her own damn fault. If she'd left him alone, he'd still be an angel, doing what he did best, instead of a human, and most likely dead in a ditch somewhere.

Unable to hold back the pain of that thought, she gave an involuntary moan.

"Are you okay?" Charity shifted, sitting up. "Did they hurt you?"

"No." Hope hated how wimpy her voice

sounded. "I'm okay." She needed to be strong for Charity, who gripped her hand, hard.

"You're not okay," her sister said, putting both her hands over hers. "You're worried about your boyfriend, aren't you?"

"He's not my boyfriend," Hope said automatically, and then burst into tears. Once begun, they wouldn't stop, and she drew up her knees, pressing her face into them as she cried and cried, both for what she'd lost, and for what she'd never had.

Charity moved, putting both arms around her and resting her head between Hope's shoulder blades. It felt strange to be the one receiving comfort instead of giving it, but Hope took it all in, unable to do anything else. And finally, when the tears became a trickle and the sobs became hiccups, she began to tell her sister about the man she loved.

"His name is Gabriel," she told her. "And he's the kindest, sweetest man I've ever met. I've caused him a lot of trouble, and cost him . . . well, I've cost him more than I can ever repay. And still, despite everything, he protected me and helped me find you." More tears threatened, but Hope shoved them down, wanting to tell Charity everything, but unsure of how. It sounded fantastic: she'd tried to kill herself and been saved by the Devil himself, then made an unholy deal with him to get her sister back. She'd been given an ancient text on how to control demons, had tried to use it for her own benefit and almost gotten herself killed, then was saved by the angel who wrote it. Then she'd corrupted the angel, simply because she couldn't keep her hands off him, and now he was dead, and they were going to die, too.

"You love him," Charity said simply.

Hope didn't deny it. "I love him."

Her sister shifted, lifting her head but keeping her arm around her as she settled them both more comfortably against the wall. "How did you meet?"

"I thought he was a mugger, and I drenched him with lavender oil."

Charity laughed, the sound of which was so incongruous with their surroundings and their situation that it made Hope laugh, too.

"Now *there's* a story to tell your grandchildren," Charity said, giving her shoulder a squeeze. "He must love you, too, if he's still around after that."

Hope didn't answer, because the possibility of such a thing happening was too painfully bittersweet to consider.

"What else? Tell me more about him."

"He's strong, and brave, and he likes cats. Sherlock follows him around like a puppy."

"Sherlock?" The skepticism in Charity's voice was completely understandable. "That furry little snot?" Then she sighed, and murmured, "I miss the little furball."

"He misses you, too," Hope told her. "He still sits by the window and watches, like he's waiting for you to come home."

"He's just watching for birds and squirrels," she said, but Hope could tell she was pleased by the thought. "What else?"

Knowing her sister was just trying to keep her mind off bad things by focusing on good ones, Hope kept talking.

"Gabriel's not like anyone I've ever met," she said slowly. "He's . . . um . . . he's very *spiritual.*"

Charity made a noise of approval. "I'm glad. You could use a little help in that area."

The remark surprised her, considering the source. "What's *that* supposed to mean?"

Another comforting shoulder squeeze made it hard to take offense. "You're just so *serious* all the time, sis. You work so hard, as though you have to do everything yourself or it won't get done. It's like you see everything in black and white, with no shades of gray, no room for fate, or chance, or luck." Charity rested her head against hers in the darkness. "You have a hard time trusting in anyone or anything except yourself, Hope. Sometimes you need to put your faith in something bigger than yourself."

An unexpected lump in her throat rendered her silent.

"You probably won't believe this, but I pray a lot, and even if I don't always get what I want, I know someone hears me," Charity murmured. "I'm not sure what His name is, whether it's God or Allah or Buddha or what—"

He has many names, thought Hope, *most of them unpronounceable, but Gabe knows them all.*

"—but I know He's there. Despite everything bad that's happened to you and me both, I know He's there."

Hope lowered her head, ashamed that after all she'd been through, all she'd seen, she still hesitated to rely on anyone but herself.

"When Mom and Dad died, and we went into foster care, I prayed all the time that you would come and get me, and you did. When Tony . . ." She hesitated, then went on. "When I found myself with Tony, doing what I was doing, I thought I'd probably never see you again—that it was probably better if I didn't, so I wouldn't have to look you in the eye—but I prayed I would anyway." Charity surprised her even more by planting a quick kiss on her hair. "And here you are."

"I missed you, Char."

"I missed you, too."

The sound of key turning in a lock made them both jump, but Hope was almost glad. If they were going to die, and if the God both Charity and Gabriel believed in actually existed, He might have just the teeniest bit of mercy on her and let her see the man she loved, one final time.

Chapter Twenty

Once Hope and Charity were taken from the bar, the Ravenai who'd overcome Gabriel had lost the appearance of humans and become their true selves—ruddy-skinned and leathery, with razor-sharp teeth, ridged backs, and hunched postures. Tony had beaten a hasty retreat, disappearing into his office, leaving the dead bodies of his men on the floor.

The Ravenai had cackled gleefully among themselves as they'd bound Gabe roughly with leather straps, straps that would never have held him if he'd been in angelic form. The body that had known so much pleasure with Hope became a torture chamber, for he couldn't free himself, no matter how he struggled. Frantic with worry for her, he kicked and fought as best he could, so much so that one of the Ravenai, losing patience, had struck him hard in the back of the head, causing him to lose consciousness. When he awoke he was still bound, this time to a chair, sitting in a room he'd never been in before.

Before him was a large mirror, and in it he saw himself, beaten and bound, dried blood on the side of his face and in his hair. His body ached, an unfamiliar sensation, as was the dizziness that assailed him. It passed quickly, however, leaving room for reason to return. With reason came worry, for he'd lost Hope, and had no idea where she might be.

Around him, the room darkened, and as it did, the mirror before him became transparent, slowly revealing the flicker of flames. As his eyes adjusted, Gabe realized he was looking down at a large chamber with a sunken floor, filled with candles, eerily lit in all four corners with torches. The candles were in the hands of people, all of them wearing hooded black robes. He could see no faces, for none of them was looking up toward where he sat. Their collective attention was on a rectangular black table in the center of the room, a coffin-sized island of darkness within a sea of flickering flames.

The walls above the torches were stained with soot, and marked with arcane symbols that made Gabriel's heart sink to his toes, for there he saw the symbol of Asmodeus, the Destroyer, and that of Behemoth, Demon of Indulgence. There, too, was the sigil of Baal, Commander of Earthly Legions, which left no doubt as to this gathering's purpose. On the table, which he now knew to be an altar, lay a gleaming silver athame, an ornate dagger used for sacrifice.

The gathering seemed to be taking place in total silence. If not for the movements of one man, who wove his way throughout the room, lighting candles as he went, Gabe would've thought the black-robed figures mannequins, so still did they appear.

A door opened at the far end of the room, and another black-robed figure came in, carrying a large, leather-bound book. He was followed by three others, one holding a large silver chalice, the other two holding gleaming golden censers from which smoke rose like steam.

The two with the censers split in opposite directions, each making a full, slow circle of the room, crossing in the middle, while the ones with the book and the chalice moved to stand at the head of the altar.

Smoke rose, and silence reigned, as Gabriel once again struggled ineffectually at his bonds. The man with the book laid it upon a lectern, opened it, and began to read. His words echoed tinnily through speakers mounted near the ceiling in the room where Gabriel was confined.

" 'Come ye, O Angel of Darkness; come hither before this assembly and accept our tribute. Come ye, O Chagadel, servants of the Lord of Flies, and feast upon our offerings. Come ye, O Satriel, servants of Lucifer, and behold the signs of power, which move the Earth and makes the heavens tremble. Come ye, O Gamichoth, who knows the corruption which lies within the breasts of women!' "

The door opened again, and Gabriel gasped in dismay as Charity was brought struggling into the room, long hair flung about her head as she thrashed in the hold of her captors.

"Let me go, you bastards," she shrieked, "let me go!"

The man reading from the book reached out and picked up the athame, ignoring Charity's shrieks. There was a rustling from the black-robed figures who'd gathered, still holding their candles, and one man stepped forward with a length of black cloth. He stepped behind Charity, and despite her struggles, gagged her quickly and mercilessly, drawing the cloth tight and knotting it behind her head, muffling her cries.

" 'Come ye, O Ravens of Death, servants of Baal.' " The man reading from the book held the dagger high, candlelight gleaming upon its razor-sharp surface.

" 'Come ye, O Anakim, servants of Nahema.' "

Charity was borne to the altar and thrust upon it, kicking and fighting. No one came to her aid, though black-robed figures swarmed over her like crows, pinning her arms and legs.

" 'Come ye, O Tagarim, servants of Behemoth,' " the man shouted, still reading from the book.

Gabriel watched, struggling fruitlessly, as Charity was bound to the altar with leather straps, just like the ones that held him. He rocked from side to side, trying to kick over the chair in which he was bound, but it was apparently bolted to the floor, for it didn't move.

" 'Come ye, O Golab, servants of Asmodeus, also known as Samael the Black!' "

Through the open door came still more black-robed figures, this time holding by the arms—though she kicked and screamed as much as her sister—his heart's desire, his one and only love, Hope.

Gabriel threw back his head and howled his former brother's name, impotent with fury, but no one heard him, for the room he was in was apparently soundproof. Maddened, he realized that he could shout until his throat was raw, but not be heard; he could watch as unholy obscenities took place before his eyes, but do nothing.

Hope's wrists were red with blood, her cuts having clearly opened during her struggles, and the sight made his Gabe's fingers itch for his sword. If Samael had been within his reach, he would've killed him with his bare hands, but such mercy was not to be granted him.

" 'May this sacrifice which we find it proper to offer unto ye be agreeable and pleasing in your sight, O Prince of Darkness. Come ye, come ye, come ye.' "

The black-robed figures took up the chant, beginning to sway in unison. "Come ye, come ye, come ye," they chanted, their voices rising in unholy communion, growing louder and louder.

Hope looked absolutely terrified, tears running down her cheeks. Charity, upon the altar, had finally given up her struggles, and lay trembling, eyes tightly shut.

Finally a black-robed figure wearing a goat mask, fantastically horned, appeared in the doorway. The bravest man's heart would've run cold at the sight, but Gabriel was not a man in the true sense of the word, and his heart ran red with righteous wrath, for he knew full well whose face was hidden behind the mask.

"Samael!" he shouted again. "Samael, don't do this!"

The man in the goat mask seemed to hear him, for he tilted his head upward, looking toward the glass behind which Gabriel was confined. The expression on the mask was set in a permanent inhuman leer, a leer that was then turned on Hope, still struggling in the hands of the two men who held her. She recoiled, but couldn't escape as the goat man came closer. She tried to kick, but the men holding her jerked her back so that her kicks fell short.

His attention on Hope, the man in the goat mask held up a hand toward the room full of chanting, black-robed figures. Like magic, the chanting stopped.

In the resultant silence, Gabe could clearly hear the frightened breathing of the two women. Closing his eyes, he began to pray as he'd never prayed in his life, desperate for help that had yet to appear.

The silence grew, as did the tension. Unable to

concentrate on his prayers because of it, Gabriel opened his eyes so that he could once again rest them on his beloved's face.

Hope took a deep breath, still staring into the eyes of the man in the goat mask. "Let my sister go," she cried. "She's been through enough. Let her go!"

The man in the goat mask tilted his head, as though considering. Then he turned, and walked toward the head of the altar. The man holding the dagger offered it to him, and he took it.

"No!" Hope shrieked, "Leave her alone. Take me! Take me instead!"

Gabe moaned in despair, his mortal heart breaking. That Hope would sacrifice herself for her sister didn't surprise him, for hadn't she sacrificed everything else for Charity already? Her happiness, her self-esteem, her very life had been offered to the Darkness because of what she considered her greatest failure: not keeping her sister safe.

"You can save her, Gabriel."

Gabe whipped his head toward the sound of the voice and saw Sammy, leaning against the wall. He glanced quickly down at the Mass taking place at his feet; the man in the goat mask was still there.

"You can save them both," Sammy said. He was clad all in black, his light hair like a beacon in the dimness. "But only if you do something for me in return."

Rage clouded Gabe's vision, turning it red. "It's not her fault she didn't keep her end of the bargain, it's mine!" he shouted.

Sammy, his face in shadow, replied, "It doesn't matter whose fault it was. You know that."

"You wanted me to suffer, didn't you? Look at me, see how I suffer! You won, you bastard, you won!" Frantic to be free, desperate to say anything that might save Hope, Gabe was not above begging. "Please, Samael, please don't do this."

"Do you love her?" Samael the Black asked the question softly, and this time, Gabe didn't have to think about the answer.

"Of course I love her!"

"Then what will you do for her?"

Chest heaving, head throbbing, Gabe stared at the man he'd once considered his brother.

"Will you lay down your life for her, as she does for her sister?"

Gabe glanced toward the black-robed figures again, seeing the gleam of candlelight play along the edge of the sacrificial dagger. The man in the goat mask was staring up at him, two reddened eyes looking directly into his. Charity was sobbing behind her gag, Hope pale with fear.

Lowering his head, Gabe surrendered to the inevitable.

"I will," he said.

When the man in the goat mask moved toward Charity again, Hope screamed, long and loud, but it did no good. The knife flashed as he held it high in both hands. He seemed to be looking upward at some point she couldn't see. Robed figures clustered around the altar, blocking her view of her sister. She screamed again as the goat man brought the knife down, her knees giving way. If it weren't for the men on either side of her, she would've collapsed under the weight of her terror.

There was a choked sound, then gasps and mutterings from the black-robed figures around the altar. Hope squeezed her eyes shut, fighting the urge to faint, as sparkles exploded behind her closed lids. The men holding her fell back, taking her with them, and she opened her eyes to see the man who'd been reading from the book stumble backward, the hilt of the dagger protruding from his throat.

Shocked murmurs arose, but no one moved to help him. His head fell back, and with it the hood of his robe, revealing his face, wide-eyed and gasping.

It was Tony. Stunned, Hope watched as he grabbed the dagger and drew it out, blood spurting from the hole in his neck. Some of it sprayed over those standing closest to him, including the man in the goat mask.

"The master accepts your sacrifice," said the goat man, in a deep, raspy voice.

The dagger fell from Tony's nerveless hand to hit the floor with a clatter. Through the cluster of black-robed figures, she could see Charity on the altar, eyes wide with terror, her chest rising and falling rapidly with her breath.

"That was not the plan!" one of the cowled men protested, stepping forward.

It was the last thing he ever said, for the goat man bent, picked up the knife, and as he rose he slashed, strong and true. The protestor fell back, clutching his own throat, his fingers rapidly turning red with blood. He, too, fell to the floor, twitching and gurgling. In moments he, too, lay still, as blood formed an ever-widening pool around him.

A circle opened around the man in the goat mask as those closest to him stepped back. To Hope, it looked like a scene from a horror movie: a fantastically horned figure in a black robe, backlit by candles and torches, holding a knife that dripped blood. He moved toward the altar again, but she had no breath left to scream, no strength left to fight. This time, when the knife flashed, it cut the leather straps that bound Charity to the altar. She rolled off in a flash, falling to the floor. Hope met her eyes, wide with panic, as Charity scrabbled toward her, still gagged.

"Let the women go," rasped the goat man, and the men who held her let go of her arms. Hope reached out to Charity, the two of them clutching each other frantically as Hope did her best to help her sister to stand.

"Go," rasped the man in the goat mask, pointing with his bloody knife toward the open door.

Not waiting to be told twice, Hope did as she was told, dragging a very wobbly Charity with her. They found themselves in a long hallway and started to run, images of the scene she'd just witnessed flashing through her mind. Charity, still gagged, had a death grip on her hand. Together they came to the end of the corridor and went the only way they could, both of them desperate to find a way out. Yet another turn, and then they both skidded to a stop, frozen in terror, as they came face-to-face with a strange woman, ornately dressed in a glittering gold gown, covered with spangles.

She was regal-looking, and very beautiful. She tilted her head, which was piled high with dark hair and woven with ribbon, and smiled, seemingly unperturbed by the sight of them, wild-eyed and panic-stricken though they were.

"You poor dears," she said, in a comforting fashion. "How frightened you must be." She held out both her hands, flashing with rings, wrists covered in bangles. "Come with me now, quickly, if you want to live."

Hope looked at Charity and Charity looked at her, the black gag an ugly slash in her pretty face. *Should we trust her?* was the question at the forefront of both their minds.

"Time is of the essence, my dears," the woman said. "You'll come to no harm with me, I swear it."

"Who are you?" Hope challenged.

"My name is Pandora, and I'm one of the good guys. Not as good as your friend Gabriel"—she gave a light tinkle of laughter—"but good nonetheless."

"You know Gabriel?"

"I've not had the pleasure," Pandora replied, "but I'm quite certain that he'd approve of you doing as I ask."

Invoking Gabriel's name had been a smart move on the woman's part. Knowing they were somewhere in the middle of nowhere, with nowhere to go, and no other options, Hope swallowed hard, and took a step toward her.

"Take my hands," Pandora said, waggling beringed fingers, "both of you."

Slowly, Hope reached out a hand, and then so did Charity. She felt the woman's fingers, surprisingly strong, close around her own. The spangles on Pandora's golden dress glittered, then became blinding, as the world around them exploded into light.

Chapter Twenty-one

"I protest," Nyx said to Pandora, "most vehemently. The master would not appreciate your interference, and neither do I." He hung the goat mask on the wall, carefully, where it leered at them both, as though finding their squabbles amusing.

"Oh, pooh," Pandora replied, choosing a plump grape from the platter in front of her. They were in an antechamber near Samael's private quarters, a place Nyx used for himself when not waiting upon his Dark Prince. "What care I for your protests?" She wrinkled her pretty nose at the black robe he was still wearing, popping the grape into her mouth. "And do take off that robe . . . the smell of blood offends me."

"What care I for your offense?" Nyx retorted,

ripping the robe from his body and tossing it on the floor. "You cannot keep humans like pets, and you most certainly cannot keep them within the inner temple."

"Why not?" Pandora asked, eyeing Nyx beneath her lashes. "There are plenty of bedrooms, and Samael can deal with them at his leisure when he returns from the Sea of Sorrows."

"The master will have more on his mind than those two when he returns," Nyx said with a frown.

"Do you think he'll be able to save the young princeling?"

"Don't call him a princeling," Nyx said absently, missing Pandora's knowing smile. It was gone from her face by the time he turned, stalking back in her direction. "And of course he'll save him. My lord can do anything."

"The Leviathan is older than time," Pandora mused, "and his ways are mysterious. I worry that he draws Samael into some kind of trap."

"I worry about that, too," Nyx confessed, in a rare show of honesty. "But His Infernal Majesty forbade me to follow him, and I must do as he bids."

"Poor Nyx," Pandora said soothingly. She patted the seat beside her. "Come, share my couch, and we'll wait together."

Nyx turned his head to give her a suspicious look, his red eyes flaring briefly.

"What?" The look Pandora gave him in return was the picture of innocence. She popped another grape into her mouth and chewed it, then swallowed. "We're on the same side, you know: Samael's." A dimple played in her cheek as she smiled up at him.

"You'll forgive me if I find that hard to believe," Nyx growled. "In all the years I've known you you've cared for no one but yourself."

Pandora gasped in mock dismay. "How you wound me!"

"Would that I could," Nyx returned darkly, "but that's something else the master has forbidden me to do."

"Now, now," she tutted, wagging a jeweled finger, "there's no need for threats of violence. I'm quite fond of Samael in my own way, and he of me, which you know quite well."

Nyx paced, a tall black shadow, unable to stay still. "He uses your body for his pleasure, that's all."

"As I use his," she admitted frankly. "If we have no problem with it, why should you?"

Nyx shot her another red-eyed glare, not deigning to answer.

Pandora selected another grape, taking her time. Once she found one to her satisfaction, she held it between her fingers, eyeing it carefully. "You're grouchier than usual today, my blackened friend, and I know why."

Nyx sneered, and continued his pacing.

Pandora popped the grape into her mouth, chewed, and swallowed. "The Mass was ruined, and you fear it will merely increase the mutterings among the legions that the Great Shaitan has grown weak, allowing emotions to rule."

A hiss of rage answered her. Nyx stopped, stock-still, and crossed his arms over his bare chest. "Have a care what you say about my master, Pandora."

Unconcerned by the demon's display of anger, Pandora shrugged a plump shoulder. "*I'm* not the one saying it, you beast, but we both know it's being said."

"It's not true," he stated emphatically. "The Great Shaitan always has a plan . . . his mind is like a labyrinth, shadowy and twisting. There is a reason for everything he does, and in this case it was to teach the Lightbringer a sorely needed lesson before handing him over to the Leviathan."

"What if the reason was mercy?" Pandora asked softly. "What if the reason was love? These are emotions, my blackened friend, and they are emotions that are dangerous to have in Sheol."

Nyx shook his horned head, stubbornly rejecting Pandora's argument. "It's not for me to question the Ruler of the Abyss, nor is it meet for the legions to do so. If I must wreak havoc among the ranks to still such rumors, I will gladly do so."

"I have no doubt of that," Pandora agreed, "for you are the most loyal of creatures."

Turning a suspicious eye once again upon the woman who sat, half reclining, upon a well-cushioned couch, Nyx asked, "And you? Are you loyal to him?"

"More than you know," she told him tranquilly, "for Samael and I share more than just a bed. We share a common history, that of being monumentally blamed for one teeny, tiny mistake, made in a moment of youthful folly. I understand his pain whether he shows openly or not, and despite the fact that he can be the biggest ass who ever lived"—she arched a perfectly tweezed brow in Nyx's direction—"present company excepted, of course—he's always been kind to me. I have nothing but his best interests at heart, which is why I brought the women here."

Nyx regarded her silently for a long moment.

"Your logic eludes me, but I expect nothing less from the female of the species."

Pandora laughed. "Since I happen to be more female than most, your confusion is completely understandable. Come"—she patted the couch beside her again—"sit with me. I'm tired of you looming over me like the Shadow of Death."

"I *am* the Shadow of Death," he snapped in reply.

"So you are, and quite fearsome, too," she agreed, not the least bit intimidated. "And yet strangely enough, the more time I spend with you, the less fearsomely ugly you appear."

Nyx made a noise that could've been construed as a bark of laughter, if such a fearsome creature as he were able to laugh.

"I've noticed the same thing about you," he told her, and joined her on the couch.

The water in the bathtub was warm, soothing, and without a hint of red. Hope stared down at the half-healed cuts she'd made just days before, marveling at how long ago it seemed. She couldn't believe she'd ever been so stupid as to try and take her own life. After what she and Charity had gone through today, she'd never take the gift of life for granted again.

The bathroom was lavish, and completely unfamiliar. While she couldn't claim that she felt completely safe in a strange woman's bathtub, she could, at least, claim to be comfortable. And Pandora was indeed a strange woman; if Hope hadn't seen stranger things with her own eyes, she'd never have believed that magic existed, much less beautiful women who looked and acted like goddesses *using* magic on her behalf. Yet there was no other explanation, for one moment she and Charity been in a corridor somewhere, and the next moment they'd been in some kind of palace, surrounded by luxury. The three rooms she'd seen so far—two bedrooms and the bathroom—were so exquisitely decorated that if she and Charity hadn't been on the verge of collapse, she'd have goggled her eyes out.

Pandora herself had been nothing but kind, helping her and Charity to calm down by assuring them over and over that they were safe, though she refused to answer any questions, turning them away with cryptic answers like, "All will be revealed, in time." Hope suspected that there'd been something in the wine Pandora had given them, because Charity had fallen asleep after just a few sips. Hope had refrained from drinking it, though the idea was tempting, mainly because she'd felt the need to be clean more than anything else. She felt tainted to her soul by what she'd seen today, even after scrubbing herself repeatedly.

Besides, if—by some miracle—Gabe showed up, she wanted to be awake and alert.

Miracle. Lying there, in the warm, quiet tub, Hope pondered the meaning of the word. These last few days, she'd been certain that being pulled from the brink of death by the Devil himself had been nothing more than a monumental curse, and yet here she was, with her sister sleeping safely in the next room. If she'd slipped into darkness the way she'd planned, she'd never have met Gabe, and that was something she couldn't bring herself to regret.

Even if she never saw him again, she'd always have the memory of how he'd looked, the sunlight streaming through her window as he sat in her living room. She'd never forget how he'd risen to her defense when the demon showed up, or how he'd tried to shield her from dealing with Sammy on the casino floor. She'd always remember their time in the hotel room, when he'd laid aside all his defenses, and let her touch him the way she'd wanted to since the moment she'd first seen him in her kitchen, wrapped in damp towels.

Laying her head back on the rim of the tub,

Hope closed her eyes, refusing, for the moment, to cry any more. It was enough, for now, to know that she'd always have those moments when passion had surged between them—so fierce, so strong—and the tenderness that followed, so gentle.

Whether Gabe had loved her at all in those moments she might never know, but there was no question that she had loved him, and always would.

And then, slowly, as the water cooled, Hope realized that mere thoughts of Gabriel were *not* enough; they would never be enough. She'd been willing to do anything to find her sister, yet for Gabriel, she'd done nothing, and was still doing nothing, because she was weak in all the places where she thought she'd been strong.

Evil wins when good does nothing, Nicki Styx had said to her.

Hope opened her eyes and sat up. She would take the only course left to her, and do it gladly.

Rising from the tub, she wrapped herself in a fluffy robe hanging from a hook on the wall, and padded quietly into the bedroom Pandora had given her to use.

There, beside the bed, she lowered herself to her knees and folded her fingers together. Scarcely knowing where to begin, for it had been so long, she began to pray to the One who'd always been there, even if she'd been too stubborn to look for Him.

"Help me, please," she prayed, "for Gabriel's sake, if not for mine. I know I don't deserve it after what I've done"—she swallowed hard, remembering how she'd agreed to cooperate with the Devil himself—"but Gabriel doesn't deserve to suffer because of me. He's served you faithfully all these years, and what happened between us was my fault, not his. Please don't punish him because of me. Please let him live . . . it doesn't matter if I ever see him again, as long as he's alive, somewhere, doing what he was meant to do."

The room was quiet. Hope leaned forward, eyes closed, hands clasped, and rested her head against the bed.

"He no longer has his flaming Sword of Righteousness. He no longer has his wings, or his powers, but he is still Gabriel, Bringer of Light, Servant of Truth. All he has is You, O Great One . . . all he has is You."

She stayed there, on her knees, for a long, long time, not knowing if her prayers would be answered, but certain, in her heart of hearts, that they had been heard.

Chapter Twenty-two

The Father of Lies stood on the shore of the Sea of Sorrows, ready to sacrifice the one person who'd never—in all these eons—lied to him. He saw no other choice, but lack of choice made it no easier. Out there, beneath the gray waves, his son waited trustfully, while here, on the gray sands, the one he'd once called brother trusted him no more.

The shades of regret had already begun to gather, drawn, Sammy knew, by the emotions within his own blackened, withered soul. They circled him and Gabriel, restless and moaning, their endless misery reflected in the leaden seas and equally somber skies.

"What is this place, and what are we doing here, Samael?"

Gabriel had been subdued since Sammy had let Hope and her sister go. Sammy had released his old friend from his bonds and brought him here, knowing that—unlike Sammy—Gabriel would keep his word and come without a struggle. He knew it the same way he'd known that Hope would offer herself in her sister's place, and that seeing his beloved about to die, Gabriel would do the same.

Lies, within lies, within lies, and he was so unutterably weary of them all.

"It's called the Sea of Sorrows." Aware he could no longer put off the inevitable, Sammy turned and looked his onetime brother in the eye. "We're waiting for the Nereids," he told him, "who will take you to the Leviathan." Coward that he was, he couldn't bring himself to dive beneath the waves with Gabriel in tow, knowing that, because of Gabe's now-mortal form, he would drown long before they reached the abyss. Let Galene and her sisters do it, for drawing mortals to their deaths beneath the sea was what they did best, and he would follow when it was done.

"The Leviathan?" Gabe frowned, puzzled. "What has he to do with anything?"

"He has my son," Samael answered simply, "and he wants to trade him for you."

Shock widened Gabriel's brown eyes.

"He's taken your son? Why didn't you come to me, why didn't you tell me . . ." Gabe trailed off, immediately recognizing that there was nothing he could've done anyway. Perhaps once, as an angel, he might've had some small bit of influence, some power, but as a mortal he had none.

To his shame, Sammy realized that he wouldn't have gone to him anyway, for he had too much pride to ask for anyone's help. Gabriel's offer of help had been instinctive, despite what he'd recently done to him—what he was *about* to do to him—and the knowledge burned like acid in the back of his throat.

If he lived another ten thousand years, he would never be the selfless soul Gabriel was. And now he must live those ten thousand years knowing he was responsible for the death of his first—and only—friend.

"You have returned." A woman's voice came from the sea, and they both looked to see Galene's sleek head, bobbing in the water. "With your brother."

"He's not my brother," Gabriel said to her coldly.

Sammy swallowed, surprised by how much the words hurt, though he'd said them himself, many times.

Galene tilted her head, her dark hair floating in the water around her. "You do not come willingly?" she asked, puzzled.

Gabriel straightened his shoulders, not looking at him. "I come willingly."

"Ah." Galene smiled, using her slender arms to tread water. "So the mighty Leviathan was right, and the brotherly bond between you and the Great Shaitan still exists, despite the evil he's done to you and yours. Love is a more powerful human emotion than even *I* realized."

Gabriel laughed, but it was a bitter laugh. "Oh, love is a powerful emotion, all right, but it is not for love of Samael the Black that I stand here before you, ready to lay down my life." He raked Sammy briefly with a scornful gaze. "It's because of my love for a mortal woman, whose feet he is not fit to kiss."

Galene frowned, her jet black eyes drawing together. "That was not the bargain," she said to Samael. "The Lightbringer was to lay down his life on *your* behalf, not for another's."

"It makes no difference," Sammy snapped, annoyed at having the Leviathan's impossible-to-meet condition revealed. "He was to come willingly, and so he has."

Beside him, Gabriel made a noise of disbelief,

followed quickly by a burst of bitter laughter. "You think to cheat the terms of your own bargain?" he asked mockingly. "How like you."

Furious, Sammy turned on Gabriel, but Gabriel wasn't finished. "Nothing is sacred to you, is it? Not life, not honor, not trust . . . you have nothing inside you but hate and hubris, Samael, nothing at all. Your body is a mere shell, your heart a blackened husk."

Not true, cried his heart, for in it nestled a young boy, who even now awaited his father's coming. There, too, was a tiny corner in which Nicki Styx still lurked, judging him in absentia with her kind brown eyes, which had seen the blackness within his soul, and forgiven him anyway.

"Gabriel, I—" The words stuck in his throat, for he knew not what to say. "Cain, he—"

"Cain will die," Galene said calmly, from her place in the water. "For you, O Great Shaitan, have not the tools to save him."

The words struck Sammy with the force of a blow, for always—*always*—he'd been able to do whatever he wished, whether by force, persuasion, or trickery. This time, what he wished for was beyond his grasp, and unlike with Nicki Styx, he did not *choose* to let Cain go.

From the rocks above the cove arose the sound

of singing, Galene's five sisters repeating the song
he'd first heard her sing, the song that had inad-
vertently lured his son to his doom:

Weep for the secrets you never revealed
The time you lost while striving,
Mourn the passing of the years
Like the dead, no hope of reviving.
Pearls on a strand were the days of your life
The string now snapped, and broken,
Mourn for the secrets you never revealed
And the words you left unspoken.

Wishing he could close his ears, Sammy closed
his eyes instead, for the sea wind made them sting
unaccountably. He'd taken his brief time with
Cain for granted, thinking he and the boy would
have years together, years in which to grow close,
to teach his child everything he knew, and how
best to avoid the mistakes he himself had made.
Instead he'd lost him when they'd barely begun,
and there was nothing he could do.

"Farewell, O Prince of Darkness," said Galene,
when the song had ended. "We will see to it that
the child does not suffer unduly."

"Wait," said Gabriel, and Sammy opened his
eyes.

Gabriel was staring at him, a strange expression on his face. Galene bobbed in the water, eyeing the two of them curiously, making no move to go just yet.

"Tell me," murmured Gabriel, for Sammy's ears alone, "and for once in your life, tell me true." His brown eyes bored into his onetime brother's, challenging him to not look away. "The boy . . . do you love him?"

There was a roaring in Sammy's ears, much like the waves themselves, yet not of them. "Yes," he heard himself say. "Yes, I do." The weight of a thousand suns was lifted off his shoulders at the words, only to crash into his heart. He staggered, and might've fallen, had not Gabriel's arm shot out to grasp his shoulder.

For a moment, the world condensed to nothing but the sea, the sand, and the touch of his brother's hand, firm upon his shoulder.

"Nereid," said Gabriel loudly, so Galene could hear. "I go willingly. I go on behalf of my brother, Samael the Fallen."

The sea wind, treacherous and salt-filled, made Sammy's eyes water. "No," he told Gabe hoarsely, but the word was lost to the wind. All he could do was put his own hand atop Gabe's where it grasped his shoulder, and squeeze, hard.

Gabriel gave him a lopsided grin, one he remembered all too well. "I'm human, now, Samael," he told him, "which means that one day I'm going to die anyway. I've waited eons for your heart to open itself to love again, and I won't be the cause of rending it asunder. If I'm to die, I might as well do it now, here, for a good cause."

"But the woman . . . Hope . . ." Shame, that most hated of all emotions, flooded him. "She still lives. You could have a life with her."

Gabriel's smile faded, but he didn't release Sammy's arm. "She has her sister back, and her own choices to make." He swallowed, his eyes going bleak. "She'll forget me in time."

"You'd do this . . ." Sammy could barely bring himself to say the words aloud. " . . . for *me*?"

"I will."

"The Leviathan will be pleased," said Galene, and her sisters began once again to sing.

Two sides of a coin are love and hate,
One side choice, one side fate.
Which side dross, which side treasure,
Which shines bright, each man must measure.

And there, on a windswept beach, Sammy bowed his head and—for the first time—accepted

that some things were beyond his power to
control. Removing his hand from Gabriel's, he
reached out and put it on his brother's shoulder,
so they gripped each other equally. "Thank you,"
he said hoarsely, "and I'm so very, very sorry."

Gabriel brushed his hand aside, and without warning, pulled him close. "I know you are,
brother," he murmured gruffly, into his ear. "I've
always known."

Unmanned, humbled for the first time in thousands of years, Sammy squeezed his eyes shut and
returned Gabriel's embrace, knowing he would
never see him again.

"Father!"

A trick of the wind brought his eyes open.

"Father, I'm here!"

It was not the wind, for Gabriel heard it, too,
pulling away to turn toward the sea.

Far beyond where the waves broke, a massive
shape was rising from the deep. Water streamed
from the head of the Leviathan, and from its coils,
writhing behind it for what seemed like miles.
And there, upon the creature's head, sat a small
figure, clutching tightly at the scaled ridge of an
ear.

"The Leviathan *is* pleased," said Galene, "for he
honors us with his presence."

As Sammy and Gabriel watched, side by side on the sand, the monstrous gray-green creature made his leisurely way to the shore, using its coils to propel it along like a snake. Water surged, cresting on either side to crash along the rocks that littered the shoreline, yet it slid onto the sand smoothly, with a resounding hiss of scales.

"That was awesome," cried Cain, and leapt to the ground as though he hadn't a care in the world. "Father, did you see?"

White blond hair plastered to his head, bright blue eyes shining, he ran to where Sammy waited, heart in his throat. Unable to speak, he grabbed the boy to him, holding him tight against his leg as he stared into the large reptilian eye of the Leviathan.

"Light and darkness, together for one cause," said the monster, deep inside Sammy's brain. "What a strange sight to see."

Beside him, Gabriel inclined his head to the creature in a gesture of respect. "Hail, O Mighty One," he said.

"Hail and well met, Lightbringer," returned the Leviathan.

Gabe stepped forward, closer to the creature, partially shielding Sammy and Cain. "Thank you for returning the boy," he said formally, "and as agreed, I offer my life in return for his."

"Of course you do," the monster replied, "for you have spent eons protecting the innocent. In this case, however, there is no need."

Sammy clutched Cain, already squirming in his grip, even closer, moving to stand beside Gabe once more. Whatever happened to his brother, it would not happen while Sammy cowered behind him.

"You, O Gabriel, Servant of Truth, have done what I hoped you would do," the Leviathan went on, "and brought Light to the Darkness."

Dumbstruck, it took Sammy a moment to realize that *he* was—quite literally—the Darkness.

"The Child of Perdition now has a child of his own, and my old friend the One wished him to know the pain of a son gone astray, as well as the lengths a father will go to bring a child home."

I'm no one's child, Sammy started to say, but he knew it was reflex only, and would make him appear even more the child he denied being.

"'Your old friend the One'?" he repeated, his normally agile mind reeling from the events of the last few minutes.

"Of course," answered the Leviathan. "He is of the heavens, and I am of the Earth, but at heart we are brothers, and always will be." His monstrous head shifted infinitesimally toward Gabriel. "As are you two."

Galene's laughter tinkled in the air, joined by that of her sisters from the rocks above the cove.

Samael the Fallen, still clutching his squirming son, cared not, for what mattered to him most was beneath his hand, and to his right. He turned his head to look at Gabriel, and saw that the lopsided grin had returned.

"Did you know about this?" he demanded.

Gabriel shook his head. "I didn't, I swear it."

And because he knew full well that Gabriel would never lie to him, he accepted the truth when he heard it.

Cain tugged at his shirt, drawing his attention. "Father?"

He looked down, into pale blue eyes so like his own. "Yes, my son?"

"Don't be mad, but I think I lost my shoes again."

Gabriel burst out laughing, the sound of it driving any lingering shades of regret away, to drift aimlessly on other sands, and other beaches.

"I'll get you another pair," Sammy told the boy gruffly, "and we'll get Tesla a pair, too."

Cain beamed up at him, while Gabriel cuffed

him playfully on the shoulder. "Aren't you going to formally introduce me to my nephew?" he asked.

"In a moment," he said, memorizing the look upon his son's face, so he would never, ever forget it.

Taking a deep breath, he then looked up at the Leviathan. "Thank you," he said, and inclined his head in a deep gesture of respect. "Thank you for the life of my son, and for the lessons I've learned here today."

"You're welcome," said the beast. "May they stay with you always."

Sammy nodded again in acknowledgment, then turned to go. "Come, Cain. Let's go home." He walked a few steps, then turned, a hand on his son's shoulder. "Wait a minute," he said to the creature. "You told me that Gabriel had the key to the magic that kept you confined to the deep, yet you came here easily enough."

"O Prince of Darkness, do you not see?" The Leviathan gave him a slow-eyed blink. "I lied."

Chapter Twenty-three

Gabriel stood over Hope, watching her sleep. Where Sammy had brought him, he hadn't asked—hadn't cared—as long as Hope would be waiting for him when he got there. He and his brother had much to talk about, and many issues to resolve (which probably never would be), but he'd been content to leave Sammy alone with his son, for his soul cried out for Hope.

Hope, with her big green eyes and even bigger heart, which had been left with a hole in it when her sister disappeared. She'd tried to fill that hole with endless searching, with work, with guilt, and when the time came that she thought Charity gone forever, the Darkness that had rushed in to fill that hole had overwhelmed her.

What would've been the outcome, he wondered, if he'd been there the night Hope had lain down in that bathtub and taken that razor in hand? He would've revealed himself to her, surely, and she'd have seen him in all his angelic glory, the way he used to be.

He would've saved her from the Darkness, but to her, he would've been a creature from another world—a brilliant, gleaming world, to be sure—as far removed from her own as the Earth from a star. Then he would've gone away, knowing he'd done the right thing, but missing everything else: the way her green eyes snapped when she was angry, and softened when she wasn't. The way her short blond hair spiked when she ran her fingers through it, and curled perfectly behind her ear. How rapt her face looked at the computer as she worked, and how she spoke to her cat as though it were a person. The warmth of her home, with its hardwood floors and eclectic furniture, the window that looked out on her neighbor's garden.

He would never have known the smooth silkiness of her skin, touched the tender curves of her breasts, felt the softness of her inner thigh. The honeyed sheath between her legs would've forever remained a mystery, as would the ecstasy that flung him into the heavens in a different—yet just as glorious way—as his wings once had.

Her determination, her strength, her tenderness, her capacity for love; all of it would've been lost to him if he'd been the one to find her as her life's blood drained away.

But Samael had found her first, and despite everything, in a strange, twisted sort of way, for that he was grateful.

A flicker of light caught his eye, drawing his attention from Hope's face. As he watched, the flicker grew, expanding to become a white ball of light that drew him like a lodestone, growing bigger and bigger until it encompassed his entire field of vision. Then he was weightless, floating, drawn toward the core of the light without any conscious effort on his part, and while his soul drank it in like water, a piece of his heart remained beside a sleeping Hope, reluctant to leave her yet again.

"Gabriel, my son." The Voice of the One was filled with warmth and kindness. "You've done well."

Near to weeping, for he'd not expected to be once again in his Father's presence this way, Gabriel bowed his head, overcome with emotion.

"During your time as a human," said the One, "you've accomplished what you, as an angel, could never have done."

"I'm glad you're pleased, O Great One," he answered. "But I'm not exactly sure what it is I've accomplished."

A soft chuckle reached his ear, like a balm to a wound he hadn't known he'd had. "You've allowed weakness to make you stronger, and better yet, you've shown your brother, by example, how to do the same."

"Samael, he . . ." Gabriel hesitated, knowing that any past arguments on Sammy's behalf had failed. "He's changing. He's not the same defiant child he was, my Father."

"Well do I know it," said the One, "but his journey isn't over. It is, in fact, barely begun. Leave my prodigal son to me, my child, and have faith that I know what I'm doing."

Gabriel bowed his head, accepting that he knew little or nothing of the One's plans for the universe, and never would.

"You, on the other hand, have ever been my faithful and dutiful child. I fear that I, like fathers everywhere, may have taken your dutifulness for granted."

"Not so," stated Gabriel staunchly, "for there is nowhere I'd rather be than at your right hand."

There was a pause, during which the Light pulsed, steadily, like the beat of a giant heart.

"Nowhere?" the One asked him softly.

Unable to help himself, Gabriel thought of Hope, sleeping peacefully somewhere far behind him. His body ached for hers, but he knew the body to be corporeal and life to be fleeting. The ache would fade. Over the years, she would grow old, and die, as she was meant to do, while he . . . he belonged to eternity, and the One whom he served.

"You have served me well, my son," said the One, clearly knowing his thoughts, "and it is past time for me to reward you."

Lost in his reverie of Hope, Gabriel waved the offer away. "I have everything I need, O Great One."

"No," said the Voice, "for you have changed, too, Gabriel. You've learned what it means to no longer be upon a pedestal, untouched by human emotion. You've felt the ground beneath your feet, and known what it's like to feel it give way. You've known powerlessness, and discovered your own power in the process. You've known love, and given it freely in return, untainted by thoughts of duty and purpose. For these things I will reward you, my son, by giving you your heart's desire."

Stunned, Gabriel said nothing, for he knew not what to say.

"Go back to your beloved, my child, and grow old together. Give the world children, and raise them to revere and respect me as you have always done. Be a lover, a friend, a protector, a brother, a father, a mentor . . ."

Gabriel felt the Light enter his soul, touching the top of his head in a kiss of benediction.

" . . . in short, my dutiful, loving child, go forth and be human, knowing we will see each other again when your life span is over."

"Thank you, O Great One." Gabriel bowed his head, deeply humbled by the gift he'd been given. "Thank you."

Despite her best efforts to stay awake, Hope couldn't manage it. After her prayers, knees stiff, she'd lain down on the bed and thought of Gabriel, wondering endlessly where he was, if he was still alive, if he thought of her. She'd fallen asleep remembering what it felt like to lie in his arms, her cheek against his bare chest, listening to the all-too-human beat of his heart. She dreamed of his face, the way the hair fell over his cheek as he leaned over her, the touch of his fingers on her skin.

"Hope," he whispered, and the sound of her name on his lips sent liquid shivers down her spine, pooling deliciously between her thighs. "Hope," he said again, "my love." She moaned in response, unable to help herself, offering her lips, her body, her heart, and wishing the dream would never end.

"Wake up, my beautiful one," said Gabriel, and she felt his lips touch hers, breaking through the clinging cobwebs of the dream and waking her to one that was far, far better.

"Gabriel," she gasped, looking into his warm brown eyes, so close to hers. "Gabriel." Throwing her arms around his neck, she clutched him tight, glorying in the way his arms went around her back, pulling her hard against him. "You're here, you're alive . . ." She kissed him, then kissed him again, running her hand through his hair, down his back, scarcely able to believe that he was really there, in her arms.

"I'm here," his said, the words muffled against her lips, "but I might not be alive much longer if you don't let me breathe."

Hope pulled away just enough to look into his dear, beautiful, smiling face, then started raining kisses on him again. "Then we'll both die happy," she said, between kisses.

He laughed, and fell into bed with her, rolling her over in one smooth motion so she lay atop him. "More than you know," he said cryptically, "more than you know."

"Where've you been? What happened? How

did you get away?" Questions flooded her mind, and she couldn't ask them fast enough, all the while staring down into his face, and the gorgeous brown eyes she thought she'd never see again.

"It's a really long story," he told her gently, tucking a short strand of her hair behind an ear, "and I think—maybe—that there will be plenty of time for me to tell it. Right now, though"—his eyes slid from her face to her neck, where her robe gaped open—"I'd much rather make love to you."

"Nothing would please me more," she told him huskily, shifting so that his growing erection pressed against the vee of her thighs, "but I have something to say to you first."

His breath caught as she shifted. "Is there a way you could say it really, really fast?"

She shook her head, shifting again, just because she wanted to hear his breath catch a second time, and see the way his eyes darkened with desire. "I want to tell you how very, very sorry I am for everything I did to you . . ."

"Everything?" he murmured, trying to reach her neck with his lips.

"Well, not everything," she amended, letting him nuzzle her neck for just a moment before dragging herself away. "I mean the way I got you thrown out of Heaven . . ."

"You didn't get me thrown out of Heaven," he murmured, merely transferring his lips lower, to her collarbone. "*This* is heaven."

She nearly melted on the spot, but despite the enticing little nibbles Gabe was giving her, she was determined to say her piece. "I dragged you into all kinds of trouble," she insisted, "and then I took shameful advantage of you . . ."

"Take advantage of me again," he urged, pressing his hips upward so she felt every long, hard inch of him.

"You're not helping," she murmured, with a groan.

"I don't want to help," he breathed, placing kisses on the swell of her breast. "I've done enough helping today." His lips moved lower. "Now I just want to help myself."

"Gabriel." With an effort, she caught his head between her hands and made him look at her. "I don't quite know how, and I don't know why, but we're safe now. Charity and I are safe, so you don't have to watch over me and protect me anymore."

Gabe quirked an eyebrow at her. "I don't?"

"You don't," she said firmly, even though she wanted him to. "You can go on and live your life without feeling like you have to babysit me anymore."

He said nothing, merely watching her with those deep brown eyes that she'd love nothing more than to drown in.

"I can take care of myself," she said, swallowing hard. "I'm done being a burden."

"So you don't want to marry me?"

Time stood still.

"What?"

Taking advantage of her stunned state, Gabe rolled, flipping her onto her back and rolling atop her in one smooth motion.

"I asked you," he said slowly, "if you'd changed your mind about marrying me?"

"You . . ." She couldn't breathe, and it wasn't because of his weight. "We've never discussed marriage."

"Do we have to?" His eyes were on her lips, which suddenly felt very dry.

"I'm pretty sure we do," she answered, licking them.

"All right, then." He settled himself more comfortably, shifting so that his length and hardness settled once more between the vee of her thighs.

She bit her lip, her eyes half closing at the sensation.

"I want to marry you," Gabriel said, matter-of-factly. "I want to have children with you, at least one boy and one girl, and I want to take them to the park and read them stories and tuck them in at night."

Hope's eyes prickled, but Gabe wasn't finished.

"I want to take you on vacations and buy you a dog and see your belly grow fat with our child—"

"Children," she whispered, correcting him.

"—our children, and I want to go to work every day just so I can come home to you at night. I want you to cook for me and laugh with me and make glorious, delicious love with me." He moved again, just to emphasize his point, and Hope gasped.

"I want to grow old with you, and watch the fine lines as the corners of your eyes deepen with age, and hear you complain about the silver in your hair. I want to kiss your wrinkled cheeks and hold your liver-spotted hand as we walk in the woods. I want to see you smile the first time you hold a grand-child of ours in your arms, and I want to lie down beside you every night for the rest of our lives."

Speechless, she could only look up at him, clutching his strong, broad shoulders, the shoulders that were meant to bear the weight of the world.

"Now." Gabriel tilted his head, giving her a lop-sided smile. "Have we talked about it enough?"

"Yes," she whispered, pulling him down for a kiss. "Yes, we have."

Chapter Twenty-four

"It was so cool," said Cain, to a wide-eyed Tesla. "Everything in the cave had like this spooky green glow to it, phospher-something—"

"Phosphorescence," interrupted Sammy dryly.

"Yeah, that was it," his son agreed, not slowing down a bit in the telling of his story. "The Leviathan was like this gigantic dragon/snake thing covered in scales, and he had all this like, treasure that the Nereids had brought him . . ."

Unnoticed, Sammy rolled his eyes at his son's bad grammar and constant use of the word "like."

" . . . and he seemed really, really scary. At first I thought he was going to like, eat me, but he turned out to be really nice . . ."

"Really," repeated Sammy under his breath,

but both the boy and the imp ignored him. Truth be told, he didn't want to interrupt Cain any more than Tesla did, for he'd rather listen to a thousand "likes" than never hear his son's voice again.

"He told me to climb on his head and hold on really tight, and then we went *whoosh* through the water"—Cain emphasized his point with a swooping motion of his hand—"just like a roller coaster."

"Wow," breathed the imp. "What's a roller coaster?"

Cain looked nonplussed, but only for a moment. "I'm not really sure, but my mom said they go up and down really fast, and that they're a lot of fun. She said she'd let me ride one one day, but she never did. Anyway . . ."

Yet another thing his son had missed out on during the nine years Sammy hadn't known of his existence, and something Sammy intended to remedy.

" . . . pretty soon we reached the surface, and he just *exploded* out of the water! I mean, water just splashed everywhere! It was awesome!"

"Awesome," repeated Tesla, suitably impressed.

The boys were sprawled on his bed, so Sammy moved to take his usual seat before the fire. Oddly, however, the Throne of Nothingness seemed a bit uncomfortable today, so he switched to another chair, one that gave him a better view of Cain and his friend.

"Where you scared?" Tesla asked Cain.

"Nah," scoffed Cain, then shot his father a guilty glance, amending it to "Well, maybe a little, at first."

"I would've been scared," said Tesla. "I probably would've cried."

"No, you wouldn't," Cain told him staunchly. "You're braver than you think."

Sammy closed his eyes for a moment, wondering how it was that a child of nine could understand friendship in a way that his father had all too easily forgotten.

"Oh, and by the way," Cain went on, "Father says he's going to buy you some tennis shoes."

Tesla's gasp of joy brought Sammy's eyes open. "Really?"

Biting back a chuckle, Sammy confirmed it. "Really."

The imp gazed at him in awe, momentarily speechless.

"A reward," he said. "For coming to tell me about Cain's foolish swim in the Sea of Sorrows. That did indeed take bravery on your part."

Tesla's small chest seemed to swell before his

eyes. "Thank you, Your Majesty," he said formally.

Samael acknowledged the imp's thanks with a nod of the head. "You're welcome."

"So anyway . . ." Cain went on to tell the rest of his adventures, though Sammy had momentarily ceased to listen. His thoughts were drawn to Gabriel, who, hopefully by now, had been reunited with the lovely Hope. He would return them to Atlanta, along with Hope's sister, once they'd had time to (and here he smiled to himself) *reunite* properly.

"Where's Nyx, Father?" Cain's question brought him from his reverie. "I wanted to tell him about the Leviathan, too."

Surprised to find that Cain wanted to tell Nyx anything that didn't involve the use of rude words, Sammy shook his head. "I don't know," he said, and began to wonder the same thing himself. Instead of summoning him mentally, however, he decided to stretch his legs and find out.

"Do *not* leave this room," he told his son sternly, then looked at Tesla. "Do you hear me?"

Two heads, one cherubically beautiful and one demonically ugly, nodded in unison.

"I'm leaving four guards outside the door just in case."

"Don't worry, Father." Cain stretched out on the

bed, making himself at home. "I'm pretty tired right now. Hungry, too."

With a flick of a finger, Sammy produced a small table, on which rested a pepperoni pizza, fresh from the oven, and two large soft drinks. "Eat," he told the boys, and ignored their lack of manners as they fell upon the food. There would be plenty of time to teach Cain the proper way to hold a fork, and today was not the day.

Then he strolled from the room, knowing that—at least until the food was gone—he needn't worry about his son's whereabouts.

Nyx's whereabouts were another matter, however, but not for long. He opened the door to a nearby antechamber to find his right-hand man engaged in what appeared to be an extremely passionate embrace with his current lover, Pandora, who—by her enthusiastic response—showed every evidence of enjoying it.

"What the—"

The two sprang apart guiltily, Nyx leaping to his feet, towering over the somewhat disheveled woman who lay, half reclining, on a cushioned couch.

"Your Majesty," Nyx said, snapping to attention, "I—"

"Spare me," Sammy snapped, raising his hand. "This is a day for surprises, it seems."

Pandora, recovering quickly, merely sighed, twitching her spangled skirt down to cover her delectably plump thighs.

"It's not what it appears," Nyx stammered.

"Yes, it is," said Pandora, lying back languorously, patting her hair into place.

The outrage Sammy should've felt was replaced by something else. His lip twitched as he addressed his second-in-command. "If I didn't know better, Nyx, I'd say you were blushing."

"Master, I—"

Pandora began to chuckle.

"She seduced me," Nyx said desperately, casting an imploring glance down at the couch. "I lost my head."

"I'm thinking you were about to lose something else," said His Satanic Majesty, beginning to grin. "It's called your virginity."

Pandora burst into full-throated laughter, catching at Nyx's taloned hand. He tried to twitch it away, but she wouldn't let him.

"Calm down," he told Nyx, joining in Pandora's amusement. " 'Needs must when the Devil drives,' as they say, and I understand this particular devil quite well."

He turned to go, pausing just before he closed the door on the two. "There's a name for it, you see. It's called desire." He gave them a satanic wink. "Quite irresistible, or so I'm told."

The next morning, Samael followed the sound of childish laughter to the library, expecting to find his son engaged in reading lessons with Pandora. The woman who sat there, however, with a child and an imp on either side, was neither plump nor dark-haired, but a golden-haired beauty who looked familiar. She was wearing an amber-colored gown that was far too large for her slender frame, belted with a gold spangled veil around her midsection. The gown was clearly Pandora's, but there any resemblance ended, for the woman wore no jewels or makeup, her long hair falling casually about her shoulders.

The three readers were deeply engrossed in a book, and didn't notice him at first, so Sammy paused in the doorway to listen.

"'I do not like green eggs and ham,'" read the blond woman, in a lilting voice. "'I do not like them, Sam-I-am.'" She put her finger on the page and tilted the book toward his son. "Your turn, Cain."

Cain, to Sammy's surprise, read the next few lines, concentrating hard on the words.

"Tesla?" She tilted the book toward the imp, trying to get him to read aloud, but Tesla shook his head shyly. He was smiling, though, keeping a knobby-knuckled hand over his mouth to hide his sharp little teeth.

She sighed at him in mock severity, apparently untroubled by the imp's ugliness, then read the next lines herself, interrupted when Cain and Tesla both broke into giggles.

"It's not *that* funny," said the woman, giggling along with them.

"But it is," Cain cried, grinning. "My father's name is Sam, and I keep picturing *him* eating green eggs and ham! Somehow I don't think he'd like it!"

The blond woman laughed, and Sammy felt his lips curl into an involuntary smile. Unused as he was at being the butt of a joke, he found that in this instance he didn't actually mind.

"Well, well," he said aloud, leaning his shoulder against the doorframe. "My taste in food is once again called into question. I wonder if green eggs and ham tastes anything like caviar?"

The woman, who'd started violently at the sound of his voice, turned eyes as amber-colored as her gown upon him. Meeting them, he suddenly, unexplainably felt a flutter in the region of his stomach, and forgot—just for a moment—how to breathe.

"Father," cried Cain, leaping to his feet, and

running over to catch his hand, "Come and meet Charity! Isn't she pretty?"

Charity, of course. Hope's sister.

She looked at him warily, not moving from her chair. Now, with her face turned toward him, he could see the resemblance clearly: the same hair, though hers was longer, the same delicate, fine-boned features. The look in her eyes was different, however, for there was nothing of the innocent about this sister. This woman had seen her share of iniquity, and had her defenses firmly in place.

"Very pretty," he said, agreeing with his son, though he himself would've used words like "beautiful," "striking," or "ravishing." Charity Henderson was a fallen angel of an entirely different kind, and somewhere deep inside, he felt an unsettling sense of kinship with her.

"Very nice to meet you, Charity," he said, extending a hand as Cain pulled him forward. "My name is . . . Sam."

She rose from the chair, leading with her chin, an unconsciously defiant gesture he recognized quite well. Her hand was small and smooth in his, her grip strong. "Nice to meet you, too," she said, her cool tone at complete odds with the warmth he'd seen her show Cain when she thought herself unobserved. "Are you a friend of Pandora's?"

Sammy smiled his most charming smile, unable to help himself. "Absolutely," he replied, feeling curiously deflated when her only response was to remove her hand from his.

"Well," she answered, the wary look still in her eye, "any friend of Pandora's is a friend of mine."

Realizing that Charity thought herself to be in Pandora's home, not his, Sammy saw no need to enlighten her. "I couldn't agree more," he said. "Pandora's been very good to me, and to my son."

"Aunt Pandy is awesome," piped in Cain.

"Awesome," repeated Tesla, nodding his bug-eyed head.

"Please"—Sammy gestured toward the seat Charity had just vacated—"keep reading. I didn't mean to interrupt."

"Father." Cain tugged at his hand again. "You promised to get Tesla and me some new tennis shoes."

"Indeed I did," Sammy replied, vaguely irritated at the interruption. He found he couldn't stop staring into Charity's eyes, an extraordinarily rich shade of brown, streaked with honey. "But not just this minute."

"When?"

Tesla, who Sammy already knew was smarter than he looked, distracted his son's attention.

"C'mon, Cain. Let's play checkers. You promised to teach me."

"Okay." Willing to be distracted, at least for the moment, Cain led the way to a nearby table, marbled in black and white squares, and began to explain the rules of the game to his friend; rules Sammy had taught Cain himself last night, just before he'd tucked him into bed.

Charity, watching them go, glanced curiously up at Sammy. "Tell me," she murmured, so the boys couldn't hear her. "What happened to Tesla? Was he burned in a fire or something?"

Sammy, his throat unaccountably dry, cleared it. "Yes," he said. "I guess you could say that."

He knew that Charity would find out who he truly was soon enough, but to his great surprise, he found himself in no hurry to enlighten her.

"Cain's adorable," she said, turning back to her chair. "You and his mother must be very proud."

Despite the innocent way she'd phrased the statement, he recognized a female lure when he heard one. The strange sense of uncertainty he felt in her presence eased somewhat as he realized she wasn't as unaffected by him as she seemed.

"His mother and I are not together," he told her, well aware of what she wanted to know. "It's just Cain and me these days, alone against the world."

Or in his case, the Underworld, but whatever.

"I'm sorry to hear that," she said, but he got the distinct feeling she wasn't.

"I have an idea," he said, taking a nearby seat. "Why don't you come shopping with us, and help me get the boys some shoes." He lifted an eyebrow, hoping he looked like a helpless male. "I find malls very confusing."

Charity eyed him beneath her lashes, but shook her head. "I couldn't," she said. "I'm waiting for my sister, and then we're heading home."

"Ah, yes," Sammy said, leaning back in his chair. "Your sister. Hope, isn't it?"

Her brown eyes widened in surprise.

"Gabriel thinks very highly of her, you know."

A genuine smile came to Charity's face, revealing white, even teeth, like pearls on a strand. "You know Gabriel?"

"We're like brothers," Sammy said, inordinately proud to finally be able to admit the truth. "We've known each other a very long time."

A very, very long time.

"He seems like a great guy."

"He is."

Charity shot him another look beneath her lashes, smoothing the pleats of Pandora's gown over her knees.

"This may sound a bit forward," Sammy said, fighting an urge to smooth those pleats himself, "but maybe the four of us could go out sometime . . . you know, like a double date." The devil inside him chuckled, laughing as the Great and Mighty Satan waited on her answer, heart in his throat.

Charity's eyes became shuttered. She looked away, her voice strained. "I—I'm not sure that's such a great idea."

"Why not?" He lifted a hand, palm up, as if the rejection meant nothing. "Just dinner, maybe a movie. Don't you like to eat?"

She smiled, just a little, at his persistence.

"Italian? Chinese? What kind of food do you like?"

"I'm a vegetarian."

Sammy grinned ruefully, more at himself than at her. "Ah," he said with a sigh. "I should've known. Tell me, what's your favorite fruit?"

The look she gave him was no longer quite as wary. She smiled again, this time revealing a tiny dimple in her right cheek.

"Apples," she replied, and Sammy began to laugh.

Next month, don't miss these exciting new love stories only from Avon Books

When a Scot Loves a Lady   by Katharine Ashe
After years in the Falcon Club, agent Lord Leam Blackwood must return to his duties in Scotland. But one temptation threatens his plan—Kitty Savege. The scandal-plagued lady warms him like a dram of whiskey and could be the key to beating a dangerous enemy who would see them both dead.

Between the Duke and the Deep Blue Sea   by Sophia Nash
Exiled to Cornwall, the Duke of Kress expects a dull existence—not a beautiful woman clinging to a cliff! Roxanne Vanderhaven's murderous husband left her for dead, and once she's back on solid ground she wants two things: a new life and revenge. She'd never imagined she'd be drawn to her unlikely champion, yet the infamous Duke of Kress isn't the scoundrel he seems . . .

Blame It on Bath   by Caroline Linden
Gerard de Lacey and Katherine Howe happen to desire the exact same thing: a marriage of convenience. Gerard's sinful good looks and penchant for scandal fit the beautiful widow's needs perfectly, and Katherine's wealth and willingness suit the rake. Now if only desire and love don't get in the way of this perfectly suitable arrangement.

The Tattooed Duke   by Maya Rodale
The Duke of Wycliff needs a rich bride if he is to save his fortune, but thanks to the *London Weekly* everyone knows to stay away from the lothario. He never suspects that Eliza, his tempting housemaid, is a Writing Girl undercover revealing his most intimate secrets to the *ton*. When passion flies . . . the truth could destroy them both.

Visit www.AuthorTracker.com for exclusive information on your favorite HarperCollins authors.

Available wherever books are sold or please call 1-800-331-3761 to order.

REL 0212

*G*ive in to your Impulses!

These unforgettable stories only take a second to buy and give you hours of reading pleasure!

Go to *www.AvonImpulse.com* and see what we have to offer.

Available wherever e-books are sold.

AVONIMPULSE

3 3132 03256 3050

IMP 0812